A SHERLOCK HOLMES WHO'S WHO
(And, of Course, Dr. Watson)

Compiled, with the occasional Comment,

by

Molly Carr

Paperback ISBN 978.1.78092.082.5
ePub ISBN 978.1.78092.083.2
PDF ISBN 978.1.78092.084.9

Published in the UK by MX Publishing
335 Princess Park Manor, Royal Drive, London, N11 3GX

www.mxpublishing.co.uk

Cover design by www.staunch.com

FOR ELIZABETH

CONTENTS

'"YOU HAVE GOT THEM!" WE CRIED.'

Introduction

Ever since A. C. Black & Co. brought out their first 'Who's Who?' of the great and good in 1849 (followed in 1897 by 'Who Was Who' after death intervened and removed their entries to a separate volume) people have been fascinated by the rich and famous. There is now, for example, a 'Who's Who' in cricket, a 'Who's Who' in Agatha Christie. and even a 'Who's Who' in a famous American cemetery.

So if you have ever wanted to know where Watson bought his boots, or where (and when) Inspectors Lestrade, Bradstreet, Athelney Jones, Hopkins and MacDonald appear in the stories then this is the book for you. How many times is Moriarty mentioned, and what was his henchman, Colonel Moran, up to in an empty house? Who on earth was Acton and, more to the point, who could possibly have been called (by the Great Detective himself) a rival to Sherlock Holmes?

Two books which I have found particularly useful are *Who's Who in Sherlock Holmes* by Scott R. Bullard and Michael Leo Collins, published by the Taplinger Publishing Company of New York in 1980, and *Sherlock Holmes* by Mark Campbell[1], published by Pocket Essentials in 2007. But in undertaking a work such as this, certain references may have been missed, and some errors crept in. So anyone who finds that

---

[1] I am indebted to this book for the idea of separating non-speaking characters (given there in italics, along with a short resumé of each 'Adventure') from those who do have something to say for themselves in the canon.

their favourite character is missing, or would like to make a comment or suggest a correction, this will be most warmly welcomed by the author.

PART ONE
(PEOPLE)

'HERE IT IS, SIR.'

"The Three Students"

<u>A Note on the Text</u>. In September 1908 Conan Doyle wrote 'A Reminiscence of Sherlock Holmes' for the *Strand Magazine*. This was in two parts and is often called 'The Adventure of Wisteria Lodge', or simply 'Wisteria Lodge' as here. Conan Doyle, however, uses the correct botanical name: Wistaria for this 'pea-flower' from China. (Bentham and Hooker, 1892)

* Denotes characters from the Sherlock Holmes canon who, as Mark Campbell says, "are not directly encountered in the narrative [but] usually feature in reported speech, flashbacks or passing references."

A

*ABERNETTY FAMILY. "The dreadful business of the Abernetty family" was first brought to Sherlock Holmes' notice by how much the parsley had sunk into the butter on a hot day. *The Six Napoleons*

*ABRAHAMS. Sherlock Holmes said he couldn't leave London while "old Abrahams is in such terror of his life". We don't know what has occasioned this fear, but nevertheless it's used as an excuse by Sherlock to send Watson to Lausanne instead of going there himself, even though he has been hired by Lady Frances' anxious relatives and turns up later disguised as a workman. *The Disappearance of Lady Frances Carfax*

*ACHMET. A merchant murdered by Jonathan Small for the sake of the Agra Treasure. *The Sign of Four*

ACTON. This man lived in the same area as Colonel Hayter, who spoke of him to Sherlock Holmes as someone who had had his house broken into. The Colonel himself had been a patient of Doctor John H. Watson during his time in Afghanistan. *The Reigate Squire*

*ADAIR, HILDA. The daughter of the Earl and Countess of Maynooth and sister of The Hon. Ronald Adair, she came from Australia to England with her mother and brother in 1894. The two women were out visiting and came home to find tragedy had struck the family. *The Empty House*

*ADAIR, RONALD. This young aristocrat, who moved in the best society, apparently had no enemies and no particular vices. He was found in their London lodgings by his mother and sister with his head "horribly mutilated" by an expanding revolver bullet. *The Empty House*

*ADAMS. A criminal in 'The Manor House Case', this investigation was solved by Holmes, but not written up by Watson. *The Greek Interpreter*

ADLER, IRENE. Sherlock Holmes described this woman as "the daintiest thing under a bonnet on this planet…She lives quietly, sings at concerts, drives out at five every day, and returns at seven sharp for dinner." She is also one of the most written about characters in the canon. A contralto and trained actress, who had once sung at *La Scala*, she became involved with 'The King of Bohemia' during a visit to Warsaw. But when His Majesty needed to marry for dynastic reasons she refused to return a 'compromising' photograph of the two of them together. Attempts by the King's agents to recover the photograph proved fruitless and he had to call in Holmes. To the detective she was ever afterwards "the woman", who eclipsed "the whole of her sex." Not, however, in any romantic sense. She had simply been the one to outwit him. She showed her mettle when, disguised as a young man, she addressed Holmes in passing one evening outside his own lodgings. *A Scandal in Bohemia* and *His Last Bow*

AGAR, DR. MOORE. A Harley Street Specialist who warns Sherlock not to work so hard if he wishes to avoid a complete breakdown. *The Devil's Foot*

*AGATHA. Holmes, disguised as a plumber and calling himself Escott, became engaged to this housemaid in order to find out about her employer, whom he called "as wicked as the Evil One and the king of all the blackmailers." *Charles Augustus Milverton*

*AINSTREE, DR. "The greatest living authority upon

5

tropical disease," he was living in London when Watson wished to consult him about Holmes' mysterious illness. *The Dying Detective*

***ALDRIDGE**. Jim Browner was "a big powerful chap, clean-shaven, and very swarthy," a little like Aldridge, who helped Holmes and Lestrade in an investigation into something called 'the bogus laundry affair'. *The Cardboard Box*

***ALEXIS**. A man who hated violence and was 'noble, unselfish and loving', he had once been a member of a Russian Nihilist group known as The Brotherhood and sometimes The Order. Anna, married to a man who later called himself Professor Coram, fell in love with him. This did not, however, save Alexis from being implicated in the killing of a police officer, a crime for which he was arrested and sentenced to work in a Siberian salt mine. Alexis had written letters to Anna which "would have saved him." But her jealous husband had hidden them out of spite. *The Golden Pince-nez*

***ALGAR**. A member of the Liverpool police force who did some investigating for Holmes into the circumstances surrounding the gruesome episode of *The Cardboard Box.*

***ALICE**. Miss Hatty Doran's maid. *The Noble Bachelor*

***ALLAN BROTHERS**. They were the most important land agents in the village of Esher. Aloysius Garcia rented a house from them. *Wisteria Lodge*

ALLEN, MRS. "A buxom and cheerful person," she helped Mrs. Jack Douglas by taking over some of her household chores. *The Valley of Fear*

ALTAMONT. The great German spy, Von Bork, said that this supposed, but independent, fellow spy was a wonderful worker. If he paid him well "he 'delivers the goods', to use his own phrase." In Von Bork's opinion Altamont (a disguised Sherlock Holmes) could not be called a traitor. His feelings towards England were those of a really bitter Irish-American. Von Bork also noted that Altamont had a nice taste in wines, and took a fancy to Tokay. Because of his goatee beard he looked like a caricature of Uncle Sam. Another point of interest is that Altamont was the middle name of Conan Doyle's father, Charles Doyle. *His Last Bow*

AMBERLEY, JOSIAH. This man was a junior partner of Brickfall & Amberley who made artistic materials. At the age of sixty-one he retired, bought a house in Lewisham and then, early in 1897, married a woman twenty years younger than himself. All seemed well. But within two years Amberley became "as broken and miserable a creature as crawls beneath the sun." He had come to Holmes because (according to him) his wife had disappeared with their neighbour and all Josiah's money. But the truth was very different. *The Retired Colourman*

AMES. The butler at Birlstone Manor in Sussex, the home of the Douglases. Watson thought he was "a gnarled, dried-up person." He was, however, able to give the police important information about the running of the household. *The Valley of Fear*

ANDAMAN ISLANDER. See Tonga. *The Sign of Four*

***ANDERSON**. During the Boer War, Anderson was in the same squadron as Godfrey Emsworth and James Dodd. In a skirmish outside Pretoria one morning, Emsworth and Anderson, along with another man, had become separated from their mates, and the latter two were killed. *The Blanched Soldier*

ANDERSON. The village constable of Fulworth, he had been called to investigate the murder of Fitzroy McPherson and asked Sherlock Holmes' advice on how to tackle the problem. *The Lion's Mane*

***ANDREWS**. Someone who lodged with Jack McMurdo, he was "Little more than a boy, frank-faced and cheerful, with the breezy manner of one who is out for a holiday, and means to enjoy every minute of it." He was sent by the Scowrers' county delegate, Evans Pott, to murder the manager of the Crow Hill Mine. *The Valley of Fear*

***ANGEL, HOSMER**. (See also James Windibank) Mary Sutherland's 'fiancé', whom she met at the gas-fitters' ball. On the morning of the wedding day Mary and her mother were waiting for him at the church; but when the cab driver arrived with the bridegroom he was as astonished as they were to find his cab empty. The inappropriately but ingeniously named Angel had disappeared completely. In reality he was Mary's step-father, who urged her to be true to him whatever the circumstances. By binding her in this way he hoped to prevent her marrying anyone and taking her small competence with her. *A Case of Identity*

ANNA. A one-time Russian Nihilist. She and her husband had belonged to a revolutionary group, along with the man she loved. In order to save his own life and to earn a great reward, her husband betrayed his wife and other comrades. But he also withheld certain letters and a diary which would have proved Alexis had no part in a murder. After she had completed her term of imprisonment in Siberia, Anna came to England to steal the letters and the diary so that 'the friend of her heart' might gain his freedom. *The Golden Pince-nez*

***ANSTRUTHER**. One of the doctors who stood in for Watson when he was away on an investigation with Holmes. *The Boscombe Valley Mystery*

ANTHONY. A manservant at Merripit House, in Devonshire, where the Stapletons lived. *The Hound of the*

Baskervilles

*APPLEDORE, SIR CHARLES. His daughter, Edith, married the Duke of Holdernesse in 1888. *The Priory School*

*APPLEDORE, EDITH. She had one son and heir, who was abducted from his school. Estranged from her husband, she lived in the south of France. *The Priory School*

*ARCHIE. He was one of John Clay's accomplices in the attempted robbery of the "Coburg branch of the City and Suburban Bank." A robbery foiled by Holmes. *The Red-Headed League*

ARMITAGE, JAMES. A bank employee convicted of embezzlement and sentenced to transportation to Australia in 1855. He took part in a successful convict uprising aboard ship and, once he got to Sydney, changed his name. He eventually came back to England a very rich man, calling himself Trevor. *The "Gloria Scott"*

*ARMITAGE, MR. He was the father of Percy Armitage, who was engaged to Helen Stoner. *The Speckled Band*

*ARMITAGE, PERCY. Second son of Mr. Armitage of Crane Water, near Reading. His fiancée, the step-daughter of Dr. Grimesby Roylott of Stoke Moran in western Surrey, was twin sister to Julia Stoner who died in mysterious circumstances. *The Speckled Band*

ARMSTRONG, DR. LESLIE. Holmes thought Dr. Armstrong "a man of energy and character." He was so impressed by him that he claimed never to have "seen a man who, if he turned his talents that way, was more calculated to fill the gap left by the illustrious Moriarty." But Armstrong's battle with Holmes was in a noble cause. Once he understood Holmes intended no harm, he capitulated. *The Missing Three-Quarter*.

*ATKINSON BROTHERS. At the time of *A Scandal in*

Bohemia, Watson, whose "own complete happiness" in his marriage to Mary Morstan at the end of the investigation into *The Sign of Four* had caused him to see less of Sherlock, had from time to time, however, heard some vague account of Holmes' doings, such as his clearing up of the singular tragedy of the Atkinson brothers at Trincomalee.

ATWOOD. He sold his Vermissa Valley ironworks to the West Wilmerton General Mining Company in order, like so many others, to escape from the Scowrers. *The Valley of Fear*

AVELING. This man taught mathematics at the Priory School and was sure that Heidegger, the missing German master, had had a particular type of tyre on his bicycle. *The Priory School*

AVENGING ANGELS, THE. This Mormon group, also known as the Danite Band, terrorized John Ferrier and ultimately destroyed his daughter, Lucy. John tried to escape from them with her and the man she loved, Jefferson Hope. But the Band caught up with them. Ferrier was killed and Lucy taken back to where she came from and forced to marry the Mormon Enoch Drebber, whose father, also Enoch, was an Elder of the Church. *A Study in Scarlet*

B

*BACKWATER, LORD. This peer recommended Holmes to Lord St. Simon who said to Sherlock, "Lord Backwater tells me that I may place implicit reliance upon your judgment and discretion." *The Noble Bachelor.* Was this the same Lord Backwater who owned Capleton Stables, on Dartmoor, where Desborough, the second favourite in the running of the Wessex Cup, was trained? *Silver Blaze*

*BAIN, SANDY. He was a jockey at Shoscombe Park,

Berkshire. Sir Robert Norberton told him to give a favourite dog belonging to his sister (Lady Beatrice Falder) to Josiah Barnes of the Green Dragon inn. This was because Sir Robert's sister had died and, for financial reasons, he wished to keep the fact secret until after an important race had been run. Meanwhile, someone else would impersonate Lady Falder on her daily ride. If her dog had spotted the impersonation, as was likely, then things would be all up for Sir Robert. *Shoscombe Old Place*

BAKER, HENRY. The owner of a battered billycock (hat) with a broken string, he had somehow lost a goose. One which was not all it seemed. *The Blue Carbuncle*

BAKER STREET IRREGULARS. Holmes used this bunch of street urchins, 'the Baker Street Irregulars', in the mystery surrounding the lonely death of Enoch J. Drebber. They were, according him, the Baker Street division of the detective police force; and there was more work to be got out of one of the ragged little beggars than out of a dozen of the proper force. The mere sight of an official-looking person caused men to keep mum. But these street arabs could go everywhere, and hear everything. They were "as sharp as needles" and all they wanted was organization. *A Study in Scarlet*. See also *The Sign of Four*

BALDWIN, TED. "A Boss of Scowrers," he later took the name of Hargrave. Using this name, he went to England in an attempt to murder Jack Douglas. "He was a handsome dashing young man" and competed with a fellow-lodger in the Vermissa Valley for the affections of his landlord's daughter, Ettie Shafter. Vicious and vindictive, he said to Jack McMurdo, "I'll get even with you without needing to dirty my hands." *The Valley of Fear*

*BALMORAL, DUKE OF. One-time Secretary for Foreign Affairs, Robert Walsingham de Vere St. Simon was his son, who sought Holmes' help in finding his wife when she vanished from her own wedding reception because (as it turned out) of someone she had spotted in the church. *The Noble Bachelor.* Was this, like Lord Backwater above, the same Duke of Balmoral who ran his horse, Iris, for the Wessex Cup? When it came in a bad third. *Silver Blaze*

*BALMORAL, LORD. With *Godfrey Milner, he had lost as much as £420 to Ronald Adair and Colonel Sebastian Moran some weeks before Adair's murder. *The Empty House*

BANNISTER. He had been Mr. Hilton Soames' servant at the College of St. Luke's for over ten years and was thought to be above suspicion when some examination papers were tampered with. *The Three Students*

*BARCLAY, COLONEL JAMES. He commanded the Royal Mallows regiment, stationed at Aldershot, and was found dead in a locked room at his house, 'Lachine', alone with his wife, who was unconscious. "Barclay's devotion to his wife was greater than his wife's to Barclay. He was acutely uneasy if he were absent from her for a day— He was a dashing, jovial old soldier in his usual mood, but there were occasions on which he seemed to show himself capable of considerable violence and vindictiveness..." *The Crooked Man*

BARDLE, INSPECTOR. An Inspector with the Sussex Police Force, he asked Sherlock Holmes for advice when Ian Murdoch was arrested for the murder of Fitzroy McPherson. *The Lion's Mane*

*BARELLI, AUGUSTO. Father of Emilia Lucca, he was the chief lawyer, and at one time the deputy, of the area around Posilippo, near Naples. Because he didn't want his daughter to marry one of his employees, the young couple eloped together and were married at Bari. *The Red Circle*

BARKER. Watson noticed a strange lounger in front of Josiah Amberley's house. Holmes later identified him as Barker, a detective who was his "hated rival upon the Surrey shore." *The Retired Colourman*

BARKER, CECIL JAMES. Of Hales Lodge, Hampstead. He was a close friend of the Douglas family and at first suspected of murdering Jack Douglas. *The Valley of Fear*

BARNES, JOSIAH. The keeper of the Green Dragon Inn at Crendall, three miles from Sir Robert Norberton's stables. After being given Lady Beatrice Falder's favourite dog he kept the animal tied up to prevent it running back to *Shoscombe Old Place*

***BARNICOT, DR**. A well-known London medical practitioner, both his residence and principal consulting-rooms in Kennington Road and his branch surgery and dispensary at Lower Brixton Road contained plaster busts of Napoleon, which were mysteriously dashed to pieces. *The Six Napoleons*

***BARRETT, POLICE CONSTABLE**. He saw, as he was patrolling Godolphin Street, that the door of number 16 was half open. After knocking and receiving no answer, he entered the front room of the house where he discovered the body of international spy Eduardo Lucas, who had been stabbed to death with a curved Indian dagger. *The Second Stain*

BARRYMORE, ELIZA. She was one of the servants at Baskerville Hall and married to the butler. Her brother was Selden, the Notting Hill murderer. *The Hound of the Baskervilles*

BARRYMORE, JOHN. The butler at Baskerville Hall, his family had served the Baskervilles for a hundred years, but the presence of his brother-in-law on the moor caused him and his wife a great deal of trouble and made them seem to act suspiciously. *The Hound of the Baskervilles*

BARTON, DR. HILL. Watson, posing as an expert in ceramics and calling himself 'Dr. Hill Barton' because, as Holmes said, he might as well be what he was, went to the house of Baron Adelbert Gruner to distract the man's attention while Holmes searched the Baron's inner study. *The Illustrious Client*

*BARTON, INSPECTOR. He took charge of the investigation into what seemed like the sudden disappearance of Neville St. Clair. *The Man with the Twisted Lip*

BASIL, CAPTAIN. "The fact that several rough-looking men called during that time and inquired for Captain Basil made me understand that Holmes was working somewhere under one of the numerous disguises and names with which he concealed his own formidable identity." *Black Peter*

*BASKERVILLE, SIR CHARLES. He had made his fortune in South African speculation, and had then returned to the family estate, Baskerville Hall, in Devonshire. His death, initially attributed to heart failure, was nevertheless surrounded by such mysterious events that Sherlock Holmes became involved. *The Hound of the Baskervilles*

*BASKERVILLE, ELIZABETH. Daughter of Hugo Baskerville (2) who set down the legend of the Hound of the Baskervilles in writing in 1742. She was kept in the dark about the legend by her brothers on their father's orders. *The Hound of the Baskervilles*

BASKERVILLE, SIR HENRY. A Canadian farmer, he was the heir to both the Baskerville estate and fortune, and also to the menacing legend of the Hound. Watson described him as "a small, alert, dark-eyed man about thirty years of age, very sturdily built, with thick black eyebrows, and a strong, pugnacious face." One of the few characters in the canon which never really 'worked'. *The Hound of the Baskervilles*

*BASKERVILLE, HUGO (1). A man "most wild, profane and godless," he lived at the time of the English Civil War, 1642-49. When he died after being viciously attacked by a huge dog this started the legend of **The Hound.** See also **Rear-Admiral Baskerville**, who served with Admiral Rodney in the West Indies and whose portrait Holmes admired while dining with Sir Henry Baskerville. Holmes also studied **Sir William Baskerville**, whose portrait hung in the family gallery at Baskerville Hall. This man had been Chairman of Committees of the House of Commons under Pitt. *The Hound of the Baskervilles*

BASKERVILLE, HUGO (2). See Elizabeth Baskerville.

*BASKERVILLE, RODGER(1). The youngest brother of Sir Charles, he was the black sheep of the family who ran off to South America, married there and had one son. He died of yellow fever in 1876. *The Hound of the Baskervilles*

BASKERVILLE, RODGER(2). Son of the above, he married Beryl Garcia of Costa Rica and, after stealing a considerable amount of money, fled with her to England. *The Hound of the Baskervilles*

BATES, MR. MARLOW. The manager of Neil Gibson's estate in Hampshire. *The Problem of Thor Bridge*

*BAXTER. Holmes in philosophical mood at the end of his investigation into the brutal slaying of Charles McCarthy said, "Why does Fate play such tricks with poor helpless worms? I never hear of such a case as this that I do not think of Baxter's words, and say. 'There, but for the grace of God, goes Sherlock Holmes." *The Boscombe Valley Mystery*

*BAXTER, EDITH. A maid at King's Pyland stables in Dartmoor, she carried a supper to the stable boy Ned Hunter. A supper which turned out to be laced with opium. *Silver Blaze*

BAYNES, INSPECTOR. A member of the Surrey Constabulary, he looked out a client of Holmes' called John Scott Eccles. This was in connection with the murder of Aloysius Garcia, at whose house Scott Eccles had very recently stayed. Holmes was most impressed with Baynes' attention to detail and thought that he had been so prompt and business-like in the way he went on that he would rise high in his profession. He had both "instinct and intuition." *Wisteria Lodge*

BECHER, DR. He lived in a house in Eyford, where Victor Hatherley went to repair Colonel Lysander Stark's hydraulic press. He was "an Englishman, and there isn't a man in the parish who has a better lined waistcoat." *The Engineer's Thumb*

BEDDINGTON. Aka Pinner. A forger and a cracksman, he impersonated a clerk (Hall Pycroft) in an attempt to rob Mawson & Williams, the financial house where Pycroft was about to start work, but was not yet known by sight. *The Stockbroker's Clerk*

*BEDDOES. Of Hampshire, he was a friend and old accomplice of the senior Mr. Trevor. Both men shared a questionable past, and this had caused them to change their names. But they were both being blackmailed by a former acquaintance named Hudson. *The "Gloria Scott"*

BELLAMY, MAUD. Fiancée of the murdered Fitzroy McPherson, she was "the beauty of the neighbourhood" around Fulworth, Sussex. Even Sherlock Holmes, for whom women had seldom been an attraction, realized "that no young man would cross her path unscathed." Maud listened to the particulars of her lover's death so composedly and with such concentration that her manner showed she possessed not only good looks, but a strong character. *The Lion's Mane*

BELLAMY, TOM. The father of William and Maud Bellamy, he had once been a fisherman. But he had built up his business to such a degree that he owned "all the boats and bathing-cots at Fulworth." His description reads as follows: "a middle-aged man with a flaming red beard. He seemed to be in a very angry mood, and his face was soon as florid as his hair." *The Lion's Mane*

BELLAMY, WILLIAM. The son and business partner of Tom Bellamy and the brother of Maud Bellamy, he was "a powerful young man, with a heavy, sullen face." And, apparently, of one mind with his father that the man who wished to marry his sister and was now dead had insulted the family with his proposal. *The Lion's Mane*

BELLINGER, LORD. Described as "austere, high-nosed, eagle-eyed, and dominant." Lord Bellinger asked Sherlock Holmes to find a stolen State document, even though at first he was reluctant to confide in the detective. *The Second Stain*

*BELMINSTER, DUKE OF. His daughter, Lady Trelawney Hope, was, in Watson's opinion, "The most lovely woman in London." *The Second Stain*

*BENDER, MR. The first person to die on the Great Alkali Plain. *A Study in Scarlet*

BENNETT, TREVOR ("JACK"). Tall, handsome, well-dressed and elegant, he was Professor Presbury's professional assistant and engaged to his daughter. Concerned about his future father-in-law's strange behaviour, he went to Sherlock Holmes. *The Creeping Man*

*BEPPO. An Italian who had once been an honest

workman in Morse Hudson's shop and at the Gelder & Company Sculpture Works, he hid the famous black pearl of the Borgias in a bust of Napoleon, and this led to at least two murders and six busts being mysteriously smashed to smithereens. *The Six Napoleons*

BERNSTONE, MRS. The housekeeper at Pondicherry Lodge, Upper Norwood, the home of Bartholomew Sholto. *The Sign of Four*

*BIDDLE. A member of the Worthingdon bank gang. They took part in a robbery in 1875, were caught, and Biddle, along with two other men, was sentenced to fifteen years in jail. The gang swore that they would take revenge on one of their former partners, Sutton, who had testified against them in court and was now lodging with a young doctor and calling himself Blessington. *The Resident Patient*

BILL. The young assistant to Mr. Breckinridge, who owned a meat seller's stall in the Covent Garden Market. *The Blue Carbuncle*

BILLY. "The young but very wise and tactful page, who had helped a little to fill up the gap of loneliness and isolation which surrounded the saturnine figure of the great detective." Billy and Dr. Watson discussed old times in *The Mazarin Stone*, written in the third person, and Billy played a significant part in the action of that adventure. In fact, Holmes worried how far he was justified in allowing the boy to be in danger. See also *The Valley of Fear* **and** *The Problem of Thor Bridge*

*BIRD, SIMON. See the Scowrers

BLACK JACK OF BALLARAT. He made his fortune by highway robbery in Australia. "There were six of us, and we had a wild, free life of it, sticking up a station from time to time, or stopping the waggons on the road to the diggings. Black Jack of Ballarat was the name I went under, and our party is still remembered in the colony as the Ballarat Gang." See also John Turner. *The Boscombe Valley Mystery*

BLACK PETER. The name given to Captain Peter Carey, "not only on account of his swarthy features and the colour of his huge beard, but for the humours which were the terror of all around him." *Black Peter*

***BLACKWATER, EARL OF**. He was one of the important people who had entrusted his son to Dr. Thorneycroft Huxtable's care in Hallamshire. *The Priory School*

***BLAKER, FOREMAN**. He earned the undying hatred of the Scowrers of Vermissa Valley by giving three of their members the sack, and would soon see "The business end of a buck-shot cartridge." *The Valley of Fear*

BLESSINGTON, MR. Aka Sutton. He provided Dr. Percy Trevelyan with the capital to set up his Brook Street practice in return for three quarters of the earnings. The doctor was to take care of him and he was to be allowed to live in the house; but Blessington was afraid to leave the building and kept himself to himself. However, the sudden arrival of a strange 'patient', accompanied by two other men, brought in Sherlock Holmes. *The Resident Patient*

BLOUNT. He was one of the students at Harold Stackhurst's coaching academy, The Gables, and discovered the dead body of Fitzroy McPherson's Airedale terrier very near the pool where its master had been brutally murdered. *The Lion's Mane*

***BOB**. Lucy Ferrier's brother, who died on the ill-fated expedition across the Great Alkali Plain. *A Study in Scarlet*.

BOHEMIA, KING OF. A note which Holmes received anonymously bore the watermark of the Egria Papier Gesellschaft. Said Sherlock, "Egria. It is in a German-speaking country – in Bohemia, not far from Carlsbad." Later, Holmes was confronted with the august person of Wilhelm Gottsreich Sigismond von Ormstein, Grand Duke of Cassel-Falstein and hereditary King of Bohemia. *A Scandal in Bohemia.* See also *A Case of Identity* and *His Last Bow*

BOONE, HUGH. A 'crippled' beggar of hideous aspect, he made his money by sitting on the pavement near the Bank of England in Threadneedle Street pretending to sell matches to get round the vagrancy laws. Morning and evening he would visit an upper room of the Bar of Gold opium den to change in and out of his rags, either before going into the City or travelling home to his house, The Cedars, at Lee in Kent in his true aspect as Neville St. Clair. A former actor, his make-up was so unusual and effective, and his line of repartee so entertaining, he made more than enough money from passers-by to abandon the idea of returning to his old job as a newspaper reporter. "A shock of orange hair, a pale face disfigured by a horrible scar, which by its contraction, has turned up the outer edge of his upper lip, a bull.dog chin, and a pair of very penetrating dark eyes, which present a singular contrast to the colour of his hair, all mark him out from amid the common crowd of mendicants." *The Man with the Twisted Lip*

BRACKENSTALL, SIR EUSTACE. One of the richest men in Kent, Sir Eustace was a tall, well-made man about forty years old. A decent enough man when sober, he turned into a fiend when drunk and had once drenched his wife's dog with petrol and set it alight. He was killed by a blow to the head with a heavy poker, and Inspector Stanley Hopkins thought the case would be "quite in [Sherlock Holmes'] line." *The Abbey Grange*

BRACKENSTALL, LADY MARY. Née Miss Mary Fraser.

Born and brought up in Adelaide, Australia, she was a beautiful blonde, golden-haired and blue-eyed. After arriving in England with her maid, Theresa Wright, she was won over by Sir Eustace Brackenstall's title, money and "London ways." However, their relationship quickly deteriorated during the few months they were married. *The Abbey Grange*

*BRACKWELL, LADY EVA. "The most beautiful debutante of last season," Lady Eva found her forthcoming marriage to the Earl of Dovercourt was being threatened by Charles Augustus Milverton. Milverton had gained possession of several imprudent letters Lady Eva had once written to "an impecunious young squire in the country," and intended to send them to the Earl, thus breaking off the match, unless seven thousand pounds were paid to him. *Charles Augustus Milverton*

BRADSTREET, INSPECTOR. He was in charge of the Bow Street police station when Holmes and Watson wanted to interview the beggar Hugh Boone about the sudden disappearance of Neville St. Clair. Bradstreet also gave evidence in the case involving the disappearance of the Duchess of Morcar's diamond. He went with Holmes, Watson, Victor Hatherley and a plain-clothes policeman to Eyford in Berkshire to investigate the brutal attack on Hatherley which resulted in the young man's thumb being cut off. *The Man with the Twisted Lip, The Blue Carbuncle* and *The Engineer's Thumb*

BRECKINRIDGE, MR. Owner of a meat stall in Covent Garden, he sold a goose to Mr. Windigate of the Alpha Inn. The landlord habitually ran a Christmas goose club and allotted this particular bird to Mr. Henry Baker with both investigative and gastronomic results. *The Blue Carbuncle*

*BREWER, SAM. A well-known Curzon Street

moneylender. He was the chief creditor of Sir Robert Norberton. Sir Robert, a man of almost ungovernable temper, had once almost come to Holmes' attention earlier when he nearly horsewhipped Brewer to death on Newmarket Heath. *Shoscombe Old Place*

*BROOKS. According to Holmes, this criminal was one of at least as many as "fifty men" who had very good reason for making attempts on the detective's life. *The Bruce-Partington Plans*

*BROWN, LIEUTENANT BROMLEY. One of three men in command of the native troops at the Blair Island penal colony in the Andaman Islands. *The Sign of Four*

BROWN, JOSIAH. Of Laburnum Lodge, Laburnum Vale, Chiswick. Holmes knew that his might be the next in the series of plaster casts of the famous Head of Napoleon by the sculptor Devine to be unaccountably smashed. *The Six Napoleons*

*BROWN, SAM. A thick-set police inspector who went with another inspector, Athelney Jones, and with Holmes and Watson, in the police launch which chased after the *Aurora*. *The Sign of Four*

BROWN, SILAS. He managed the Capleton Stables, on Dartmoor, where Desborough, the second favourite for the Wessex Cup, was trained. Holmes said of him, "A more perfect compound of the bully, coward and sneak than Master Silas Brown I have seldom met with." *Silver Blaze*

*BROWNER, JIM. This rather morose sailor married Mary Cushing in Liverpool. He first worked as a steward on a South American line, but later transferred to the Liverpool, Dublin and London Steam Packet Company aboard the *May Day*. His involvement with two of the Cushing sisters eventually led to a double murder. *The Cardboard Box*

*BRUNTON, RICHARD. The butler at Hurlstone, the

ancestral home of a branch of the Musgrave family, in Sussex. He disappeared in mysterious circumstances after he'd been caught going through the Musgrave family papers and dismissed. He was later found dead, shut into a cellar by a vengeful housemaid. *The Musgrave Ritual*

BURNETT, MISS. An Englishwoman of about forty, her face was both "aquiline and emaciated" and her character was such that there could be no 'love interest' between her and Aloysius Garcia. Her job was ostensibly that of governess to the Henderson children. But she was part of a plot to murder *Don Juan Murillo ('The Tiger of San Pedro'), also known as *Dictator Murillo, with a secretary named *Lucas or *Lopez. Both men (now calling themselves *The Marquess of Montalva and *Signor Rulli) were later found murdered in their rooms at The Hotel Escorial in Madrid. *Wisteria Lodge*

*BURNWELL, SIR GEORGE. Arthur Holder's false friend. Alexander Holder, Arthur's father, said of Burnwell. "He is older than Arthur, a man of the world to his finger-tips, one who has been everywhere, seen everything, a brilliant talker, and a man of great personal beauty. Yet when I think of him in cold blood... far away from the glamour of his presence, I am convinced....that he is one who should be deeply distrusted." Holmes heartily agreed with this opinion and said, " He is one of the most dangerous men in England —a ruined gambler, an absolutely desperate villain; a man without heart or conscience." *The Beryl Coronet*

C

CAIRNS, PATRICK. A harpooner, he was lured to 221B Baker Street by a newspaper advertisement put in by Holmes posing as Captain Basil. Cairns had been in the business for twenty-six years and had sailed out of Dundee aboard the *Sea Unicorn,* Captain Peter Carey's vessel. Sherlock, however, suspected him of murdering Carey and, while pretending to get Cairns to sign a contract, clapped handcuffs on him. *Black Peter*

*CALHOUN, JAMES. Captain of the sea-going vessel *Lone Star*, out of Savannah, Georgia. He was the leader of the gang that hounded two generations of Openshaws to their deaths. *The Five Orange Pips*

CANTLEMERE, LORD. He was helping to manage the recovery of a very precious jewel and was opposed to Holmes' involvement in the affair. *The Mazarin Stone*

CARBONARI. The "old" Italian organization, to which a Neapolitan secret society was connected. *The Red Circle*

*CARERE, MLLE. The full explanation of the present case had to wait until Holmes concluded two other investigations of "the utmost importance." In the second of these he had defended "the unfortunate Mme Montpensier from the charge of murder which hung over her in connection with the death of her step-daughter, Mlle Carere, the young lady who, as it will be remembered, was found six months later alive and married in New York." *The Hound of the Baskervilles*

*CAREY, MISS. Daughter of the murdered Captain Peter Carey. "A pale fair-haired girl, whose eyes blazed defiantly at us as she told us that she was glad that her father was dead, and that she blessed the hand which had struck him down." *Black Peter*

*CAREY, MRS. Wife of the murdered Captain Peter Carey. "A haggard grey-haired woman...whose gaunt and deep-lined face, with the furtive look of terror in the depths of her red-rimmed eyes, told of the years of hardship and ill-usage which she had endured." *Black Peter*

*CAREY, CAPTAIN PETER. Of Woodman's Lee, Sussex.

The very obscure circumstances surrounding his death caused Inspector Stanley Hopkins to call Holmes into the case. *Black Peter*

*CARFAX, THE LADY FRANCES. Holmes believed that "One of the most dangerous classes in the world is the drifting and friendless woman. She is the most harmless, and often the most useful of mortals, but she is the inevitable inciter of crime in others." And Lady Frances, was just such a person. When her old governess hadn't heard from her for several weeks, Holmes was called in to find out the reason why. *The Disappearance of Lady Frances Carfax*

*CARNAWAY, JIM. A Scowrer killed in an attempt to murder Chester Wilcox. His widow received a pension from the Vermissa Valley Lodge. *The Valley of Fear*

CARRUTHERS, BOB. "He was a dark, sallow, clean-shaven, silent person; but he had polite manners and a pleasant smile." When he, a widower, invited Violet Smith to accept the job of music teacher to his only daughter she, being very poor, was pleased to do so. Unfortunately, Carruthers was a good friend of the bully, Jack Woodley, and they both had ulterior motives for involving Miss Smith in the household. Carruthers fell in love with Violet, and his subsequently strange behaviour decided her to consult Sherlock Holmes. *The Solitary Cyclist*

*CARRUTHERS, COLONEL. At the time Holmes received a telegram from Scott Eccles, who wanted to consult him about a "grotesque experience", the detective was complaining of being bored "since we locked up Colonel Carruthers" and so was more than eager to take up any promising case. *Wisteria Lodge*

CARTER. Treasurer of the Vermissa Valley Lodge of The Ancient Order of Freemen. A capable organizer, his was the plotting brain which thought up the details of every outrage committed by the Scowrers. *The Valley of Fear*

*CARTWRIGHT. A member of the Worthingdon bank gang who was hanged on Blessington's evidence. *The Resident Patient.*

CARTWRIGHT. "A lad of fourteen, with a bright, keen face," he had shown some ability during the investigation of the case which had saved the good name, and perhaps the life, of Wilson the manager of the district messenger office where the boy worked. Holmes used the boy on occasions, to search for a newspaper from which a warning message to Sir Henry Baskerville had been clipped, to bring food and other supplies to the detective when he hid upon the moor and to keep track of Dr. Watson's activities at Baskerville Hall. *The Hound of the Baskervilles.*

*CASTALOTTE, TITO. An experienced and somewhat charitable Italian businessman, he was "saved...from some ruffians in a place called the Bowery" by Gennaro Lucca. Castalotte was a senior partner in the firm of Castalotte & Zamba, the chief fruit importers of New York. But he was the one who had the power within the firm and, as a reward, he made Lucca head of a department and acted kindly towards him in every way, treating him as the son he might have had if he'd ever married. So it's no surprise that Gennaro balked when the boss of a Neapolitan terrorist society, with an off-shoot in New York, ordered him to blow up Castalotte with dynamite because the fruit importer refused to give in to its violent threats. *The Red Circle*

*CAUNTER. The elder of the two boys occupying the bedroom adjacent to that of the young Lord Saltire. He was a light sleeper but heard no disturbance on the night that the son of the Duke of Holdernesse mysteriously disappeared. *The Priory School*

*CHANDOS, SIR CHARLES. Ames, the butler of Birlstone Manor, had been in service with this man for ten years before being employed by John Douglas. *The Valley of Fear*

*CHARPENTIER, ALICE. Her brother thrashed Enoch J. Drebber for making improper advances towards her. Inspector Tobias Gregson thought she was "an uncommonly fine girl." *A Study in Scarlet*

*CHARPENTIER, ARTHUR. A sub-lieutenant in the Royal Navy, his thrashing of Enoch Drebber unfortunately took place on the very night Drebber was found murdered so a suspicious Tobias Gregson took him into custody. *A Study in Scarlet*

*CHARPENTIER, MADAME. The late Enoch J. Drebber and his secretary, Joseph Stangerson, had stayed at Madame Charpentier's boarding-house, in Torquay Terrace, Camberwell. The name implies that her husband may have been French. *A Study in Scarlet*

*CHOWDER, LAL The faithful servant of Major John Sholto. When Major Morstan returned to England from India and called on Sholto to claim his share of the Agra treasure, it was this man (since dead) who admitted him to the house. *The Sign of Four*

CLAY, JOHN. Jabez Wilson engaged a young man, who called himself 'Vincent Spalding', as an assistant in his shop. In reality, he was the leader of a gang and devised an ingenious plan to decoy his master from the premises every day for a time so that an audacious robbery could be set up. Holmes said that Clay, a thief and a murderer who had been educated at Eton and Oxford and claimed to be the grandson of a Royal Duke, was the fourth smartest man in London. *The Red-Headed League*

CLAYTON, JOHN. A rough-looking cab driver who picked

up a fare in Trafalgar Square and was offered two guineas to go where he was told all day. *The Hound of the Baskervilles*

*COBB, JOHN. A groom at Charles McCarthy's Hatherley Farm. He went with McCarthy to Ross on the day McCarthy's son came back from Bristol. *The Boscombe Valley Mystery*

*COLONNA, PRINCE OF. The famous black pearl of the Borgias had been stolen from his bedroom at the Dacre Hotel. At first the Princess of Colonna's maid was suspected, but...*The Six Napoleons*

COOKE, POLICE CONSTABLE. He was on duty when he heard a splash and a cry for help from the direction of Waterloo Bridge. The night was so dark and stormy, however, that in spite of help from passers-by Cooke was unable to attempt a rescue. *The Five Orange Pips*

CORAM, PROFESSOR. An elderly man, he was the resident of Yoxley Old Place in Kent. A very heavy smoker, he consumed a thousand Alexandrian cigarettes per fortnight, and his addiction proved to be his downfall when Holmes spilled a box of them on the floor and then deduced from that where his wife was hidden. His name, however, was an *alias* and he was responsible for his wife's lover and many other 'revolutionaries' being put in prison. 'Mrs Coram' too had served a prison sentence. *The Golden Pince-nez*

*CORMAC, TIGER. "A thick-set, dark-faced, brutal-looking young man," it was this brutality which had earned him his nickname and he was one of a group of murderers called Scowrers. *The Valley of Fear*

CORNELIUS, MR. An *alias* used by Jonas Oldacre to swindle his creditors because things were going badly for him. He was also putting large sums of money into a bank in another town in this name. If his ruse involving the young McFarlane had been successful, Sherlock Holmes had no doubt Oldacre would have assumed this name permanently, moved to this town and vanished. *The Norwood Builder*

COVENTRY, SERGEANT. Of the local Hampshire police, he was examining the affair surrounding the death of Maria Pinto Gibson, wife of Neil Gibson the Gold King. *The Problem of Thor Bridge*

*COWPER. Jefferson Hope learned from this man, a Mormon who he had helped at different times, that Lucy Ferrier had been forced to marry Enoch Drebber. *A Study in Scarlet*

*CRABBE, OLD MAN. Two Scowrers, Lander and Egan, claimed the head-money for the shooting of this man at a place called Stylestown. *The Valley of Fear*

CROKER, JACK (CAPTAIN). A very tall young man, with blue eyes and a golden moustache, he was remarkably quick-witted, strong as a lion, and active as a squirrel. Formerly first officer of the *Rock of Gibraltar,* he fell in love with Mary Fraser as she travelled from Australia to England on board that ship. But Miss Fraser could only return his love with friendship. Later however, after her disastrous marriage, he visited her home and recued her from the ill-treatment of her husband. Unfortunately, the husband was killed in the struggle. But later Holmes and Watson acted as 'judge and jury' in the case, when they 'acquitted' the sailor of any crime. *The Abbey Grange*

*CROSBY. A banker, he met a "terrible death" in 1894. Watson connected this death with what he called "the repulsive story of the red leech." *The Golden Pince-nez*

*CROWDER, WILLIAM. A gamekeeper on John Turner's

Boscombe Valley estate, he saw Charles McCarthy, followed by his son, walking down to the Boscombe Pool. Later, Charles McCarthy was found murdered. *The Boscombe Valley Mystery*

CUBITT, HILTON. Of Ridling Thorpe Manor, Norfolk. He came to Holmes with a problem about some curiously drawn stick figures which were appearing inside and outside the house. His wife, who seemed to have some idea of their meaning, would say nothing. *The Dancing Men*

*CUBITT, MRS. HILTON. (Born Elsie Patrick). She made her husband promise not to inquire into her past life in America. *The Dancing Men*

CUMMINGS, MR. JOYCE. The barrister hired to defend Grace Dunbar, who had been accused of shooting her employer's wife. *The Problem of Thor Bridge*

CUNNINGHAM, ALEC. His smiling expression and showy dress were in strange contrast to the business which had brought Holmes and Watson to Reigate. He was the son of the Squire, with whom he concocted a note with each writing a word in turn, and nearly succeeded in finishing Holmes off. *The Reigate Squire*

CUNNINGHAM, MR. "An elderly man, with a strong deep-lined, heavy-eyed face." Father of the above. *The Reigate Squire*

*CUSACK, CATHERINE. The Countess of Morcar's maid when a fabulous jewel was stolen from the Countess's dressing room. *The Blue Carbuncle*

*CUSHING, MARY. Youngest sister of Susan Cushing, she married Jim Browner, and had been missing for some little time before her sister received an extremely gruesome and upsetting package in the post. *The Cardboard Box*

*CUSHING, SARAH. The younger sister of Susan

Cushing, she had lived for a time with her married sister in Liverpool, and later with her older sister in Croydon. After some sort of a row, Sarah moved out of Susan's house and went to live in New Street, Wallington. When Holmes called on her there, she could not see him because she was suffering from an attack of 'brain fever'. *The Cardboard Box*

CUSHING, SUSAN. An unmarried woman of fifty, she led a most retiring life in Cross Street, Croydon, knowing few people and receiving hardly any post. So it was a surprise to her to receive a parcel one day. Not, however, a very pleasant one since it contained two human ears. *The Cardboard Box*

D

*D'ALBERT, THE COUNTESS. Milverton, the master blackmailer, thought that one of the Countess's servants had come to sell him five compromising letters about her. But it was the Countess herself in disguise, and she had come to murder him. *Charles Augustus Milverton*

DAMERY, COLONEL SIR JAMES. He consulted Holmes about the notorious Baron Adelbert Gruner for a client who he refused to name. Damery, however, had "rather a reputation for arranging delicate matters which are to be kept out of the papers." When he drove away from Baker Street and Watson spotted a certain half-hidden coat-of-arms on the carriage door, both men then knew Holmes would be working for *The Illustrious Client*

*'DARBYSHIRE, WILLIAM'. An account for thirty-even pounds, fifteen shillings from Madame Lesurier's millinery shop in Bond Street was found on John Straker's dead body. Holmes said, "When I returned to London I called upon the milliner, who at once recognized Straker as an excellent customer, of the name Darbyshire." *Silver Blaze*

*DAVENPORT, J. He answered Mycroft Holmes' newspaper advertisement asking for information about the whereabouts of Sophy Kratides. *The Greek Interpreter*

*DAWSON. A book-keeper on Abel White's indigo plantation. Jonathan Small was an overseer there. Both Dawson and his wife were killed in the Indian Mutiny. *The Sign of Four*

DAWSON. A groom at the Capleton stables, on Dartmoor, where Desborough, the second favourite for the Wessex Cup, was trained. *Silver Blaze*

*DE MERVILLE, GENERAL. "Of Khyber fame". His daughter was literally enthralled by the notorious Baron Adelbert Gruner, and the General could do nothing about it. "De Merville is a broken man. The strong soldier has been utterly demoralized by this incident. He has lost the nerve which never failed him on the battlefield and has become a weak, doddering old man, utterly incapable of contending with a brilliant, forceful rascal like this Austrian." *The Illustrious Client*

DE MERVILLE, VIOLET. She was, according to Holmes, "young, rich, beautiful, accomplished, a wonder-woman in every way." He went on to enlarge on her attractions as follows. "She is beautiful, but with the ethereal other-world beauty of some fanatic whose thoughts are set on high. I have seen such faces in the pictures of the old masters of the Middle Ages." And now she was determined to marry the man suspected of murdering a former wife, the notorious Baron Adelbert Gruner. *The Illustrious Client*

*DENNIS, SALLY. Someone posing as a Mrs. Sawyer picked up the wedding ring that Holmes had advertised about by saying it had been found in the roadway between the White Hart Tavern and Holland Grove on the night that Enoch J. Drebber was murdered. 'Mrs. Sawyer' claimed that the ring belonged to her daughter, Sally, who had been married to Tom Dennis only a year before. *A Study in Scarlet*

DENNIS, TOM. Falsely said, since he didn't exist, to be a steward aboard a Union ship. *A Study in Scarlet*

*DESMOND, JAMES. The presumed heir to Sir Henry Baskerville, he was an elderly clergyman living in Westmorland. *The Hound of the Baskervilles*

DEVINE, MISS MARIE. The Lady Frances Carfax's maid. Watson chased her as far as Montpelier, hoping to find some trace of the woman's mistress. *The Disappearance of Lady Frances Carfax.*

DEVOY, NANCY. The daughter of a Colour-Sergeant in the Royal Mallows, she later married James Barclay of the same regiment. Although there was more love on her husband's side than on hers (according to a brother officer) they were happy for many years, until an old lover suddenly turned up. *The Crooked Man*

DIXIE, STEVE. Black fighter and member of the Spencer John gang, he burst into Holmes' rooms to bully him into staying out of the Harrow Weald case but was soon cowed. However, there are parts of the dialogue between him and the detective which point to an innate racism in Holmes. *The Three Gables*

*DIXON, JEREMY. A resident of Trinity College, Cambridge, he owned the 'canine detective' Pompey, a dog Sherlock Holmes considered to be an eminent specialist in the science of tracking. *The Missing Three-Quarter*

*DIXON, MRS. A housekeeper who had been engaged by Bob Carruthers to look after his house, Chiltern Grange. *The Solitary Cyclist*

*DOBNEY, SUSAN. This woman was Lady Frances Carfax's former governess. Lady Frances kept in touch with her, writing a letter every two weeks. After she hadn't heard from her former pupil for almost five weeks, Miss Dobney asked Sherlock Holmes to investigate where she might be. *The Disappearance of Lady Frances Carfax*

DODD, JAMES M. He had recently returned to England from South Africa, where he had served with the Imperial Yeomanry, Middlesex Corps. He wore a short beard, and worked as a stockbroker. While in the Army, Dodd had been Godfrey Emsworth's best friend, and was upset at not hearing from him for more than six months. *The Blanched Soldier*

***DOLORES**. A maid who had been with Mrs. Ferguson before her marriage to Bob Ferguson and was "a friend rather than a servant." Because she had known her longer, Dolores had a better understanding of her mistress's character than her husband did. *The Sussex Vampire*

***DOLSKY**. See Leturier. *A Study in Scarlet*

***DORAK**. This man kept a general store in London, and acted as an agent for Lowenstein of Prague, selling drugs to the clients Lowenstein had in England. *The Creeping Man*

***DORAN, ALOYSIUS, ESQ.** An astute businessman and San Francisco millionaire, he had made his fortune mining in the Rockies. He had one daughter, who suddenly disappeared from her own wedding breakfast. *The Noble Bachelor*

DORAN, MISS HATTY. Her new husband, Lord St. Simon, consulted Holmes after his bride disappeared at the Reception held after their marriage in St. George's, Hanover Square. *The Noble Bachelor*

***DORKING, COLONEL**. The victim of a rogue's blackmailing activities, he saw his wedding to the Honourable Miss Miles called off only two days before it was due to take place. *Charles Augustus Milverton*

DOUGLAS, JOHN ("JACK"). Aka 'McMurdo' and 'Edwards'. "Douglas was a remarkable man both in character and in person; in age he may have been about fifty, with a strong-jawed, rugged face, a grizzling moustache, peculiarly keen grey eyes, and a wiry, vigorous figure which had lost nothing of the strength and activity of youth." He was thought to have been murdered - a faceless body was presented as his - but in fact the killing didn't take place until much later. *The Valley of Fear*

DOUGLAS, MRS. IVY. She was an English woman who had met Mr. Douglas, an American widower twenty years her senior, in London. But the difference in age did not seem to mar their family life in any way. *The Valley of Fear*

*DOVERCOURT, EARL OF. He was engaged to marry Lady Eva Brackwell, But an arch-blackmailer felt quite certain he was the type of man who would call off the wedding if he knew about some lively letters Lady Eva had once written to another man. *Charles Augustus Milverton*.

*DOWNING, CONSTABLE. He belonged to the Surrey Police, and was badly bitten on the thumb in the struggle to capture a half-caste cook. *Wisteria Lodge*

*DOWSON, BARON. Holmes remarked to Count Negretto Sylvius that "Old Baron Dowson said the night before he was hanged that in my case what the law had gained the stage had lost." *The Mazarin Stone*

*DREBBER. One of the four principal Mormon Elders in Utah, father of Enoch Drebber. *A Study in Scarlet*

*DREBBER, ENOCH J. The body of a gentleman (later identified as the son of the above) well dressed, and having cards in his pocket bearing the name of Enoch J. Drebber, was found by a constable in a lonely house at 3 Lauriston Gardens. The one word, RACHE, was found scrawled in blood on the wall. In the days when he competed with Joseph Stangerson as to who should marry the captured Lucy Ferrier, Drebber was "a bull-necked youth with coarse, bloated features." His father had given his mills over to him, and eventually compelled Lucy to marry his son. The word on the wall made Inspector Lestrade suspect there was a woman involved but that the murderer hadn't had time to complete it. *A Study in Scarlet*

*DUBUQUE, MONSIEUR. Watson retained an almost verbatim report of Holmes' interview with Monsieur Dubuque, of the Paris police, and Fritz von Waldbaum, the well-known specialist of Danzig, in the affair of The Second Stain. *The Naval Treaty*

DUNBAR, GRACE. Governess to Neil and Maria Gibson's two children, Gibson pressed his attentions on her and was rebuffed. However, she stayed on because she felt she could influence the man's mind when it came to using his fortune for good and so remained in his service. But when Gibson's wife was discovered shot dead and the murder weapon found on the floor of Grace Dunbar's wardrobe, suspicion naturally fell very heavily on her. *The Problem of Thor Bridge*

*DURONDO, VICTOR. The San Pedro Minister in London, he met and married his wife there. She said. "A nobler man never lived upon earth". Unfortunately, the Dictator Murillo (See Miss Burnett) heard of his excellence, recalled him on some excuse and had him shot. Having some idea of what might happen to him once he returned to his native country, Durando refused to let his wife come with him and she was left in England "with a pittance and a broken heart."

DURONDO, SIGNORA VICTOR. See Miss Burnett. *Wisteria Lodge*

E

ECCLES, JOHN SCOTT. Tall, stout, grey-whiskered, heavy featured, pompous in manner and "conventional to the last degree", this wonder of outraged respectability consulted Holmes about a "most incredible and grotesque experience." *Wisteria Lodge*

EDMUNDS, MR. Of the Berkshire Constabulary, he was a thin, yellow-haired young man. Sometime after he concluded his investigation into the Abbas Parva tragedy, he was sent to Allahabad. See the entry in Part Two for more about this city. *The Veiled Lodger*

EDWARDS, BIRDY. Pinkerton's 'best man', he was instrumental in breaking up the Scowrers, having joined them by pretending to be one of them from another Lodge. *The Valley of Fear*

EGAN. See Crabbe.

*****ELISE**. A woman living in Colonel Lysander Stark's house who warned Victor Hatherley to run away from the strange job he was offered there. Later she was probably instrumental in saving his life. *The Engineer's Thumb*

ELMAN, J. C., M.A. Of Little Purlington, Essex, Vicar of Mossmoor cum Little Purlington. The scheming villain, Josiah Amberley, received a telegram supposedly sent by this man. It read. 'Come at once without fail. Can give you information as to your recent loss.' After Amberley (very reluctantly) and Dr. Watson had hastened to Little Purlington to see him, Elman denied ever sending such a message. The implication, of course, is that it was one of Sherlock's ruses. *The Retired Colourman*

*****ELRIDGE**. He owned the isolated farmhouse in Norfolk where Abe Slaney stayed while getting in touch with Elsie Patrick. *The Dancing Men*

THE ANCIENT ORDER OF FREEMEN. See the

Scowrers.

EMSWORTH, COLONEL. A "huge, bow-backed man with a smoky skin and a straggling grey beard," he had won the Victoria Cross in the Crimean War. His hot temper cowed nearly everyone, but Holmes was able to force the old soldier's hand by scrawling a single word on a loose sheet of paper. *The Blanched Soldier*

EMSWORTH, GODFREY. The only son of the Colonel, Godfrey was a fighter and had volunteered for service in the Boer War, when he was hit by a bullet from an elephant gun in the action near Diamond Hill outside Pretoria. *The Blanched Soldier*

*EMSWORTH, MRS. COLONEL. She was "A gentle little white mouse of a woman," in complete contrast to her fiery husband, and responded eagerly to James Dodd's description of her son's bravery in the Boer War. *The Blanched Soldier*

*ERNEST, DR. RAY. Chess-playing neighbour of Josiah Amberley, falsely accused by him to Holmes of running away with his wife and fortune. Ernest's family hired the detective, Barker, to seek out the truth of the matter. A truth which was most distressing. *The Retired Colourman*

ESCOTT. One of Holmes' disguises, that of a swaggering plumber. 'Escott' became engaged to Milverton's housemaid, Agatha, so that he could find out information about her employer. *Charles Augustus Milverton*

*ETHEREGE, MRS. She advised Mary Sutherland to consult Sherlock Holmes in the matter of the disappearance of her fiancé. Her own husband had once been found very easily by the detective when everyone else had given him up for dead. *A Case of Identity*

*EVANS. Convicted of forgery, he was sentenced to be sent to the colonies in 1855. He took part in an uprising on board ship, made his own way to Australia, prospered there and eventually returned to England a wealthy man under an assumed name. See Beddoes. *The "Gloria Scott"*

*EVANS. A police officer who was shot because he had been brave enough to arrest two members of The Ancient Order of Freemen. *The Valley of Fear*

EVANS, CARRIE. Also known as **Carrie Norlett**, she was the personal maid of Lady Beatrice Falder. *Shoscombe Old Place*

EVANS, "KILLER". Aka 'Morecroft' and 'Winter'. His dossier at Scotland Yard showed the following about this dangerous man. "Aged forty-four. Native of Chicago. Known to have shot three men in the States. Escaped from penitentiary through political influence. Came to London in 1893. Shot a man over cards in a night club in the Waterloo Road in January, 1895. Man died, but he was shown to have been the aggressor in the row. Dead man was identified as Rodger Prescott, famous as forger and coiner in Chicago. Killer Evans released in 1901. Has been under police supervision since, but so far as known has led an honest life." That is, up until the time of *The Three Garridebs* when he called himself John Garrideb.

F

*FAIRBAIRN, ALEC. "He was a man with winning ways, and he made friends wherever he went. He was a dashing, swaggering chap, smart and curled, who had seen half the world and could talk of what he had seen." But he paid the highest price possible for falling in love with Mary Browner. *The Cardboard Box*

*FALDER, LADY BEATRICE. The sister of Sir Robert Norberton, with whom she lived on her deceased husband's estate. She was especially fond of the famous Shoscombe spaniels and also took an interest in Sir Robert's Shoscombe

Park Stables. Sir Robert's strange and seemingly cruel attitude toward her aroused the suspicion of John Mason, who came to Holmes with the problem. *Shoscombe Old Place*

*FALDER, SIR DENIS (18TH CENTURY). Buried in the crypt of the ruined chapel in the grounds of Shoscombe Park. *Shoscombe Old Place*

*FALDER, SIR JAMES. Of Shoscombe Old Place. He left his estate to his widow, Lady Beatrice, for her lifetime. After she died it was to revert to Sir James' brother. *Shoscombe Old Place*

*FALDER, SIR WILLIAM. Buried in the crypt of the ruined chapel in Shoscombe Park. *Shoscombe Old Place*

*FARINTOSH, MRS. She went to Holmes about the theft of an opal tiara, and later recommended him to Helen Stoner who wanted to discover the facts behind the tragic death of her sister. *The Speckled Band*

*FARQUHAR, MR. Watson bought his medical practice in the Paddington district from old Mr. Farquhar, who had had an excellent number of patients at one time. but age, and the St. Vitus dance from which he suffered, had caused their number to drop. *The Stockbroker's Clerk.*

*FERGUSON. The retired sea captain who owned The Three Gables before the Maberleys bought it. When Isadora Klein was so anxious to buy it *and all its contents* from a somewhat unwilling Mrs. Maberley, Holmes speculated that Ferguson might have buried his treasure there. *The Three Gables,*

FERGUSON, JACK. Elder son of Robert Ferguson, by his first marriage. He was "a remarkable lad, pale-eyed and fair-haired, with excitable blue eyes which blazed into a sudden flame of emotion and joy [whenever] they rested upon his father." An unfortunate fall as a child, and a twisted spine, meant that the fifteen-year-old's mobility was affected, but he was "very developed in mind." Given his physical problems, however, to say nothing of his psychological ones, for Holmes to suggest a year at sea for him seems somewhat fatuous. *The Sussex Vampire*

FERGUSON, MR. A partner of Colonel Lysander Stark, he was also known as Becher, which see. *The Engineer's Thumb*

*****FERGUSON, MR.** Neil Gibson's Secretary. *The Problem of Thor Bridge*

FERGUSON, ROBERT. In his youth, Big Bob Ferguson had been the finest three-quarter Richmond ever had. In later years, however, the "great frame had fallen in, his hair was scanty, and his shoulders were bowed." It was Ferguson's opinion that he was prematurely aged by the bizarre events which had taken place in his household. His second wife had twice assaulted Ferguson's son by his first marriage, and had twice been caught behaving like some sort of monster, sucking at a small wound in the neck of her own child. *The Sussex Vampire*

*****FERRIER, DR.** He lived near the unfortunate Percy Phelps in Woking, and took charge of him when Phelps returned home after the mysterious disappearance of a top.secret naval treaty from his office. The Doctor's services were very necessary because at the time Phelps, by his own admission, was "practically a raving maniac." *The Naval Treaty*

*****FERRIER, JOHN.** "His face was lean and haggard, and the brown parchment-like skin was drawn tightly over the projecting bones; his long, brown hair and beard were all flecked and dashed with white; his eyes were sunken in his head, and burned with an unnatural lustre; while the hand which grasped his rifle was hardly more fleshy than that of a skeleton." But, after this man and his daughter were rescued from the Great Alkali Plain by the Mormon band, he prospered in Utah. *A Study in Scarlet*

*FERRIER, LUCY. John Ferrier's adopted daughter. When she was rescued by the Mormons from the Great Alkali Plain, she was "a little child, with her round, white arms encircling [Ferrier's] brown, sinewy neck, and her golden-haired head resting upon the breast of his velveteen tunic." As the years went by she grew more beautiful each day, and was known as 'The Flower of Utah'. Lucy fell in love with Jefferson Hope, but was wanted in marriage by both Drebber and Stangerson. *A Study in Scarlet*.

*FISHER, PENROSE. "One of the best doctors in London" according to Watson, who wanted to consult him about Holmes' strange illness. *The Dying Detective*

*FOLLIOTT, SIR GEORGE. His large house, Oxshott Towers, was near the one rented from ***Marx & Co** by Aloysius Garcia. Others belonged to ***Lord Harringby**, ***Mr. Hynes Hynes**, ***James Baker Williams**, ***Mr. Henderson** and the ***Rev. Joshua Stone.** Of these, the most significant name is that of Mr. Henderson because, among other reasons, his house was within walking distance of *Wisteria Lodge*

FORBES, MR. The detective in charge of the investigation into the disappearance of the top-secret naval treaty from Percy Phelps' office. He began by being hostile towards Holmes, but later welcomed his advice. *The Naval Treaty*

*FORDHAM. A Horsham lawyer, he prepared the will which left Elias Openshaw's estate ("with all its advantages and all its disadvantages") to his brother, Joseph. *The Five Orange Pips*

*FORDHAM, DR. Victor Trevor's father ('Old

Trevor') employed this man as his physician. *The "Gloria Scott"*

FORRESTER, INSPECTOR. When Mr. Acton's house was burgled, it was this man who carried out the investigation into who was responsible. He also investigated another more serious crime, the murder of William Kirwan who was employed as a coachman by *The Reigate Squire*

FORRESTER, MRS. CECIL. Mary Morstan, who later married Dr. Watson, was employed by her as a governess, and she suggested seeking Holmes' help when Mary began receiving mysterious messages and highly valuable pearls from an unknown correspondent. *The Sign of Four*

*FOURNAYE, HENRI. A certain international spy "lived a double life" and posed as an unmarried man when in London. He was really **Eduardo Lucas**. In Paris, however, he was 'Henri Fournaye'. He met an untimely death at the time Holmes was involved in the investigation into *The Second Stain*

*FOURNAYE, MME. HENRI. The woman to whom Eduardo Lucas was secretly married in Paris. She was "of Creole origin, of an extremely excitable nature, and suffered...from attacks of jealousy which amounted to frenzy." One such attack caused her to follow her husband to London, with fatal results for that gentleman. *The Second Stain*

*FOWLER, MR. Alice Rucastle met Mr. Fowler at a house she was visiting and fell in love with him. When she mysteriously disappeared, he proved a faithful friend. *The Copper Beeches*

FRANKLAND, MR. Of Lafter Hall, Devonshire. "He is an elderly man, red-faced, white-haired, and choleric. His passion is for British law, and he has spent a large fortune in litigation." He also kept close tabs on any activity on the moor, using a high-powered telescope, and was the father of Laura Lyons, of Coombe Tracey. *The Hound of the Baskervilles*

*FRASER. He became friendly with Rodger Baskerville (a man of many *aliases*) on board ship during a voyage from Central America to England, and joined with him in establishing a school in East Yorkshire. But later he died of consumption. *The Hound of the Baskervilles*

FRASER, ANNIE. She posed as the bogus Dr. Shlessinger's wife, and was his 'companion in crime'. "A tall, pale woman, with ferret eyes." *The Disappearance of Lady Frances Carfax*

FRASER MARY. The maiden name of Lady Brackenstall. She found English life irksome because of its propriety and primness. *The Abbey Grange*

*FREEBODY, MAJOR. On the day of his death Joseph Openshaw had left home to visit an old friend, Major Freebody, a man who had been in command of one of the forts on Portsdown Hill. Is this Ports Down, the site of Nelson's Monument, four miles from Fareham, an area of many chalk-pits? Rather significant, in the light of what happened to Openshaw. *The Five Orange Pips*

G

*GARCIA, ALOYSIUS. He lived near Esher, in Surrey. Scott Eccles said of him, when speaking to Holmes, that he was of "Spanish descent and connected in some way with the Embassy. He spoke perfect English, was pleasing in his manner, and as good-looking a man as ever I saw in my life." After inviting Eccles to visit him, both Garcia (and his servants) had mysteriously disappeared by the time his guest woke up in the morning. *Wisteria Lodge*

GARCIA, BERYL. She was one of the beauties of Costa Rica and married Rodger Baskerville, *alias* Vandeleur. *The*

Hound of the Baskervilles

*GARRIDEB, ALEXANDER HAMILTON. According to 'John Garrideb,' this wealthy landowner had left a most unusual will, in which his estimated fortune of fifteen million dollars could be dispersed only when three other persons named Garrideb were found to inherit his estate. *The Three Garridebs*

*GARRIDEB, HOWARD. This man was supposedly the third person of that unusual surname needed to fulfil the terms of the will left by Alexander Hamilton Garrideb. John (see below) was first; Nathan, a reclusive London collector, was second; and Howard, reputedly a "constructor of agricultural machinery" from a place near Birmingham, appeared to be the third. *The Three Garridebs*

GARRIDEB, JOHN. This man said he was a 'Counsellor at Law' from Moorville, Kansas when he called on Nathan Garrideb with what seemed like an attractive piece of news. But, although Holmes quickly detected that he wasn't all he claimed to be, he couldn't work out what his game was at first. *The Three Garridebs*

GARRIDEB, NATHAN. A recluse with an extremely unusual name, he was "a very tall, loose-jointed, round-backed person, gaunt and bald, some sixty.odd years of age— The general effect, however, was amiable, though eccentric." He was interested in a wide variety of topics, about which he was also very knowledgeable, and he maintained extensive collections of the objects relating to such interests. A man calling himself John Garrideb told him that, if they could locate a third man with the same surname, they stood to inherit five million dollars each from the estate of Alexander Hamilton Garrideb. *The Three Garridebs*

GIBSON, J. NEIL. The American Senator and Gold King.

He had bought a considerable estate in Hampshire, and lived there with his family and servants. When his wife was found shot dead on Thor Bridge, suspicion fell upon his children's governess, and Gibson (who had earlier made advances to her which were rejected) came to Holmes asking him to find out if she really was guilty of murder. The detective said of him, "This man is the greatest financial power in the world, and a man, as I understand, of most violent and formidable character." *The Problem of Thor Bridge*

GIBSON J. NEIL, MRS. See Pinto, Maria. *The Problem of Thor Bridge*

GILCHRIST, MR. A scholar at the College of St. Luke's, in one of England's great university towns, he was a candidate for the Fortescue Scholarship and said to be "a fine scholar and athlete; plays in the Rugby team and the cricket team for the college, and got his Blue for the hurdles and the long jump. He is a fine, manly fellow…very poor, but he is hard-working and industrious." *The Three Students*

*GILCHRIST, SIR JABEZ. "The notorious Sir Jabez Gilchrist, who ruined himself on the Turf," was the father of Mr. Gilchrist, the student who was expected to do well at the College of St. Luke's mentioned above. *The Three Students*

GORGIANO, GIUSEPPE. Known variously as 'Gorgiano of the Red Circle,' 'Black Gorgiano' and—more simply but ominously—'Death' he "was red to the elbow in murder" in the south of Italy, and was "at the bottom of fifty murders" in America. Born in Posilippo, near Naples, as were the Luccas, he was "a huge man... [and] everything about him was grotesque, gigantic, and terrifying." As such, he was an ideal agent for the Red Circle, a Neapolitan terrorist society. Fleeing to New York to avoid the Italian police, he started a branch of the society in his new surroundings. *The Red Circle*

*GOROT, CHARLES. A clerk in the Foreign Office, he was alone in Percy Phelps' office at the very time a top.secret naval treaty disappeared. Phelps, however, said to Holmes, "His people are of Huguenot extraction, but as English in sympathy and tradition as you and I are. Nothing was found to implicate him in any way...and there the matter dropped." *The Naval Treaty*

*GOWER. A Scowrer, he took part in an attack on the newspaper editor James Stanger. *The Valley of Fear*

*GRAFENSTEIN, COUNT VON UND ZU. Holmes saved this man, who was the uncle of the German spy Von Bork, from being murdered by the Nihilist Klopman. *His Last Bow*

*GREEN, ADMIRAL. He had commanded the Sea of Azov fleet in the Crimean War and his son, who had been "a wild youngster," went to South Africa, where he made his fortune. *The Disappearance of Lady Frances Carfax*

GREEN, THE HON. PHILIP. Son of the above, Jules Vibart described him as "Un sauvage . un veritable sauvage," and the landlord of the Englischer Hof in Baden called him "a bulky, bearded, sunburned fellow, who looks as if he would be more at home in a farmers' inn than in a fashionable hotel. A hard, fierce man, I should think, and one whom I should be sorry to offend." He had been following the Lady Frances Carfax, who had suddenly vanished and with whom he had been (and indeed still was) in love. *The Disappearance of Lady Frances Carfax*

GREGORY, INSPECTOR. He invited Holmes to look into the disappearance of a horse, and also the mysterious death of the animal's trainer. Holmes told Watson that Gregory was an extremely competent officer but   lacking in imagination. *Silver Blaze*

GREGSON, INSPECTOR TOBIAS. He sought Holmes' help in the case of Enoch J. Drebber, and the detective thought of him as "the smartest of The Yarders; he and Lestrade are the pick of a bad lot. They are both quick and energetic, but conventional—shockingly so. They have their knives into one another, too. They are as jealous as a pair of professional beauties." *A Study in Scarlet*. See also *The Greek Interpreter, Wisteria Lodge* and *The Red Circle*

*GREYMINSTER, DUKE OF. He was, as Holmes said, deeply involved in the case of the 'Abbey School' – perhaps The Priory School? *The Blanched Soldier*

*GRICE PATERSONS, THE. "The year '87 furnished us with a long series of cases of greater or less interest, of which I retain the records," said Watson. One of the investigations which took place during this twelve-month period concerned the "singular adventures of the Grice Patersons in the island of Uffa." But, unfortunately for the curious, the Doctor didn't find time to tell us more. *The Five Orange Pips*

*GRIGGS, JIMMY. He was a clown employed by Ronder's wild beast show. However, because the outfit was declining due to Ronder's behaviour, he "had not much to be funny about, but he did what he could to hold things together." Indeed, the little man possessed such a large spirit that, when Mrs. Ronder was attacked by a dangerous lion, he helped to drive the creature off. *The Veiled Lodger*

GRUNER, BARON ADELBERT. Sir James Damery said of this person that "There is no more dangerous man in Europe." He was known as the "Austrian murderer," having apparently engineered the death of his wife in the Splugen Pass. Now, he planned to marry the infatuated ("enthralled") Violet de Merville.

"The fellow is, as you may have heard, extraordinarily handsome, with a most fascinating manner, a gentle voice, and that air of romance and mystery which means so much to a woman." Damery didn't seem to have come to Holmes on behalf of the woman's father, or any other member of her family, but for someone who Watson called *The Illustrious Client*

H

HAINES-JOHNSON. A crooked auctioneer who offered a very good price to Mrs. Maberley for her house and its contents on behalf of Isadora Klein, who wished to recover a manuscript which would ruin her chances of re-marriage if it fell into the wrong hands. *The Three Gables*

*HALES, WILLIAM. Of Stake Royal, he was one of the most popular and best-known mine-owners in the Gilmerton district. He had been marked for death by the Scowrers, and it was Ted Baldwin who undertook to murder him. *The Valley of Fear*

*HARDEN, JOHN VINCENT. A tobacco millionaire, he had been subjected to a peculiar persecution which Sherlock Holmes saw as "a very abstruse and complicated problem." The detective was so engrossed in the research connected with the Harden case that he had to postpone any personal involvement in Violet Smith's case. *The Solitary Cyclist*

HARDING, MR. Founder and manager of Harding Brothers emporium, Kensington. His firm had sold plaster casts of Devine's head of Napoleon to Horace Harker, Josiah Brown, and Mr. Sandeford. *The Six Napoleons*

*HARDY, MR. A foreman who carried on the Sutherland plumbing business with Sutherland's widow until her remarriage to James Windibank. He was the man who escorted Mrs. Sutherland and her daughter, Mary, to the gas-fitters' ball, where Mary met and fell in love with 'Hosmer Angel'. *A Case of Identity.*

*HARDY, SIR CHARLES. The Right Honourable Trelawney Hope had a valuable State document taken from among the papers he kept in a locked dispatch.box in his bedroom. Another of those papers was a "report from Sir Charles Hardy." *The Second Stain.*

*HARDY, SIR JOHN. In the afternoon of March 30th 1894, he had, along with two other gamblers, played whist with Ronald Adair who was murdered later that same day. *The Empty House*

HARGRAVE. See Baldwin, Ted.

*HARGREAVE, WILSON. Holmes' friend of the New York Police Bureau, "who has more than once made use of my knowledge of London crime" and gave Holmes important information by cable in the affair of *The Dancing Men*

HARKER, MR. HORACE. A newspaper correspondent, he was upset because he was so flustered by a particularly horrible event that he could not cover his own story. *The Six Napoleons*

*HAROLD, MRS. Holmes had all the facts, in a squat notebook, concerning the death of old Mrs. Harold, who had left the crooked Count Negretto Sylvius her estate. *The Mazarin Stone*

*HARRAWAY. Secretary of the Vermissa Valley branch of the Scowrers, he was "a lean, bitter man, with a long scraggy neck and nervous jerky limbs — a man of incorruptible fidelity where the finances of the Order were concerned, and with no notion of justice or honesty to anyone beyond." *The Valley of Fear*

HARRIS, MR. Sherlock Holmes posed as an accountant, Mr. Harris, of Bermondsey, in his interview with Hall Pycroft's employer, Mr. Harry Pinner, of the Franco-Midland Hardware Company. As the detective had suspected, and later discovered, there was no Company and no employment. Pycroft was simply being kept out of the way to facilitate a fraud. *The Stockbroker's Clerk*

HARRISON, ANNIE. The bride-to-be of the unfortunate Percy Phelps. She nursed the young Phelps back to health from a bout of brain fever, after he had suffered a dreadful blow to his career when an important document disappeared one night from the Foreign Office. Joseph Harrison, the culprit, was her villainous brother. *The Naval Treaty*

HARVEY. A young stable boy at Shoscombe Park, he was in charge of the central heating furnace which was in the cellar below Lady Beatrice Falder's bedroom. One morning, while raking out the cinders, he found a charred bone which he showed to Sir Robert Norberton's trainer. This man took the bone to Baker Street where Watson identified it as "the upper condyle of a human femur." *Shoscombe Old Place.*

HATHERLEY, VICTOR. He was an hydraulic engineer, of 16A Victoria Street. He came to Watson's surgery near Paddington Station suffering from a brutally severed thumb. The tale he told was so strange, Watson took him immediately to Baker Street. *The Engineer's Thumb*

HAYES, REUBEN. Owner of the Fighting Cock Inn, in Hallamshire. He had been the head coachman at Holdernesse Hall, but the Duke of Holdernesse had sacked him, according to Hayes, "without a character on the word of a lying corn-chandler." *The Priory School*

HAYES, MRS. REUBEN. A kindly woman, but entirely under the thumb of her brutal husband. *The Priory School*

*HAYLING, MR. JEREMIAH. This advertisement appeared in the papers about a year before Victor Hatherley's employment to fix Colonel Lysander Stark's hydraulic press. 'Lost on the 9th inst., Mr. Jeremiah Hayling, aged 26, a hydraulic engineer. Left his lodgings at ten o'clock at night, and has not been heard of since.' This implies that the hydraulic press needed fixing more than once or that the unfortunate Hayling was unable to fix it, and in any case wasn't allowed to leave the premises alive. *The Engineer's Thumb*

HAYTER, COLONEL. He had been looked after by Dr. Watson

in Afghanistan and had a house near Reigate. Holmes and Watson were his guests there when investigating a particular incident. Watson said of their host, "Hayter was a fine old soldier, who had seen much of the world, and he soon found, as I had expected, that Holmes and he had plenty in common." *The Reigate Squire*

*HAYWARD. A member of the Worthingdon bank gang. They pulled a job in 1875, but were caught, and Hayward was sentenced to fifteen years. The gang swore, and eventually took, revenge on their former partner, Sutton, who had testified against them. *The Resident Patient*

*HEBRON, LUCY. The daughter of Effie Hebron Munro who, first married to the black Mr. John Hebron, an Atlanta lawyer with a good practice who had died of yellow fever, claimed that the only child of the marriage had also died of yellow fever in Atlanta. But the little girl was alive and well and being kept in America. When she came to England, her existence was still kept secret from her mother's second husband, Grant Munro. *The Yellow Face*

*HEBRON, MR. JOHN, and HEBRON, MRS. EFFIE. See above.

HEIDEGGER, MR. The German master at a school in Hallamshire, he mysteriously disappeared on the same night Lord Saltire (legitimate heir to the Duke of Holdernesse) vanished. He had been at the school for two years and "came with the best references; but he was a silent, morose man, not very popular either with masters or boys." Heidegger was found later, brutally murdered. *The Priory School*

*HEINRICH. He was the German spy Von Bork's cousin, and an Imperial Envoy. *His Last Bow*

*HENDERSON, MR. Of High Gable, near Oxshott, in Surrey. Holmes was able to show that Henderson was involved in the death of Aloysius Garcia and the attempted abduction of Miss Burnett. *Wisteria Lodge*

*HIGGINS, TREASURER. He belonged to the Merton County Lodge of The Ancient Order of Freemen. *The Valley of Fear*

*HILL, INSPECTOR. He made it his business to know all the prominent criminals of Saffron Hill and the Italian quarter in London. *The Six Napoleons*

*HOBBS, MR. FAIRDALE. A lodger of Mrs. Warren's of Great Orme Street, he had brought a simple matter to Sherlock Holmes' attention in the year immediately prior to his landlady's own need of Sherlock's services. Although Holmes was at first reluctant to consider her problem, he was eventually won over when she told him that Hobbs never stopped talking of how the detective had "brought light into the darkness." *The Red Circle*

*HOBY, SIR EDWARD. Old Mr. Trevor helped him to break up a poaching gang, whose members then threatened to knife both of them, even going so far as to attack Sir Edward on one occasion. *The "Gloria Scott"*

HOLDER, ALEXANDER. A renowned City banker of Holder & Stevenson, he accepted a national treasure as security for a short-term loan, and then was thrown into fits when it was stolen. *The Beryl Coronet*

*HOLDER, ARTHUR. The dissipated son of Alexander Holder, Arthur was found by his father holding part of a precious tiara in his hands. Holder immediately suspected his son of trying to steal it and called the police, who arrested the young man. But Arthur remained strangely silent to avoid incriminating a certain person and was later shown to be innocent. *The Beryl Coronet*

*HOLDER, JOHN. Jonathan Small's company sergeant in the 3rd Buffs. He saved Small's life when he rescued him from the River Ganges after an attack from a crocodile, during which Small lost a leg. *The Sign of Four*

HOLDER, MARY. Niece of Alexander Holder. He took her into his family after the death of her father. But she later became involved with an aristocratic rogue and disappeared with him after the theft of a unique jewel. *The Beryl Coronet*

HOLDERNESSE, DUKE OF. His son, Lord Saltire, had disappeared from Dr. Thorneycroft Huxtable's Priory School. The Duke had offered a large reward for any information as to the whereabouts of his son, and an additional sum for the identity of the kidnappers. The Principal of the School, Dr. Huxtable, came to Holmes in a state of nervous exhaustion to ask his help; and it was Holmes who, somewhat uncharacteristically, ended up pocketing an enormous cheque at the end of the investigation. *The Priory School*. See also *Black Peter*

HOLDHURST, LORD. This great Conservative politician was the uncle of Percy Phelps and (through his influence and his nephew's skill) the young man obtained a good position at the Foreign Office. When a naval treaty of vital importance was lost from Phelps' office, Phelps wrote to his old school friend, Watson, for help, and Watson in turn involved Sherlock. Holmes. *The Naval Treaty*

*HOLLIS. One of the agents of the German spy, Von Bork. He was captured before the outbreak of the First World War. Von Bork showed little concern, and his comment was that the man was mad. *His Last Bow*

HOLMES, MYCROFT. Sherlock Holmes said of his brother, seven years older than himself, "If the art of the detective began and ended in reasoning from an arm-chair, my brother would be the greatest criminal agent that ever lived. But he has no ambition and no energy. He would not even go out of his way to verify his own solutions, and would rather be considered wrong than take the trouble to prove himself right. Again and again I have taken a problem to him and have received an explanation which has afterwards proved to be the correct one. And yet he was absolutely incapable of working out the practical points which must be gone into before a case could be laid before a judge or jury." *The Greek Interpreter*. See also *The Final Problem, The Empty House* and

The Bruce-Partington Plans

HOLMES, SHERLOCK. Holmes described his investigation into the death of Justice of the Peace Trevor as "the first in which I was ever engaged." And Victor Trevor (the son) was the only friend the future 'consulting detective' ever made during the two years he was at college. Never very sociable, and always rather fond of moping in his rooms working out his own methods of thought, Sherlock never mixed much with the men of his year. Apart from fencing and boxing, he had few athletic tastes, and his "line…of study was quite distinct from that of the other fellows, so that we had no points of contact at all." Holmes had become friends with the younger Trevor through an 'accident', when the latter's bull-terrier fastened onto his ankle one morning as he went down to the College chapel. *The "Gloria Scott"*. But since he occupies the whole canon it seems invidious to single out one 'Adventure' above another. Except, perhaps, the two tales he wrote up himself - *The Blanched Solider* and *The Lion's Mane*

"**HOLMES, SHERLOCK**". A man using this name hired a cab to shadow Sir Henry Baskerville and Dr. James Mortimer. *The Hound of the Baskervilles*

*HONES, JOHNNY. Another of the casualties of the expedition across the Great Alkali Plain. *A Study in Scarlet*

HOPE, LADY HILDA TRELAWNEY. Youngest daughter of the Duke of Belminster and wife of Britain's Secretary for European Affairs, she had come to Sherlock Holmes asking for details of the case which her husband had earlier presented to him. Holmes refused to satisfy her request, pleading "professional secrecy." At this, Lady Hilda abruptly departed, leaving Holmes to say, "Now, Watson, the fair sex is your department. What was the fair lady's game? What did she really want?" *The Second Stain*

HOPE, JEFFERSON, JUNIOR. A scout, a trapper, an explorer searching for silver and a rancher, Hope had done them all and had many exciting adventures. He became a favourite of John Ferrier and his adopted daughter, Lucy, and before he left for the Nevada Mountains (the site of his diggings) Lucy had promised to marry him. *A Study in Scarlet*

*HOPE, JEFFERSON, SENIOR. He and John Ferrier had been good friends in St. Louis. *A Study in Scarlet*

HOPE, THE RIGHT HONOURABLE TRELAWNEY. Secretary for European Affairs under Lord Bellinger. A very important State document had been stolen from his home. When Holmes managed to get it back, Hope thought him "a wizard, a sorcerer". *The Second Stain*

*HOPKINS, EZEKIAH. Of Lebanon, Pennsylvania, he was the supposed founder of a particular society. A red-head himself, and sympathetic to all men with hair of that colour, when he died it was found that he had left his enormous fortune in the hands of trustees, with instructions to use the interest to provide some kind of easy work for such fellows. *The Red-Headed League*

HOPKINS, INSPECTOR STANLEY, OF SCOTLAND YARD. "Our visitor was an exceedingly alert man, thirty years of age, dressed in a quiet tweed suit, but retaining the erect bearing of one who was accustomed to official uniform. I recognized him at once as Stanley Hopkins, a young police inspector for whose future Holmes had high hopes, while he in turn professed the admiration and respect of a pupil for the scientific methods of the famous amateur." This paragon of police activity had asked Holmes to help investigate the circumstances surrounding the death of Captain Peter Carey. *Black Peter*. See also *The Abbey Grange* and *The Golden Pince-nez*

*HORNER, JOHN. A plumber, aged 26, he was arrested in connection with the disappearance of the Countess of Morcar's famous jewel. *The Blue Carbuncle*

HORSOM, DR. Of 13, Firbank Villas, he had signed the death certificate of Rose Spender, a woman Henry Peters and Annie

Fraser had brought to their home for nefarious purposes from the Infirmary in Brixton Workhouse. *The Disappearance of Lady Frances Carfax*

*HOWELLS, RACHEL. She was second housemaid in the Musgrave household and had once been engaged to the butler, Brunton. He jilted her, for which she took a terrible revenge. *The Musgrave Ritual*

HUDSON. A young seaman on board a convict ship in 1855, he was the only survivor of an explosion which happened after it had been taken over by convicts. Some of them, however, had left in a rowboat just before the disastrous event, and they pulled Hudson (badly burned and completely exhausted) out of the water, where he had been marooned on a raft. It was this man who turned up many years later and proceeded to blackmail Old Trevor and his friend Beddoes. *The "Gloria Scott"*

HUDSON, MORSE. Owner of a shop in the Kennington Road which sold pictures and statues. When one of his plaster busts of Napoleon was smashed in the shop, Hudson put it down to hooliganism. *The Six Napoleons*

HUDSON, MRS. Patient, long-suffering and helpful landlady to Holmes and Watson in their rooms at 221B Baker Street, who paid her the rent. See *The Empty House*, *The Naval Treaty*, *The Dancing Men*, *Wisteria Lodge*, *The Dying Detective* etc.

*HUNT. A police officer who was shot because he dared to arrest two Scowrers. *The Valley of Fear*

*HUNTER, NED. A stable.lad on guard the night a race.horse disappeared. The theft was made easy because the boy had been drugged. *Silver Blaze*

HUNTER, VIOLET. Of Montague Place. She dressed in a very plain but neat way, and had a bright, quick face, freckled like a plover's egg. Her manner was that of a woman who had her own way to make in the world, and she came to Baker Street after she (a governess) had accepted a well-paid job with little to do but wear a particular dress and sit in a window reading a book. *The Copper Beeches*

*HURET. In 1894, Sherlock Holmes tracked and arrested Huret, the Boulevard assassin, for which he received an autographed letter of thanks from the French President and also the Legion of Honour. *The Golden Pince-nez*

HUXTABLE, DR. THORNEYCROFT. "We have had some dramatic entrances and exits upon our small stage at Baker Street, but I cannot recollect anything more sudden and startling than the first appearance of Dr. Thorneycroft Huxtable." Dr. Huxtable arrived at the Baker Street rooms in a state of nervous exhaustion over the disappearance of Lord Saltire, the Duke of Holdernesse's son, from *The Priory School*

I

*INDIAN PETE. One of the casualties of the expedition across the Great Alkali Plain. *A Study in Scarlet*

*IONIDES OF ALEXANDRIA. Not an Ancient Greek Philosopher but an Egyptian cigarette maker, he prepared Alexandrian cigarettes for Professor Coram, who smoked them at the rate of a thousand a fortnight. *The Golden Pince-nez.*

J

*JACKSON. Watson had no doubt that Jackson could take over his practice while he went with Holmes to Aldershot to investigate the circumstances surrounding the death of Colonel James Barclay. *The Crooked Man*

JACOBS. He was butler to the Right Honourable Trelawney Hope and his wife. *The Second Stain*

*JACOBSON. Mordecai Smith's steam launch, *Aurora,* had been removed to Jacobson's shipyard, on the Surrey side of the Thames, outwardly to receive minor repairs to her rudder. *The Sign of Four*

JAMES. Son of the postmaster in the hamlet of Grimpen, Devonshire. He delivered a telegram to Baskerville Hall to John Barrymore. *The Hound of the Baskervilles*

*JAMES, JACK. An American captured and sentenced to death for spying for the Germans before World War 1. Von Bork felt that "He was too self-willed for the job." *His Last Bow*

*JOHN. Irene Adler's coachman, he drove her to her wedding at the Church of St. Monica in the Edgware Road. Later he kept watch on Holmes who, disguised as an injured clergyman, gained access to Adler's sitting-room. *A Scandal in Bohemia*

*JOHN. The coachman who picked up Holmes and Watson near the Bar of Gold opium den. *The Man with the Twisted Lip*

*JOHN. "A pompous butler" employed by Dr. Leslie Armstrong, he saw Holmes and Watson to the door on his angry master's orders. *The Missing Three-Quarter*

*JOHNSON. One of the two "Oxford fliers" who, in the opinion of the worried Captain of the Cambridge rugby team (whose star player had disappeared), "could romp round" Moorhouse the slow first reserve in the Cambridge line.up. *The Missing Three-Quarter*

JOHNSON, "PORKY" SHINWELL. A valuable assistant to Sherlock in the early years of the twentieth century. He had first made his name as a very dangerous villain, and served two prison terms. Repenting of his misdeeds he allied himself to Holmes, acting as his agent in the huge criminal underworld of London, and obtaining information which often proved to be of great importance. Huge, coarse, red-faced and scorbutic, the only outward sign of his cunning mind was a pair of vivid black eyes. He had much to do with Kitty Winter, and was useful in helping Holmes counter the vile schemes of Baron Adelbert Gruner. *The Illustrious Client*

JOHNSON, SIDNEY. One of two men who had a key to the

safe from which certain Plans were stolen, this senior clerk and draughtsman was a man of forty who, though taciturn and moody, had by and large an excellent record in serving the public. *The Bruce-Partington Plans*

*JOHNSON, THEOPHILUS. A coal owner of Newcastle, very active and not much older than Holmes. He and his family were staying at the Northumberland Hotel at the same time as Sir Henry Baskerville. *The Hound of the Baskervilles*

*JOHNSTON. One of four principal Mormon Elders in Utah. *A Study in Scarlet*

JONES, ATHELNEY. Stout, red-faced, burly, and plethoric, with a pair of very small, twinkling eyes, Jones was in charge of the official investigation into the murder of Bartholomew Sholto. *The Sign of Four*

JONES, PETER. The official police agent in the mystery of *The Red-Headed League.* Holmes thought it was just as well to have Jones on this case. He wasn't a bad fellow, "though an absolute imbecile in his profession." The man's one positive virtue, however, was that he was as brave as a bulldog and as tenacious as a lobster.

*JOSÉ. Personal manservant of Mr. Henderson of High Gable, he delivered the note which led to the death of Aloysius Garcia. *Wisteria Lodge*

K

*KEMBALL. Like the father of the murdered man Drebber, he was one of the four principal Mormon Elders in the Church in Utah. *A Study in Scarlet*

*KEMP, WILSON. "A man of the foulest antecedents," he was Harold Latimer's partner in attempting to gain the property of Sophy and Paul Kratides. *The Greek Interpreter*

KENT, MR. A medical man who shared secluded lodgings with a patient whose health was a worry. *The Blanched Soldier*

*KESWICK. On inquiring for Mrs. Sawyer at 13, Duncan Street, Houndsditch, Holmes "found that the house belonged to a respectable paper-hanger, named Keswick, and that no one of the name of Sawyer. had ever been heard of there." *A Study in Scarlet*

*KHALIFA. After his supposed death at the Reichenbach Falls, Sherlock Holmes travelled for two years in Tibet. Leaving Tibet, he had a series of adventures, one of which involved "a short but interesting visit to the Khalifa at Khartoum." *The Empty House*

*KHAN, ABDULLAH. A tall and fierce-ooking Sikh trooper, he was one of the men bound by an important oath, along with *Mohamet Singh and *Dost Akbar. *The Sign of Four*

*KHIDMUTGAR. An Indian servant (male) who waits at table, mentioned by one of the Sholto brothers as a member of his household. *The Sign of Four*

KING, MRS. The cook at Ridling Thorpe Manor, Norfolk, where Mr. Hilton Cubitt was found shot through the heart and his wife with a bullet lodged in her brain. Mrs. King and the housemaid gave the alert after being woken up by what they thought were a series of explosions. *The Dancing Men*

*KIRWAN, WILLIAM. A coachman who had been in the service of the Cunninghams for many years on their estate near Reigate. He was killed in a false burglary, which Holmes investigated, and which gave rise to a conversation about powder-blackening. *The Reigate Squire*

*KLEIN. The wealthy German sugar king, he was the first husband of Isadora Klein. *The Three Gables*

KLEIN, ISADORA. Of Grosvenor Square. The celebrated beauty of her day and still very good-looking but nevertheless nearing the time when subdued lighting was the kindest. The richest woman in the world, an ex-lover had written a romantic novel about their affair, an account which threatened to prevent her marriage to the young Duke of Lomond. *The Three Gables*

*KLOPMAN. This Nihilist had threatened to kill Von Bork's uncle, but Holmes prevented the murder. See Grafenstein. *His Last Bow*

*KNOX, JACK. McMurdo suspected that Lawler and Andrews might be after Knox. They lodged with McMurdo and had been sent by the Scowrers' county delegate, Evans Pott, to murder this manager of the Crow Hill Mine. *The Valley of Fear*

*KRATIDES, PAUL. He came to England from Athens to rescue his sister Sophy from a potentially disastrous alliance. *The Greek Interpreter*

*KRATIDES, SOPHY. Like her brother, Paul, she belonged to a wealthy Grecian family, and had been on a visit to some friends in England. While there she met a young man (Harold Latimer) who acquired an ascendancy over her, and eventually persuaded her to fly with him. *The Greek Interpreter*

L

*LA ROTHIERE, LOUIS. Living at Campden Mansions, Notting Hill, he was one of the three foreign spies in England whom Mycroft Holmes thought capable of handling so big an affair as the theft of some vital submarine papers. *The Bruce-Partington Plans*. See also *The Second Stain*

LANCASTER, JAMES. Captain Basil (Sherlock Holmes in disguise) did not want him as a harpooner for his fictitious exploring expedition. He was part of the trap the detective was busy laying for the man he did want, Cairns. *Black Peter*

*LANDER. A Scowrer, both he and Egan claimed the head-money for shooting Old Man Crabbe at a place called Stylestown. *The Valley of Fear*

LANNER, INSPECTOR. He was in charge of the investigation into Mr. Blessington's death. He didn't agree at first with Holmes' statement that the death was not a suicide but murder. Later, however, he acknowledged that the facts presented by Sherlock were in favour of this hypothesis. *The Resident Patient*

*LARBEY. He was almost beaten to death by the Scowrers, and his wife was shot while nursing him. *The Valley of Fear*

*LASCAR. This unnamed man, who ran the Bar of Gold opium den, forcibly prevented Neville St. Clair's wife from entering the building after she had seen her husband's startled face at an upper window. *The Man with the Twisted Lip*

*LATIMER, HAROLD. This man, fashionably dressed, powerful and broad-shouldered, gained control over Sophy Kratides. When Sophy's brother came from Athens to rescue her from her involvement with him, Latimer and a rascally associate needed the services of Mr. Melas to act as an interpreter to trick the young man. It was Mr. Melas who relayed most of the information about the affair to Holmes in reported speech. *The Greek Interpreter*

*LAWLER. See Knox

*LE BRUN. Baron Adelbert Gruner warned Holmes that his fate might be the same as Le Brun's, a French agent who was beaten up by some Apaches in the Montmartre district and crippled for life after making inquiries into the Baron's affairs only a week before. *The Illustrious Client*

*LEE. He sold his Vermissa Valley mine to the 'State and Merton County Railroad Company'. *The Valley of Fear*.

*LEFEVRE. Holmes felt his discovery of the infallible test for blood stains would have been decisive in the cases of Muller and Lefevre of Montpellier, among others. *A Study in Scarlet*

*LE VILLARD, FRANCOIS. He had lately come rather to the fore in the French detective service, and had all the Celtic power of quick intuition. But he was deficient, according to Holmes, in the wide range of exact knowledge which was an essential ingredient for the higher development of a detective's art. Le Villard consulted Holmes in a case concerning a will, a case which the detective thought "possessed some features of interest," and he was also translating Holmes' works into French. *The Sign of Four*

*LEONARDO. He was 'The Strong Man' in Ronder's Circus and murdered Mrs. Ronder's bully of a husband. *The Veiled Lodger*

LESTRADE, INSPECTOR. He worked with Inspector Tobias Gregson on the murder of Enoch J. Drebber in an empty house off the Brixton Road. Gregson had called in Holmes to help him to unravel the mystery and the detective said, according to Watson, "Gregson is the smartest of the Scotland Yarders; he and Lestrade are the pick of a bad lot. They are both quick and energetic, but conventional — shockingly so. They have their knives into one another, too. They are as jealous as a pair of professional beauties." Later, Watson wrote that Lestrade was as "lean and ferret-like as ever." One of the mysterious visitors to Baker Street before the Doctor discovered his fellow-lodger's profession. *A Study in Scarlet*. See also *The Sign of Four, The Boscombe Valley Mystery, The Noble Bachelor, The Hound of the Baskervilles, The Empty House, The Norwood Builder, Charles Augustus Milverton, The Six Napoleons, The Second Stain, The Cardboard Box, The Bruce-Partington Plans, The Disappearance of Lady Frances Carfax* and *The Three Garridebs*

*LESURIER, MADAME. A milliner's account, made out by Madame Lesurier of Bond Street to William Darbyshire, was found in the pocket of a dead trainer named John Straker, whose body was found on the moor. *Silver Blaze*

*LETURIER. Holmes, in analyzing his successful investigation of the mysterious death of Enoch J. Drebber, said, "The forcible administration of poison is by no means a new thing in criminal annals. The cases of Dolsky in Odessa, and of Leturier in Montpellier, will occur at once to any toxicologist." *A Study in Scarlet*

*LEVERSTOKE, LORD. He had entrusted his son to Dr.

Thorneycroft Huxtable's care at the Priory School in Hallamshire. *The Priory School*

LEVERTON. A detective employed by Pinkerton's American Agency. In London, Leverton was disguised as a cabman on the greatest trail of his life when he was introduced to Sherlock Holmes by Gregson, the Scotland Yard detective. Like any other young detective, Leverton was greatly flattered when he received praise from Holmes – who said he was quite pleased to meet the hero of the 'Long Island Cave mystery'. *The Red Circle*

*LEWIS, SIR GEORGE. Sir James Damery had managed the delicate negotiations with Sir George Lewis over the Hammerford Will case. *The Illustrious Client*

LEXINGTON, MRS. Housekeeper to Jonas Oldacre. She said she had let John Hector McFarlane into the house; and then gone to bed, hearing nothing of what transpired between the two men. Holmes felt that she was concealing vital information, however, because of a certain sulky defiance in her eyes. This only went, in his opinion, with guilty knowledge. *The Norwood Builder*

*LINDER, MAX AND CO. They paid 500 dollars to the Scowrers to be left alone. *The Valley of Fear*

LOMAX. Sub-Librarian of the London Library in St. James's Square and a friend of Watson's, he supplied the book on "Chinese pottery" that the Doctor studied in his attempt to fool Baron Gruner. *The Illustrious Client*

*LOMOND, DUKE OF. Isadora Klein's prospective young bridegroom, provided she kept free of scandal before the marriage. *The Three Gables*

*LOWENSTEIN. Of Prague. A scientist striving to find the elixir of eternal youth. Which was why he attracted the attention of Professor Presbury. *The Creeping Man*

*LUCAS, EDUARDO. Watson says he was well-known in society circles on account of his charming personality, and that he was an unmarried man, thirty-four years of age. He was also an international spy responsible for engineering the theft of a valuable State document which was stolen from the bedroom of Britain's Secretary for European Affairs, the Right Honourable Trelawney Hope. Watson, however, was deceived about Lucas' bachelor status. See Fournaye. *The Second Stain*

LUCCA, GENNARO. In his youth, this man had joined a Neapolitan secret society dedicated to terrorism and then found it was impossible to escape from it, not even by moving to New York. The man who had initiated him into the society came to America to open a branch of it, and then tricked Lucca into either killing his benefactor or facing the vengeance of the organisation. This vengeance would extend to Lucca's wife, Emilia, who had fled with him after marrying against her father's wishes. *The Red Circle*

*****LYNCH, VICTOR**. Sherlock Holmes' "good old index" contained many records of old cases, mixed with the gathered information of a lifetime. The volume devoted to the letter V was especially interesting. Somewhat surprisingly, and one which ought to have been difficult to find, an item concerned a forger named Victor <u>Lynch</u>. *The Sussex Vampire*

*****LYONS**. An artist who married Laura Frankland, of Coombe Tracey in Devonshire, and then left her. *The Hound of the Baskervilles*

LYONS, LAURA. (See above). She had had a mysterious assignation with Sir Charles Baskerville on the night he died. Her father refused to have anything to do with her, because she had married without his consent, and maybe for one or two other reasons as well. So she had been forced to turn to paid typewriting. *The Hound of the Baskervilles*

M

*****MABERLEY, DOUGLAS**. Son of Mary and Mortimer Maberley. Holmes remembered him as a "magnificent creature." But Douglas's mother had seen him turn into a "moody, morose, brooding creature" in the time before he left for Rome as an Attaché . *The Three Gables.*

*MABERLEY, MORTIMER. He had once consulted Holmes in "some trifling matter," and his widow sought Holmes' help when she was in difficulty. *The Three Gables*

MABERLEY, MRS. MARY. "A most engaging elderly person, who bore every mark of refinement and culture," she contacted Holmes because of the strange events surrounding an attempt by someone to buy her house. *The Three Gables*

MACDONALD, INSPECTOR ALEC. Watson writes, "He was a young but trusted member of the detective force, who had distinguished himself in several cases which had been entrusted to him...He was a silent, precise man, with a dour nature and a hard Aberdonian accent. Twice already in his career had Holmes helped him to attain success, his own sole reward being the intellectual joy of the problem." 'Mr. Mac', as Holmes called him, assisted the detective in what looked at first like a grisly tragedy at Birlstone Manor. *The Valley of Fear*

*MACNAMARA, WIDOW. Mike Scanlan and Jack McMurdo boarded at her lodgings in Vermissa, after Jacob Shafter kicked McMurdo out of his boarding-house because of the latter's connection with the Scowrers. *The Valley of Fear*

MACPHAIL. Professor Presbury's coachman. The uproar caused by Presbury's faithful wolfhound's attack on his own master brought the sleepy and astonished man out of his room above the stables. *The Creeping Man*

*MCCARTHY, CHARLES. An acquaintance of John Turner in Australia, he once drove a waggon in the gold fields there. Having met up with Turner again in England, he began to live on one of his farms and was found brutally murdered, apparently by his own son. *The Boscombe Valley Mystery.*

*MCCARTHY, JAMES. Son of the above, he was seen looking for his father shortly before the latter's body was found.

Although there was strong evidence pointing to the young man's guilt, Holmes felt that he might be innocent and managed to clear him. *The Boscombe Valley Mystery*

*MCCAULEY. Elias Openshaw's notebook for March, 1869, contained the entries. "7th. Set the pips on McCauley, Paramore, and Swain of St. Augustine. 8th. McCauley cleared." It also contained a mysterious entry for 'Hudson'. *The Five Orange Pips*

MCFARLANE, JOHN HECTOR. "…a bachelor, a solicitor, a Freemason, and an asthmatic," he stormed into Baker Street, hoping Holmes could prove him innocent of murder. In the opinion of the police, McFarlane's tale was weak, for he claimed that Jonas Oldacre had decided to leave almost all his property to him on condition that McFarlane visit him to inspect a number of documents. This the younger man did; but he swore that, in spite of all the evidence against him, he had left his host healthy and whole, not as "charred remains." *The Norwood Builder*

MCFARLANE, MRS. Mother of the above. She had once been sought in marriage by Jonas Oldacre, whom she described as a 'cunning ape' . and rejected him for someone she said was a better, but poorer, man. *The Norwood Builder*

*MCGINTY, BOSS JOHN ("BLACK JACK"). He was "a black-maned giant, bearded to the cheekbones, and with a shock of raven hair which fell to his collar." Usually referred to at meetings as 'Eminent Bodymaster', he controlled Lodge 341 of The Ancient Order of Freemen in Vermissa Valley. As well as being the Leader of the Scowrers, he owned the Union House hotel and saloon in Vermissa. In addition to the secret powers which he was believed by everyone to exercise so ruthlessly, he was also an important public official, a municipal councillor, and a commissioner for roads, elected to the office by the votes of ruffians who, because of their support, expected to receive favours from him in return. *The Valley of Fear*

*MCGREGOR, MRS. Another of the casualties of the

expedition across the Great Alkali Plain. *A Study in Scarlet*

MCKINNON, INSPECTOR. A smart young police inspector who was in charge of the investigation into the disappearance of Josiah Amberley's wife and fortune. *The Retired Colourman*

*MCLAREN, MILES. A scholar at the College of St. Luke's. He was a candidate for the Fortescue Scholarship. Brilliant when he chose to work, but wayward, dissipated and (more suspicious of all perhaps in the light of what had recently taken place) unprincipled. *The Three Students*

MCMURDO. An ex-prize-fighter, employed as porter at Pondicherry Lodge, Upper Norwood. He recognized Sherlock Holmes as the amateur who had fought three rounds with him at Alison's rooms on the night of his (McMurdo's) benefit. He said to the detective, "If instead o' standin' there so quiet you had just stepped up and given me that cross-hit of yours under the jaw, I'd ha' known you without a question." *The Sign of Four*

MCMURDO, JACK. Aka Birdy Edwards. "Fresh-complexioned, middle-sized and young, he was not (one would guess) far from his thirtieth year. He had humorous grey eyes which twinkled as he looked through his spectacles at the people about him. Sociable, and with a seemingly simple disposition, he appeared anxious to be friendly to everybody. But those who studied him more closely might discern (from a certain firmness of jaw and grim tightness about the mouth) warnings of hidden depths." No wonder, for he wasn't the villain he seemed. *The Valley of Fear*

MCPHERSON. A "big constable," he had been in charge of guarding 16, Godolphin Street after the murder of international spy Eduardo Lucas. So it was understandable that he seemed "very hot and penitent" after Lestrade, acting on instructions from Sherlock Holmes, carpeted him for allowing an inquisitive female into the relevant room. McPherson was also amazed when Holmes was able to show him a picture of this 'unknown' woman. *The*

Second Stain

MCPHERSON, FITZROY. "Fitzroy McPherson was the science master, a fine upstanding young fellow whose life had been crippled by heart trouble following rheumatic fever." He was engaged to Maud Bellamy at the time of his brutal murder. She was certain that "no single person could ever have inflicted such an outrage upon him." *The Lion's Mane*

*****MANDERS**. A Scowrer, he was a reckless youngster who accompanied Jack McMurdo in a predictably unsuccessful attempt on the life of Chester Wilcox. *The Valley of Fear*

*****MANSEL**. Also a Scowrer, he took part in the assault on James Stanger, editor of the Vermissa *Herald*. *The Valley of Fear*

*****MANSON**. He sold his Vermissa Valley ironworks to the West Wilmerton General Mining Company. *The Valley of Fear*

MARKER, MRS. An elderly housekeeper, she was employed by Professor Coram of Yoxley Old Place. Of excellent character, she was understandably shaken when Holmes questioned her after the murder of Coram's secretary. *The Golden Pince-nez*

MARTHA. Housekeeper for the German spy, Von Bork, just before the outbreak of World War I. It was said she might almost personify Britannia [and was possibly Holmes' housekeeper in disguise, especially as he asked her to meet him outside Claridge's Hotel at the end of the case]. *His Last Bow*

MARTIN, INSPECTOR. Of the Norfolk Constabulary. He was investigating the tragic death of Hilton Cubitt of Ridling Thorpe Manor and welcomed Holmes' interest in the case. *The Dancing Men*

*****MARTIN, LIEUTENANT**. He remained loyal to his captain during a convict uprising at sea in 1855 and was killed trying to put down the rebellion. *The "Gloria Scott"*

*****MARVIN, CAPTAIN TEDDY**. Of the Coal and Iron Police, in the Vermissa Valley. He pretended to know Jack McMurdo from the latter's gangster days in Chicago, and was instrumental in getting rid of the Scowrers from the area. *The Valley of Fear*

*MARY. She prepared the fire in Elias Openshaw's room, in which he burned most of the evidence of his days in Florida. *The Five Orange Pips*

MARY. The "little maid-servant" to Mrs. Mary Maberley. Her screams scared away some robbers and brought the police to Mrs. Maberley's help. *The Three Gables*

*MARY JANE. The Watsons' incorrigible servant girl, who had scarred the Doctor's shoes when removing mud from the soles. *A Scandal in Bohemia*

*MASON. Holmes was jubilant over his discovery of an 'infallible test for blood stains.' He felt it would have been decisive in the case of Mason of Bradford. *A Study in Scarlet*

*MASON. A platelayer, he had discovered the dead body of Arthur Cadogan West lying just outside Aldgate Station on the District Railway at six o'clock on Tuesday morning. *The Bruce-Partington Plans*

MASON, JOHN. The head trainer at Sir Robert Norberton's Shoscombe Park Stables. He had come to Holmes because of the exceedingly strange behaviour of his master prior to the running of the Derby. *Shoscombe Old Place*

*MASON, MRS. "A tall, gaunt woman...who seemed to be a sour, silent kind of creature," she was engaged to look after Robert Ferguson's younger son, to whom she was devoted. Her love for the child brought her to tell Ferguson that his wife had been seen sucking a small wound in the boy's neck. She then began to guard the baby day and night. *The Sussex Vampire*

MASON, WHITE. The local officer in charge of the investigation carried out at Birlstone Manor. He called in Inspector Alec MacDonald, who then called in his friend Sherlock Holmes. Mason described the case as "a real downright snorter." And it was White Mason who spoke of them all finding a place eventually in Watson's 'book'. *The Valley of Fear*

*MATHEWS. Holmes felt that his index of biographies was especially useful for finding names beginning with the letter M. One of those was Mathews, who knocked out Sherlock's left canine in the waiting-room at Charing Cross Station. See also Merridew and Morgan. *The Empty House*

*MAUDSLEY. "I had a friend once called Maudsley, who went to the bad, and has just been serving his time in Pentonville. One day he had met me, and fell into talk about the ways of thieves and how they could get rid of what they stole. I knew that he would be true to me, for I knew one or two things about him, so I made up my mind to go right on to Kilburn, where he lived, and take him into my confidence." This was said by James Ryder when confessing his crime to Sherlock Holmes. There followed another example of the detective 'compounding a felony' by allowing the man to get away. *The Blue Carbuncle*

*MAUPERTUIS, BARON. Watson wrote, "The whole question of the Netherland-Sumatra Company and of the colossal schemes of Baron Maupertuis is too recent in the minds of the public, and too intimately concerned with politics and finance, to be a fitting subject for this series of sketches." *The Reigate Squire*

*MAYNOOTH, EARL OF. Governor of one of the Australian colonies. In the spring of 1894 his wife needed an operation for cataract and the Earl had sent her back to England, along with their son, Ronald, and daughter, Hilda. *The Empty House*

*MAYNOOTH, LADY. Wife of the above, when she came to London with her children they all three lived together at 427 Park Lane. Coming home one night with her daughter, after spending the evening with a relation, Lady Maynooth tried to enter her son's room to say good-night. She found the door locked on the inside. When it was forced open the unfortunate woman found the young man dead, "his head horribly mutilated from an expanded revolver bullet." *The Empty House*

*MEEK, SIR JASPER. According to Watson, he was another of the best medical practitioners in London and he intended to consult the man about Holmes' strange sickness. *The Dying Detective*

MELAS MR. Mycroft Holmes said, "Mr. Melas is a Greek by extraction...and he is a remarkable linguist. He earns his living partly as interpreter in the law courts, partly by acting as guide to any wealthy Orientals who may visit the Northumberland Avenue hotels." He also lived above Mycroft's rooms in Pall Mall, although later he quitted them for the country after his strange and, to him, very frightening adventure. *The Greek Interpreter*

*MELVILLE. A retired brewer who lived at Albemarle Mansions, Kensington. John Scott Eccles was a guest at his table when he met Aloysius Garcia. Garcia later visited Eccles at his own home and then, rather surprisingly considering the difference in age and temperament between the two men, invited him to *Wisteria Lodge*.

*MENZIES. See the Scowrers

*MERCER. Second mate, he was in league with Jack Prendergast in a convict rebellion aboard ship. *The "Gloria Scott"*

MERCER. A man who looked up routine business for Holmes and was a general factotum, he was said to have been employed by the Great Detective since Watson's time. A telegram from Mercer about Dorak helped Holmes clear up a case. *The Creeping Man*

MERIVALE. Of Scotland Yard. He asked Holmes to look into the St. Pancras murder case. Holmes, using his microscope, positively connected a suspect with a cap found at the scene of the crime. *Shoscombe Old Place*

*MERRIDEW. Holmes felt that his "index of biographies" was especially "illustrious" in the section devoted to those persons whose names began with the letter M. One such was "Merridew of abominable memory." *The Empty House*

MERRILOW, MRS. "An elderly, motherly woman of the buxom landlady type," she came to Sherlock Holmes on behalf of her "terribly mutilated" lodger, Mrs. Eugenia Ronder. The lodger's night-time cries had so alarmed Mrs. Merrilow that she suggested consulting either the clergy or the police. Then, when Mrs. Ronder rejected both of those options, Mrs. Merrilow suggested Holmes, and the lodger "fair jumped" at the idea. *The Veiled Lodger*

*****MERROW, LORD.** The Right Honourable Trelawney Hope had had a valuable State document taken from among the papers he kept in a locked dispatch.box in his bedroom, along with a letter from Lord Merrow. *The Second Stain*

MERRYWEATHER, MR. Chairman of directors of the City and Suburban Bank. He went with Holmes, Watson and a police inspector into a bank vault and saw them prevent a burglary. *The Red-Headed League*

MERTON SAM. A boxer, he was Count Negretto Sylvius' companion in the filching of a very valuable jewel. Holmes said, "Not a bad fellow, Sam, but the Count has used him. Sam's not a shark. He is a great big silly bull-headed gudgeon. But he is flopping about in my net all the same." However, even if he wasn't a bad fellow, it was Sam who suggested to the Count that they go into Holmes' bedroom and "do him in." *The Mazarin Stone*

*****MEYER, ADOLPHE.** He resided at 13, Great George Street, Westminster, and was one of the three foreign spies in England whom Mycroft Holmes thought capable of handling so big an affair as the theft of *The Bruce-Partington Plans*

*****MICHAEL.** Although a   stable-hand in the employment of Robert Ferguson, he slept in his master's house. *The Sussex Vampire*

MIDIANITES. See Dr. Shlessinger, aka 'Holy Peters'.

*****MILES, THE HONOURABLE MISS.** A victim of Charles

Augustus Milverton's machinations, she saw her wedding to Colonel Dorking called off only two days before it was due to take place. *Charles Augustus Milverton*

*MILLAR, FLORA. Once a dancer at the Allegro, she had been an intimate companion of Lord St. Simon, who eventually married Hatty Doran. Millar "endeavoured to force her way into the house after the bridal party, alleging that she had some claim upon Lord St. Simon. It was only after a painful and prolonged scene that she was ejected by the butler and the footman." Later, she was arrested because she was the last person seen in the company of the bride, who had mysteriously disappeared. *The Noble Bachelor*

*MILMAN. See the Scowrers.

*MILNER, GODFREY. With Lord Balmoral, he had lost as much as £420 in a sitting of cards to Ronald Adair and Colonel Sebastian Moran, some weeks before Adair's murder. *The Empty House*

MILVERTON, CHARLES AUGUSTUS. "The king of all the blackmailers," Milverton was considered "the worst man in London" by Holmes. "A genius in his way," Sherlock compared him to the benevolent Mr. Pickwick, except that the effect was spoiled by a perpetually frozen smile and deadly eyes. This man was in the process of blackmailing Lady Eva Brackwell, when Holmes took on the case. *Charles Augustus Milverton*

*MITTON, JOHN. Valet to the international spy Eduardo Lucas, he had been out for the evening, visiting a friend at Hammersmith the night his master was "stabbed to the heart." Though the authorities arrested Mitton "as an alternative to absolute inaction," no case could hold up against him because he had an alibi, apparently visiting friends in Hammersmith. *The Second Stain*

*MOFFAT. A member of the Worthingdon bank gang. They

pulled their heist in 1875, but were caught, and Moffat was sentenced to fifteen years. The gang swore, and achieved, revenge on their erstwhile partner, Sutton, who had testified against them. *The Resident Patient*

*MONTGOMERY, INSPECTOR. Jim Browner made his statement before Inspector Montgomery at the Shadwell Police Station. *The Cardboard Box*

*MONTPENSIER MME. As far as Holmes was concerned, the full explanation of all the mysterious happenings in Devon had to wait until he had concluded two cases of "the utmost importance." The second concerned Mme. Montpensier, charged with the murder of her step-daughter, Mlle. Carere, "the young lady who, as it will be remembered, was found six months later alive and married in New York." *The Hound of the Baskervilles*

*MOORHOUSE. 'First reserve' on the rugby team of Cambridge University, he was the logical choice to replace Godfrey Staunton, the three-quarter who had vanished just before Cambridge's big match with Oxford. However, the captain of the Cambridge side, Cyril Overton, questioned Moorhouse's abilities, saying that he was trained as a half, and always edged right in on to the scrum instead of keeping out on the touch-line. The man was a fine place-.kick it was true, but he had no judgment, "and he can't sprint for nuts." *The Missing Three-Quarter*

MORAN. The lodge-keeper on the Boscombe Valley Estate. Holmes had a word with him at the conclusion of his investigation into the brutal slaying of Charles McCarthy. *The Boscombe Valley Mystery*

MORAN, COLONEL SEBASTIAN. "The second most dangerous man in London," after Professor Moriarty, he had been educated at the best schools, had written two books, and — for a time, at least — lived the life of "an honourable soldier." But when he began to go wrong he was sought out by Professor Moriarty. Sherlock Holmes had had tangible proofs of Moran's evil nature, for it had been the Colonel who'd hurled boulders down at him when he lay on a ledge above the pathway overlooking the Reichenbach Falls, where Professor Moriarty had fallen to his death. So, when the detective heard that a young aristocrat, Ronald Adair, had been murdered he felt the crime bore the stamp of Colonel Sebastian Moran and he hastened back to London in such an open way that he also brought Moran out in the open. *The Empty House*. See also *The Valley of Fear, The Illustrious Client* and *His Last Bow*.

MORAN, PATIENCE. A girl of fourteen, daughter of the lodge-keeper at John Turner's Boscombe Valley Estate. She was picking flowers in the woods when she saw Charles McCarthy and his son, James, having a violent quarrel. Soon afterwards James McCarthy's father was found murdered on the same spot. *The Boscombe Valley Mystery*.

*MORAN, SIR AUGUSTUS. Once British Minister to Persia, and father of the Colonel. *The Empty House*

*MORCAR, COUNTESS OF. The owner of a fabulous jewel of an unusual colour. *The Blue Carbuncle*

MORECROFT. The criminal who called himself John Garrideb was a man of many names. He was also known as James Winter, *alias* Morecroft, *alias* Killer Evans. *The Three Garridebs*

*MORGAN. Holmes felt that his index of biographies was especially illustrious in the section devoted to those persons whose names began with the letter M. One of those persons was Morgan, the poisoner. *The Empty House*

*MORIARTY, COLONEL JAMES. His letters defending the memory of his brother, Professor Moriarty, who had apparently plunged to his death over the Reichenbach Falls, forced Watson "to lay the facts before the public exactly as they occurred." [A third man, brother to the Colonel and the Professor, and also called *James, was employed as a stationmaster.] *The Final Problem*

MORIARTY, PROFESSOR JAMES. Holmes said that his career has been an extraordinary one. "He is a man of good birth and excellent education, endowed by Nature with a phenomenal mathematical faculty. At the age of twenty-one he wrote a treatise upon the Binomial Theorem, which had a European vogue. On the strength of it, he won the Mathematical Chair at one of our smaller Universities, and had, to all appearance, a most brilliant career before him. But the man had hereditary tendencies of the most diabolical kind. A criminal strain ran in his blood, which, instead of being modified, was increased and rendered infinitely more dangerous by his extraordinary mental powers. Dark rumours gathered round him in the University town, and eventually he was compelled to resign his Chair and to come down to London, where he set up as an Army coach. For years past I have continually been conscious of some power behind the malefactor, some deep organizing power which forever stands in the way of the law, and throws its shield over the wrongdoer. Again and again in cases of the most varying sorts — forgery cases, robberies, murders —I have felt the presence of this force, and I have deduced its action in many of those undiscovered crimes in which I have endeavoured to break through the veil which shrouded it, and at last the time came when I seized the thread and followed it until it led me, after a thousand cunning windings, to ex-Professor Moriarty." Holmes called him "the Napoleon of crime", the organizer of half that was evil and of nearly all that went undetected in London. Watson had never heard of the man and neither, at that point, had the reader. *The Final Problem*. See also *The Empty House, The Norwood Builder, The Missing Three-Quarter, The Valley of Fear,* and *His Last Bow*

*MORPHY, ALICE. "A very perfect girl both in mind and body," she was the daughter of Professor Morphy, holder of the Chair of Comparative Anatomy at Camford University. She became engaged to one of her father's colleagues, Professor

Presbury, in spite of the great difference in age. But he had beaten his younger rivals by his frenziedly youthful courtship. *The Creeping Man*

*MORPHY, PROFESSOR. See above.

*MORRIS. "An elderly, clean-shaven man, with a kindly face and a good brow," he was in favour of some moderation and conciliation on the part of the Scowrers. This was partly because, with so many mines being sold to large corporations outside the Valley, he feared the ordinary workers would suffer. He also had more conscience than his fellow Scowrers and told McMurdo that he once had a religion but was now lost in this world and the next. He had come from Philadelphia, where his Lodge was simply a benefit club, and been forced to join the Scowrers. Now he feared not only for his life but for that of his wife and three children. *The Valley of Fear*

*MORRIS, WILLIAM. Not the writer and artist, but a red-headed gentleman who temporarily occupied rooms at Pope's Court, Fleet Street.To Jabez Wilson, he was known as *Duncan Ross, manager of the offices of a somewhat strange group. To the landlord at Pope's Court, however, he was known as William Morris, a solicitor using a room as a temporary convenience until his new (non-existent) premises were ready. *The Red-Headed League*

*MORRISON, ANNIE. She had some sort of relationship with the murdered William Kirwan. *The Reigate Squire*

*MORRISON, MISS. The Barclays' next-door neighbour at Aldershot, she went with Mrs. Barclay to a meeting of the Guild of St. George and on the way home saw the confrontation with *The Crooked Man*

*MORSTAN, CAPTAIN ARTHUR. When he returned to London from India in 1878 after serving in an Indian regiment for many years, this widower asked his daughter, Mary, to come down from her school in Edinburgh to be with him. But when she arrived she found that he had mysteriously disappeared. A close friend of Major John Sholto, he had served with him at the Blair Island penal colony in the Andaman Islands. A significant clue in *The Sign of Four*

MORSTAN, MISS MARY. Daughter of Captain Morstan, she asked for Holmes' help to solve the strange events surrounding the disappearance of her father. Later, she married Dr. Watson, who said of her, "She was a blonde young lady, small, dainty, well gloved, and dressed in the most perfect taste. There was, however, a plainness and simplicity about her costume which bore with it a suggestion of limited means. Her face had neither regularity of feature nor beauty of complexion, but her expression was sweet and amiable, and her large blue eyes were singularly spiritual and sympathetic. In an experience of women which extends over many nations and three separate continents, I have never looked upon a face which gave a clearer promise of a refined and sensitive nature." After the end of the adventure Watson, having said more about Mary than he ever would later, told the detective that she had done him the honour of accepting him as "a husband in prospective." *The Sign of Four*

*MORTIMER. The gardener at Yoxley Old Place, he was "an Army pensioner—an old Crimean man of excellent character." He did not live in the main house, but in a cottage at the other end of the garden. Other duties besides gardening included pushing his incapacitated employer round the grounds in a bath-chair. *The Golden Pince-nez*

MORTIMER, JAMES. Grimpen, Dartmoor, Devon. A house-surgeon from 1882 to 1884 at Charing Cross Hospital. Winner of the Jackson Prize for Comparative Pathology, with an essay entitled 'Is Disease a Reversion?' Corresponding member of the Swedish Pathological Society. Author of 'Some Freaks of Atavism' (Lancet, 1882), 'Do We Progress?' (Journal of Psychology, March, 1883). Medical Officer for the parishes of

Grimpen, Thorsley, and High Barrow. He was a close friend of Sir Charles Baskerville as well as the administrator of his estate, and e brought Holmes the story of that friend's death. He also mentioned some of the problems facing Sir Henry Baskerville, the heir. *The Hound of the Baskervilles*

*MORTON. One of the two "Oxford fliers" who, in the opinion of Cyril Overton, captain of the Cambridge rugby team, "could romp round" Moorhouse, the slow first reserve on Cambridge's squad. *The Missing Three-Quarter*

*MORTON, CYRIL. An electrical engineer employed by the Midland Electric Company, at Coventry, he was engaged to marry Miss Violet Smith. *The Solitary Cyclist*

*MORTON, INSPECTOR. An old acquaintance of Holmes', from Scotland Yard, he took part in this particular investigation in "unofficial tweeds." *The Dying Detective.*

MOSER, M. Watson was searching for some clues as to the whereabouts of the vanished Lady Frances Carfax and found himself at the National Hotel at Lausanne, "where I received every courtesy at the hands of M. Moser, the well-known manager." *The Disappearance of Lady Frances Carfax*

MOULTON, FRANCIS HAY. He made the acquaintance of Hatty Doran in 1881. They were engaged, and he eventually married her secretly in San Francisco. He was presumed dead when a miners' camp in New Mexico, where he was prospecting, was attacked by Apaches. *The Noble Bachelor*

MOUNT-JAMES, LORD. Godfrey Staunton's uncle, he was thought to be his nearest living relative. He was also one of the richest men in England and "an absolute miser." *The Missing Three-Quarter*

*MUNRO, COLONEL SPENCE. Miss Violet Hunter, whose acceptance of a position as governess with the Rucastles in Hampshire involved Holmes in a most odd mystery, had been a governess in the family of Colonel Spence Munro for five years, until he accepted a post in Halifax, Nova Scotia. *The Copper Beeches*

MUNRO, EFFIE. See Hebron

MUNRO, GRANT ("JACK"). He came to Holmes because he was worried about his wife's strange behaviour. *The Yellow Face*

***MURCHER, HARRY**. On the night that Constable John Rance discovered the dead body of Enoch J. Drebber in an empty house just off the Brixton Road, he had met with Harry Murcher, of the Holland Grove beat, at the corner of Henrietta Street. Murcher later came to his help when the body was discovered. *A Study in Scarlet*

MURDOCH, IAN. Mathematical coach at The Gables, "a tall, dark, thin man, so taciturn and aloof". At first Holmes thought him quite friendless., saying "He seemed to live in some high, abstract region of surds and conic sections with little to connect him with ordinary life." A man of "ferocious" temper, Murdoch had once hurled Fitzroy McPherson's dog "through a plate-glass window." *The Lion's Mane*

MURDOCH, JAMES. See the Scowrers.

***MURILLO, DON JUAN**. The Tiger of San Pedro. "The whole history of the man came back to me in a flash. He had made his name as the most lewd and bloodthirsty tyrant that had ever governed any country with a pretence to civilization. Strong, fearless, and energetic, he had sufficient virtue to enable him to impose his odious vices upon a cowering people for ten or twelve years." An uprising against the man forced him to flee the country, taking his two children, his secretary and his wealth with him. "From that moment he had vanished from the world, and his identity had been a frequent subject for comment in the European press." *Wisteria Lodge* See also *The Norwood Builder*

***MURPHY**. A gypsy horse-dealer, on the moor at the time of the death of Sir Charles Baskerville. He had been drinking, but declared that he heard cries. However, he was unable to say which direction they had come from. *The Hound of the Baskervilles*

*MURPHY. Jack McMurdo told Jacob Shafter that a man of the name of Murphy had given him the address of his Vermissa boarding-house while he was in Chicago. *The Valley of Fear*

*MURPHY, MAJOR. Of the Royal Mallows regiment, he was stationed at Aldershot. He gave Holmes the most information about Colonel James Barclay and his wife, born Nancy Devoy. *The Crooked Man*

*MURRAY. Dr. John H. Watson, newly attached to the Berkshires during the second Afghan War, was seriously wounded in the battle of Maiwand; and would "have fallen into the hands of the murderous Ghazis had it not been for the devotion and courage shown by Murray, my orderly, who threw me across a packhorse, and succeeded in bringing me safely to the British lines." *A Study in Scarlet*

*MURRAY, MR. On March 30th, 1894 he had played whist with the murdered Ronald Adair. *The Empty House.*

*MUSGRAVE, SIR RALPH. A prominent Cavalier, and the right.hand man of Charles II in his wanderings. *The Musgrave Ritual*

*MUSGRAVE, REGINALD. Holmes said. "In appearance he was a man of an exceedingly aristocratic type, thin, high-nosed, and large-eyed, with languid and yet courtly manners. He was indeed a scion of one of the very oldest families in the kingdom, though his branch was a cadet one which had separated from the Northern Musgraves sometime in the sixteenth century, and had established itself in Western Sussex, where the manor house of Hurlstone is perhaps the oldest inhabited building in the county." Musgrave had been the detective's "only friend" at college and now brought him an intriguing adventure. *The Musgrave Ritual*

N

*NED, UNCLE. Of Auckland, New Zealand, he left his niece, Mary Sutherland, some New Zealand Stock valued at two thousand five hundred pounds. *A Case of Identity*.

NELIGAN, JOHN HOPLEY. Son of the Neligan of Dawson & Neligan who disappeared after the failure of this West Country banking firm. He had traced the securities that his father was said to have stolen back to Captain Peter Carey, who was subsequently found murdered. Neligan naturally came under suspicion for the murder, and Holmes was called in by Inspector Stanley Hopkins. *Black Peter*

*NEWTON, MR. HEATH. He ran a horse called The Negro for the Wessex Cup against *Silver Blaze*.

NICHOLSON FAMILY. See the Scowrers. *The Valley of Fear*

NORBERTON, SIR ROBERT. He lived with his sister, Lady Beatrice Falder, who had only a life interest in the property under the terms of her late husband's will. A man of the most violent temper, and so much in debt that he went to truly bizarre lengths to save himself from ruin. *Shoscombe Old Place*

NORLETT, MR. "A small, rat-faced man with a disagreeably furtive manner," he was employed by Sir Robert Norberton for a most unusual, not to say bizarre, assignment. *Shoscombe Old Place*

NORLETT, MRS. CARRIE. See Carrie Evans

NORTON, GODFREY. A close friend of Irene Adler, whom he finally married. A lawyer of the Inner Temple, "he was a remarkably handsome man, dark, aquiline." He asked Holmes, disguised at the time as an unemployed groom, to witness the wedding ceremony, which took place very quietly at the Church of St. Monica. *A Scandal in Bohemia*

O

OAKSHOTT, MRS. MAGGIE. A purveyor of poultry who lived in the Brixton Road and sold the goose which figured so prominently in a particular case to a Mr Breckinridge (which see) of Covent Garden Market. *The Blue Carbuncle*

OAKSHOTT, SIR LESLIE. A famous surgeon who treated Holmes after he had been viciously attacked outside the Café Royal on the orders of Baron Gruner. *The Illustrious Client*

*OBERSTEIN, HUGO. One of only three foreign spies Mycroft Holmes thought capable of stealing so important a document as *The Bruce-Partington Plans*

*OLD RUSSIAN WOMAN. One more of Watson's untold tales. *The Musgrave Ritual*

OLDACRE, JONAS. The man thought to have been murdered by the young Hector McFarlane, tempted by the knowledge that, according to Jonas, he had been left money in the older man's will. *The Norwood Builder*

OLDMORE, MRS. She and her maid were staying at The Northumberland Hotel at the same time as Sir Henry Baskerville. *The Hound of the Baskervilles*

OPENSHAW, ELIAS. He had emigrated to America as a young man, made his fortune as a planter in Florida, fought in Jackson's army and been made a colonel. but then he returned to Britain (buying a small estate at Horsham) because he disliked the emancipation of the negroes. A mysterious letter from India, bearing the letters 'K K K' and containing dried seeds, terrified him. Apparently with good reason as, according to his nephew, John Openshaw, "We found him face downwards in a little green scummed pool" not long after. A verdict of suicide was returned, but the younger Openshaw thought otherwise. *The Five Orange Pips*

OPENSHAW, JOHN. His father having inherited his uncle's fortune and estate, John then inherited in his turn from his father. But he had a strange dread of dried orange pips and met his death after leaving Baker Street. *The Five Orange Pips*

OPENSHAW, JOSEPH. Father of John Openshaw and brother of Elias Openshaw, Joseph "had a small factory at Coventry, which he enlarged at the time of the invention of bicycling. He was the patentee of the Openshaw unbreakable tire,[sic] and his business met with such success that he was able to sell it, and to retire upon a handsome competence." He became even more wealthy when he inherited his brother's estate, but later met his death in a chalk-pit after having received a letter from Scotland. The envelope contained the dried seeds mentioned above, and the mysterious message, "Put the papers on the sundial." *The Five Orange Pips*

OVERTON, CYRIL. Skipper of the Cambridge University rugby team. An excellent player himself, Overton nevertheless conceded that another man, Godfrey Staunton, was the best in the squad. So he was understandably upset when Staunton disappeared just before to an important match against Oxford. Overton had been referred to Sherlock Holmes by Inspector Stanley Hopkins, and hoped the detective could find Staunton before the match. *The Missing Three-Quarter*

P

*****PARAMORE**. Elias Openshaw's notebook for March, 1869, contained the cryptic entries. "7th. Set the pips on McCauley, Paramore, and Swain of St. Augustine...12th. Visited Paramore. All well." *The Five Orange Pips*

*PARKER. Arthur Pinner, claimed that this man, once the manager at Coxon & Woodhouse, raved about Hall Pycroft's financial ability. *The Stockbroker's Clerk*

*PARKER. A look-out for the Moriarty gang, he was said by Sherlock Holmes to be "a harmless enough fellow." This, even though he was "a garrotter by trade." Holmes also thought it was worth reporting that Parker was "a remarkable performer upon the jews' harp." *The Empty House*

PARKER. The vicar of Hilton Cubitt's parish in Norfolk, he was staying at a boarding house in Russell Square, and when Cubitt came up to London for the Jubilee he stayed at the same place. *The Dancing Men*

*PARR, LUCY. Second waiting-maid at Fairbank, the home of Alexander Holder, a banker. One of the most precious treasures of the Empire was stolen from his house and Lucy was suspected of the crime, having been employed there for only a few months. *The Beryl Coronet*

*PATRICK, ELSIE. She married Hilton Cubitt after meeting him at a Russell Square boarding house. She was very much in love, but made him promise not to inquire into her previous life in America. Cubitt kept his promise, even after certain writings in code began to appear in and around the house. *The Dancing Men*

*PATRICK, OLD. Father of Elsie Patrick and boss of a 'Chicago Joint'. He invented the writings mentioned above. *The Dancing Men.*

*PATTERSON, INSPECTOR. In charge of the investigation that was working towards capturing Professor Moriarty and his gang. In a final note to Watson, left under a silver cigarette-case above the Reichenbach Falls, Holmes wrote, "Tell Inspector Patterson that the papers which he needs to convict the gang are in pigeon-hole M., done up in a blue envelope and inscribed 'Moriarty.'" *The Final Problem*

PATTINS, HUGH. Captain Basil (Sherlock Holmes in disguise) refused to have him as harpooner for his (mythical) expedition. *Black Peter*

PERKINS. The groom at Baskerville Hall, he was sent to fetch Dr. James Mortimer after the body of Sir Charles Baskerville was found. *The Hound of the Baskervilles*

*PERKINS. Holmes accused the fighter, Steve Dixie, of killing young Perkins outside the Holborn Bar. *The Three Gables*

*PERSANO, ISADORA. One of Holmes' unfinished tales, mentioned by Watson, involved "Isadora Persano, the well-known journalist and duellist, who was found stark staring mad with a match-box in front of him which contained a remarkable worm, said to be unknown to science." A slight problem here, as a man would not normally be named 'Isadora'. *The Problem of Thor Bridge*

PETER. A groom employed by Bob Carruthers, he was driving Miss Violet Smith to Farnham Station in a dog-cart when they were attacked. Peter was clubbed and Violet kidnapped. *The Solitary Cyclist*

PETERS, HENRY ("HOLY"). "One of the most unscrupulous rascals that Australia has ever evolved," he posed as the good Dr. Shlessinger, and won Lady Frances Carfax's confidence. So much so that she went off with him and his 'wife'. *The Disappearance of Lady Frances Carfax*

PETERSON. A commissionaire, he brought a mysterious goose and a battered billycock hat to Holmes, which led to an interesting investigation. *The Blue Carbuncle*

PHELPS, PERCY ("TADPOLE"). An old school friend of

Watson's, "he was a very brilliant boy, and carried away every prize which the school had to offer, finishing his exploits by winning a scholarship, which sent him on to continue his triumphant career at Cambridge." Phelps' family had good connections and this, combined with his great skill, landed him a position at the Foreign Office. Watson heard nothing more of Phelps until he received a letter from him imploring help in the "horrible misfortune" which had come to "blast his career." A top-secret naval treaty had disappeared, under strange circumstances, from Phelps' office. *The Naval Treaty*

*PHILLIMORE, JAMES. A man in yet another mysterious investigation which Watson didn't write up. "Mr. James Phillimore, who, stepping back into his own house to get an umbrella, was never more seen in this world." *The Problem of Thor Bridge*

"PIERROT". A pseudonym used in The Daily Telegraph's 'agony column' by Holmes for the time it took to trap 'his' partner in crime. *The Bruce-Partington Plans*

*PIKE, LANGDALE. Holmes' human book of reference upon all matters of social scandal. He spent his waking hours in the bow window of a St. James' Street club, and both received and transmitted all the gossip of the Metropolis. Holmes discreetly helped Pike to obtain such gossip, and was himself helped in turn. *The Three Gables*

PINNER, ARTHUR. Supposedly a financial agent, he said that his brother, Harry Pinner, was promoter and managing director of the fictitious Franco-Midland Hardware Company, and was looking for "a young, pushing man" to add to the organization. Harry had asked Arthur to find someone who could fit the job, and Arthur lighted upon Hall Pycroft, offering him what sounded like a good position. Arthur Pinner also went under the name

Beddington. *The Stockbroker's Clerk*

PINNER, HARRY. He very closely resembled his brother, except that he was clean shaven and his hair was not so dark. Pycroft noticed, however, that both brothers had a second tooth (on the left-hand side of the mouth) which had been very poorly filled with gold. Presumably this enabled him to identify them later. *The Stockbroker's Clerk*

*****PINTO, JONAS** . He was supposedly shot dead in the Lake Saloon, Market Street, Chicago, in the first week of January, 1874. Jack McMurdo said as a blind, "I was helping Uncle Sam to make dollars. Maybe mine were not as good gold as his, but they looked as well and were cheaper to make." Pinto helped him to put the fake dollars out into circulation at first. But later he said he would split on him. Said McMurdo, "Maybe he did split. I didn't wait to see. I just killed him and lighted out for the coal country." *The Valley of Fear*

*****PINTO, MARIA**. The maiden-name of the Brazilian wife of Neil Gibson, the Gold King. She became so jealous of her husband's attentions towards their children's governess that she killed herself in a way which would throw suspicion on the young woman. *The Problem of Thor Bridge*

*****POLLACK, CONSTABLE**. He and *Sergeant Tuson together succeeded in arresting the forger Beddington, aka Pinner) following the latter's attempted robbery of Mawson & Williams, the famous financial house. *The Stockbroker's Clerk*

*****PORLOCK, FRED**. Holmes said, "Porlock, Watson, is a *nom-de-plume*, a mere identification, but behind it lies a shifty and evasive personality. In a former letter he frankly informed me that the name was not his own, and defied me ever to trace him among the teeming millions of this great city. Porlock is important, not for himself, but for the great man with whom he is in touch. Led on by some rudimentary aspirations towards right, and encouraged by the judicious stimulation of an occasional ten-pound note sent to him by devious methods, he has once or twice given me advance information which has been of value." It was a letter in cipher from this man which first drew Holmes' attention to The *Valley of Fear*

PORTER, MRS. The elderly Cornish housekeeper who, helped by a girl, looked after the wants of the Tregennis family. *The Devil's Foot*

*****POTT, EVANS.** He was a County delegate of The Ancient Order of Freemen and lived at Hobson's Patch. *The Valley of Fear*

*****PRENDERGAST, JACK.** "He was a man of good family and of great ability, but of incurably vicious habits, who had…obtained huge sums of money from the leading London merchants." In 1855 he was caught and sentenced to transportation to the Australian colonies on board the "Gloria Scott". He bribed the crew, and led a successful uprising with the help of two fellow convicts, Armitage and Evans. He was killed in an explosion which destroyed the ship shortly afterwards. *The "Gloria Scott"*

*****PRENDERGAST, MAJOR.** John Openshaw had heard of Holmes from Major Prendergast, whom Holmes had saved from disgrace in the Tankerville Club Scandal. *The Five Orange Pips*

PRESBURY, PROFESSOR. A man whose bizarre behaviour was brought to Holmes' attention by the Professor's Assistant. A sixty-one-year-old widower, Presbury was a man of European reputation, who, in a "passionate frenzy of youth," had become engaged to Alice Morphy, daughter of one of his colleagues and a woman about the same age as Presbury's own daughter, Edith. It wasn't, however, the difference in age between Presbury and Alice that led Edith's fiancé to ask Holmes' advice. Though the Professor was naturally "combative," he had turned quite savage in his courtship of the girl—so savage, in fact, that his faithful wolfhound, Roy, had tried to bite him. *The Creeping Man*

*PRESCOTT, RODGER. Once famous as a forger and coiner in Chicago, and the greatest counterfeiter London had ever seen, he was shot by Killer Evans in the Waterloo Road in January, 1895. The man died but, as he was shown to be the aggressor in the row, Evans got off with a relatively light sentence. *The Three Garridebs*

PRICE, MR. Doctor Watson posed as a clerk, Mr. Price of Birmingham, when he went with Holmes to interview Harry Pinner. *The Stockbroker's Clerk*

*PRINGLE, MRS. She was Eduardo Lucas' elderly housekeeper at 16, Godolphin Street. *The Second Stain*

*PRITCHARD. Holmes is perhaps a little mistaken in his assessment of certain members of the medical fraternity when he says, "Palmer and Pritchard were among the heads of their profession." But maybe not when he says that when a doctor does go wrong he is the first of criminals. "He has nerve and he has knowledge." *The Speckled Band*

*PROSPER, FRANCIS. Greengrocer for Alexander Holder's household in Streatham, he was the sweetheart of the second maid at Fairbank. He had a wooden leg, a fact which became important during the investigation. *The Beryl Coronet.*

PYCROFT, HALL. An unemployed clerk, he accepted a seemingly good berth with the Franco-Midland Hardware Company, but was puzzled over some of the terms of his employment, and this caused him to come to Holmes for a solution. *The Stockbroker's Clerk*

R

*RAE, ANDREW. See Windle. *The Valley of Fear*

RALPH. The Emsworth family's butler. *The Blanched Soldier*

RALPH, MRS. Wife of the above. She had been Godfrey Emsworth's nurse at Tuxbury Old Hall and "second only to his mother in his affections." *The Blanched Soldier*

RANCE, JOHN. A constable on night patrol, he discovered the dead body of Enoch J. Drebber. He had narrowly missed capturing the murderer and Holmes and Watson visited him at his home 46, Audley Court, Kennington Park Gate, when the detective told him he would never rise in his profession if he didn't use his head. *A Study in Scarlet*

*RANDALL. Surname of a Lewisham gang of burglars — a father and his two sons. The Randalls had committed a burglary at Sydenham a fortnight before the murder of Sir Eustace Brackenstall, and they became suspects. *The Abbey Grange*

RAO, LAL. Bartholomew Sholto's Indian butler. Both lived at Pondicherry Lodge, Upper Norwood. *The Sign of Four*

RAS, DAULAT. An Indian student at the College of St. Luke's, in one of England's great university towns. He lived on the same staircase as the tutor Hilton Soames and was a candidate for the Fortescue Scholarship. *The Three Students*

*REILLY. A reckless youngster, he went with Jack McMurdo to help murder Wilcox. *The Valley of Fear*

*REILLY. Lawyer for the Scowrers, he succeeded in freeing the men jailed for the assault on James Stanger. *The Valley of Fear*

*RICHARDS, DR. He went on an urgent call to Tredannick Wartha, the house of the Tregennis family, in Cornwall. The three persons for whom he had been summoned were so far beyond any assistance he could offer, that he fell fainting into a chair. *The Devil's Foot*

ROBINSON, JOHN. An alias of James Ryder, the man who stole *The Blue Carbuncle*

*RONDER. "One of the greatest showmen of his day" before he took to drink. But now a ruffian and a bully, he deserted his wife for others, tying her down and lashing her with his riding whip when she complained. *The Veiled Lodger*

RONDER, MRS. EUGENIA. Once "a very magnificent woman," she had been terribly mutilated by "a very fine North African lion" which was one of the primary exhibits in the wild beast show she ran with her husband. Her face was now a "grisly ruin," but her spirit had been even more disfigured by the awful incident, and to ease her mind she wanted someone to know the truth before she died. It was in this tale that Holmes showed his greatest sympathy for a victim. *The Veiled Lodger*

ROSS, COLONEL. Owner of a wonder horse, and the King's Pyland stables on Dartmoor from which the animal disappeared. He invited Holmes to look into the matter with Inspector Gregory. *Silver Blaze*

*ROSS, DUNCAN. Manager of the offices of The Red-Headed League in London, he claimed to be a member himself. He set Jabez Wilson on the arduous task of copying the *Encyclopaedia Britannica.* Also known as William Morris (which see). *The Red-Headed League*

ROUNDHAY, MR. "The vicar of the parish" centred in the Cornish hamlet of Tredannick Wollas, Mr. Roundhay "was something of an archaeologist, and as such Holmes had made his acquaintance." *The Devil's Foot*

ROYLOTT, DR. GRIMESBY. Step-father of Helen and Julia Stoner; last of the Roylott family of Stoke Moran, in Surrey. His family had been at one time among the richest in England. But the estate had declined through bad management and Grimesby Roylott, seeing that he must fend for himself, took a medical degree and went to Calcutta where he established a large practice. In a fit of anger, however, Dr. Roylott beat his native butler to death, and narrowly escaped hanging. After a long term of imprisonment he returned to England morose and disappointed. While in India he had married a widow, Mrs. Stoner. *The Speckled Band*

*RUCASTLE, ALICE. Daughter of Jephro Rucastle. She was apparently away in Philadelphia at the time Jephro hired Miss Violet Hunter, who bore a remarkable resemblance to his daughter, as governess at a very generous salary. Miss Rucastle's fiancé was nevertheless convinced that she still remained at home. *The Copper Beeches*

*RUCASTLE, EDWARD. Son of Jephro Rucastle, who said of his son, "One child —one dear little romper just six years old. Oh, if you could see him killing cockroaches with a slipper! Smack! smack! smack! Three gone before you could wink!" But the governess, Miss Violet Hunter, said, "I have never met so utterly spoilt and so ill-natured a little creature... Giving pain to any creature weaker than himself seems to be his one idea of amusement, and he shows quite remarkable talent in planning the capture of mice, little birds, and insects." This gave Holmes the chance to air some of his theories. "My dear Watson, you as a medical man are continually gaining light as to the tendencies of a child by the study of the parents. Don't you see that the converse is equally valid. I have frequently gained my first real insight into the character of parents by studying their children. This child's disposition is abnormally cruel…and whether he derives this from his smiling father, as I should suspect, or from his mother, it bodes evil for the poor girl who is in their power." *The Copper Beeches*

RUCASTLE, JEPHRO. He sought out Miss Violet Hunter ostensibly as a governess for his young son, Edward. However, his and his wife's peculiar whims and fancies regarding Miss Hunter's dress, appearance, and what she was asked to do in addition to her duties as governess very quickly involved Holmes. *The Copper Beeches*

*RUCASTLE, MRS. JEPHRO. Violet Hunter described her as "a nonentity", silent, pale and considerably younger than her husband. But it had been easy to see she was passionately devoted to him, and to their child. *The Copper Beeches*

*RUFTON, EARL OF. The Lady Frances Carfax, whom Holmes rescued from 'Dr. and Mrs. Shlessinger', was the sole survivor in the direct line of the late Earl of Rufton. *The Disappearance of Lady Frances Carfax*

RYDER, JAMES ("JEM"). Upper attendant at the Cosmopolitan Hotel, from where the Countess of Morcar's fabulous jewel was stolen. See Maudsley. *The Blue Carbuncle*

S

ST. CLAIR, NEVILLE. He disappeared into the wretched beggar Hugh Boone's room at the Bar of Gold opium den. All that was found of him there were his clothes. Holmes said of him that he "had no occupation, but was interested in several companies, and went into town as a rule in the morning, returning by the 5.14 from Cannon Street every night. Mr. St. Clair is now 37 years of age, is a man of temperate habits, a good husband, a very affectionate father, and a man who is popular with all who know him." *The Man with the Twisted Lip*

ST. CLAIR, MRS. NEVILLE. On her return from the Aberdeen Shipping Company, Mrs. St. Clair saw her husband in a second-floor window of the Bar of Gold opium den. When she reached the room, however, he had mysteriously disappeared. *The Man with the Twisted Lip*

*ST. SIMON, LADY CLARA. Sister of Lord Robert St. Simon, whose bride mysteriously disappeared. *The Noble Bachelor*

*ST. SIMON, LORD EUSTACE. Younger brother of Lord Robert St. Simon. *The Noble Bachelor*

ST. SIMON, LORD ROBERT. Robert Walsingham de Vere St. Simon, second son of the Duke of Balmoral. Born in 1846. Once Under-Secretary for the Colonies. He came to Holmes to ask if he would find a missing bride. *The Noble Bachelor*

*SALTIRE, LORD. The heir (and only legitimate son) of the Duke of Holdernesse, he disappeared mysteriously from Dr. Huxtable's Educational Establishment. *The Priory School*

*SAMSON. Yet again Holmes is shown as jubilant over his discovery of "an infallible test for blood stains." This time he felt it would have been decisive in the case of Samson of New Orleans. *A Study in Scarlet*

SANDEFORD, MR. He possessed the sixth significant plaster cast of Devine's bust of Napoleon, which Holmes bought from him for the large sum of £10 and then smashed. *The Six Napoleons*

*SANDERS, IKEY. He refused to cut up the stolen Crown diamond for Count Negretto Sylvius, and testified against the Count to the detective. *The Mazarin Stone*

SAUNDERS. Housemaid at Ridling Thorpe Manor, Norfolk, where Hilton Cubitt was found fatally shot through the heart, and his wife barely alive with a bullet lodged in her brain. The housemaid gave the alarm, after having been aroused from her sleep by the explosion. *The Dancing Men*

SAUNDERS, MRS. Caretaker of the house in which Nathan Garrideb lived, she remained on the premises each day up to four o'clock. *The Three Garridebs*

SAUNDERS, SIR JAMES. A great dermatologist for whom Holmes had once done a professional service. *The Blanched Soldier*

*SAVAGE, VICTOR. "A strong, hearty fellow" who somewhat surprisingly contracted an out-of-the-way Asiatic disease in the heart of London and died a horrible death. *The Dying Detective*

SAWYER, MRS. A person using this name came for the wedding ring which Holmes had advertised (falsely) as found in the roadway between the White Hart Tavern and Holland Grove on the night Drebber was murdered. She appeared to be "a very old and wrinkled woman" but, in reality, was an actor hired by Jefferson Hope – who prized the ring highly but had accidently lost it. *A Study in Scarlet*

*SCANLAN, MIKE. He met Jack McMurdo and later became his roommate, even though some policemen warned McMurdo against getting in with "that man and his gang." McMurdo was able to pass as a fellow gangster because he could respond correctly to certain signals, i.e. the special hand-shake; and when 'Brother Scanlan' raised his right hand to his right eyebrow McMurdo responded immediately by raising his left hand to his left eyebrow, etc. *The Valley of Fear*

SCOTT, J. H. Body-master of Lodge 29, Chicago, of The Ancient Order of Freemen. In applying to join the Lodge controlling Vermissa Valley, Jack McMurdo claimed (falsely) to have belonged to the Chicago Lodge. *The Valley of Fear*

SCOWRERS. Aka The Ancient Order of Freemen. A secret society which spread terror throughout a coal-mining area known as Vermissa Valley in an attempt to organise and rule the mineworkers. It exacted a harsh penalty from anyone who violated the oath of secrecy; and its methods of control included assault, wife-murder, mutilation, random killings and demands for protection money. **Simon Bird**, **Josiah H. Dunn, Hales**, **Hyam**, **Little Billy James**, the young **Jenkins** brothers, **Menzies** the engineer of the Crow Mine, also **Harringby** of the same mine, **Milman**, **Murdock, The Nicholson Family, Old man Crabbe, Andrew Rae, Stanger** (the editor of the Vermissa *Herald*, who was viciously beaten),**The Staphouse family** (which was blown-up), the **Stendals**, **Van Shorst**, the **Walker brothers** and **Charlie Williams**, all suffered in one way or another, along with many others. Jack McMurdo became a member to suit his own purposes, leading to a conclusion which was something of a surprise. *The Valley of Fear*

SELDEN. The Notting Hill murderer, and brother-in-law of the butler at Baskerville Hall. He committed such a ferocious crime that there was some doubt as to his sanity. He escaped from Princetown [Dartmoor] prison, and later hid on the moor near the Hall. He died a horrible death at the jaws of what appeared to be the "enormous hound" of the Baskerville legend. *The Hound of the Baskervilles*

SERGIUS. The real name of the man who called himself "Professor Coram". *The Golden Pince-nez*

SHAFTER, ETTIE. She helped run her father's boarding-house on Sheridan Street in Vermissa, where Jack McMurdo stayed. An extremely beautiful girl who quite captivated McMurdo, she "had a pleasing little touch of a German accent." *The Valley of Fear*

SHAFTER, JACOB. He asked Jack McMurdo to leave his house when the latter became active in The Ancient Order of Freemen (the Scowrers). *The Valley of Fear*

SHERMAN. A bird-stuffer, who lived at 3, Pinchin Lane, Lambeth. His hound, Toby, was given to Watson, at first called an 'ill-dressed vagabond' from an upstairs window, to help Holmes track down Bartholomew Sholto's killers. *The Sign of Four*

SHLESSINGER, DR. Supposedly a missionary from South America who was recuperating at the Englischer Hof in Baden from a disease caught while carrying out his apostolic duties. "He was preparing a map of the Holy Land, with special reference to the kingdom of the Midianites, upon which he was writing a monograph." While at Baden, he met Lady Frances Carfax, and he and the woman posing as his wife left in her company for London. His left ear was jagged or torn. This was what gave Holmes the clue to the man's real identity. He was the notorious 'Holy Peters'. *The Disappearance of Lady Frances Carfax.*

SHLESSINGER, MRS. The *alias* used by Annie Fraser to dupe a lonely traveller. *The Disappearance of Lady Frances Carfax*

SHOLTO, BARTHOLOMEW. Brother of Thaddeus Sholto, he spent much time and expense trying to find where the great Agra treasure was, and this led indirectly to his murder. *The Sign of Four*

*SHOLTO, MAJOR JOHN. Of the 34th Bombay Infantry, retired. Once a close friend of Captain Arthur Morstan, who mysteriously disappeared in December, 1878, Sholto's death some four years later was part of a number of sensational events which involved Holmes in the mystery of *The Sign of Four*

SHOLTO, THADDEUS. "A small man with a very high head, a bristle of red hair round the fringe of it, and a bald, shining scalp which shot out from among it like a mountain-peak from fir-trees. He writhed his hands together as he stood, and his features were in a perpetual jerk— now smiling, now scowling, but never for an instant in repose. Nature had given him a pendulous lip, and a too visible line of yellow and irregular teeth, which he strove feebly to conceal by constantly passing his hand over the lower part of his face. In spite of his obtrusive baldness, he gave the impression of youth. In point of fact, he had just turned his thirtieth year." His kindness to Mary Morstan, orphaned daughter of Captain Morstan, though anonymous, led to Holmes and Watson becoming involved in a most dangerous case. So involved that, when all was over, Watson went so far as to marry the lady. *The Sign of Four*

*SHUMAN. He sold his Vermissa Valley ironworks to the West Wilmerton General Mining Company. *The Valley of Fear*

SIGERSON. Accounts of this Norwegian's explorations were so remarkable that news of them reached London but, as this was Holmes under an assumed name, Watson hadn't known that he was receiving news of the friend he thought dead. *The Empty House*

SIMPSON. A "small street Arab," he kept a watch on Henry Wood's lodgings for Sherlock Holmes. *The Crooked*

Man

*SIMPSON, "BALDY". In the Boer War, Simpson was in the same squadron as Godfrey Emsworth and James M. Dodd. However, during the morning fight at Buffelsspruit, outside Pretoria, Emsworth, Simpson, and one Anderson were separated from their mates, and the latter two were killed. *The Blanched Soldier*

*SIMPSON, FITZROY. He had been arrested upon circumstantial, but convincing, evidence for the murder of Silver Blaze's trainer, John Straker. Simpson "was a man of excellent birth and education, who had squandered a fortune upon the turf, and who lived now by doing a little quiet and genteel bookmaking in the sporting clubs of London." *Silver Blaze*

*SINCLAIR, ADMIRAL. Admiral Sinclair entertained Sir James Walter at the former's house at Barclay Square during the whole of the evening when the theft of some important papers took place. *The Bruce-Partington Plans*

*SINGH, MAHOMET. A Sikh trooper, he was one of the men bound by an oath. *The Sign of Four*

*SINGLEFORD, LORD. He ran Rasper against Colonel Ross's horse for the Wessex Cup. *Silver Blaze*

SLANEY, ABE. "The most dangerous crook in Chicago" his great love for Elsie Patrick drove him to follow her to England with catastrophic results. *The Dancing Men*

*SLATER. A stonemason who, while walking from Forest Row about one o'clock in the morning, stopped as he passed Peter Carey's cabin at Woodman's Lee and saw the shadow of a strange man outlined against the light in the window. *Black Peter*

SMALL , JONATHAN. One of the men bound by The Sign of the Four oath, he was responsible for the deaths of Major

John Sholto and Bartholomew Sholto. Without seeing him, Holmes correctly deduced that Small was "a poorly educated man, small, active, with his right leg off, and wearing a wooden stump which is worn away upon the inner sole. He is a middle-aged man, much sunburned, and has been a convict." *The Sign of Four*

SMITH, CULVERTON. Of 13, Lower Burke Street. A planter and well-known resident of Sumatra, he was unmatched in his knowledge of the tropical disease that appeared to have struck down Sherlock Holmes. *The Dying Detective*

SMITH, JACK. Son of Mordecai Smith of the *Aurora,* he was "a curly-headed lad of six." *The Sign of Four*

*****SMITH, JAMES**. Deceased father of Violet Smith, he had conducted the orchestra at the old Imperial Theatre. *The Solitary Cyclist*

SMITH, JIM. Eldest son of Mr. and Mrs. Mordecai Smith, he accompanied his father on their steam launch, *Aurora,* which had been chartered by Jonathan Small. *The Sign of Four*

SMITH, MORDECAI. Of Smith's Wharf. He was the owner of the steam launch *Aurora,* which was hired by Jonathan Small. *The Sign of Four*

SMITH, MRS. MORDECAI. She shared Holmes' concern over her husband's disappearance. *The Sign of Four*

*****SMITH, RALPH**. Uncle of Miss Violet Smith, he had gone to Africa twenty-five years prior to the death of James Smith, his brother and Violet's father, and Violet and her mother had never had a word from him since. Thus, they were greatly surprised when, after answering an advertisement in *The Times* inquiring for their whereabouts, they were met by two men who claimed that

Ralph Smith's dying wish had been that his sister-in-law and niece should experience no want, if the men could help it. Further, the men, Carruthers and Woodley by name, contended that Violet's Uncle Ralph had died in poverty. *The Solitary Cyclist*

SMITH, MISS VIOLET. She was a "young and beautiful woman, tall, graceful, and queenly, who presented herself at Baker Street late [one] evening and implored [Holmes'] assistance and advice." It seemed that Miss Smith, a music teacher, found herself beset by several persons, the most bizarre of whom was a "middle-aged man, with a short, dark beard" who rode after her whenever she went cycling. Holmes took on her case, even though he believed, at first, that her problem was nothing more than "some secretive lover." He was quick to discern, however, that there was "some deep intrigue going on." *The Solitary Cyclist*

*SMITH, WILLOUGHBY. The third secretary retained by Professor Coram, Willoughby Smith was "a quiet, hard-working fellow, with no weak spot in him at all." Thus, there seemed to be "no reason on earth why anyone should wish him harm." Yet Smith had been fatally stabbed in the neck with a small sealing-wax knife. However, this was accepted as an accident by Holmes when told it was the act of a panic-stricken woman who was trying desperately to escape from the house. *The Golden Pince-nez*

SMITH-MORTIMER CASE, THE. This was 'a famous Succession Case' Holmes handled in 1894 and Watson didn't find time (or was too grief-stricken) to write up. *The Golden Pince-nez*

SOAMES, HILTON. Tutor and lecturer at the College of St. Luke's in one of the great university towns, he came to

Holmes with a painful problem concerning the Fortescue Scholarship examination. *The Three Students*

*SOAMES, SIR CATHCART. He entrusted his son to Dr. Thorneycroft Huxtable's care at the educational establishment in Hallamshire. *The Priory School*

*SOMERTON, DR. "A fast, sporting young chap," he was the surgeon at the penal colony at Blair Island, where Jonathan Small was imprisoned. His card parties managed to get Major Sholto and Captain Morstan hopelessly in debt. *The Sign of Four*

*SOUTHERTON, LORD. The woods that surrounded the Rucastle's domain on three sides were part of Lord Southerton's property. *The Copper Beeches*

SPAULDING, VINCENT. The *alias* used by John Clay to dupe Jabez Wilson. *The Red-Headed League*

*SPENDER, ROSE. Henry ('Holy') Peters and Annie Fraser brought her from the Brixton Workhouse Infirmary to their home, where she died three days later of senile decay. They claimed that she was an old nurse of Annie Fraser's, the woman who posed as Peters' wife, but her dead body and a double coffin were intended to serve a really villainous, if ingenious, purpose. *The Disappearance of Lady Frances Carfax*

STACKHURST, HAROLD. His well-known coaching establishment, The Gables, was half a mile from Sherlock Holmes' retirement villa in Sussex. "Stackhurst himself was a well-known rowing Blue in his day, and an excellent all-round scholar." He was also the one man in the vicinity who was on such friendly terms with Holmes that they "could drop in on each other in the evenings without an invitation." *The Lion's Mane*

STAMFORD. Dr. John H. Watson, recently invalided

home from the second Afghan War, ran into "young Stamford", his former dresser at Bart's, in the Criterion Bar. Watson was looking for lodgings cheaper than his hotel room in the Strand, and Stamford introduced him to Sherlock Holmes, who needed someone he could share rooms with in Baker Street. *A Study in Scarlet*

*STAMFORD, ARCHIE. Sherlock Holmes felt that the area near Farnham, on the borders of Surrey, was "a beautiful neighbourhood, and full of the most interesting associations." But the most memorable one was its proximity to where he and Watson captured Archie Stamford, the forger. *The Solitary Cyclist*

*STANGERSON, ELDER. One of the four principal Mormon elders, he was given the job by Brigham Young of teaching the Faith to John Ferrier. *A Study in Scarlet*

STANGERSON, JOSEPH. As a young Mormon, with "a long, pale face," he had competed with Enoch J. Drebber for the hand of Lucy Ferrier. When Lucy and her adoptive father fled from their home rather than have her marry either of them, Stangerson and Drebber, part of the Danite Band (aka The Avenging Angels) chased after them and Stangerson shot her father. Drebber, however, was the one who finally married Lucy, who later died of grief and ill-treatment. *A Study in Scarlet*

STAPLES. The "solemn" butler of Mr. Culverton Smith. *The Dying Detective*

'STAPLETON', (GARCIA) BERYL. Aka as 'Mrs. Vandeleur'. Supposed sister of Jack Stapleton, of Merripit House, in Devonshire. She tried to warn Sir Henry Baskerville away from the moor, and he later fell in love with her. *The Hound of the Baskervilles*

'STAPLETON, JACK'. Aka as 'Vandeleur', "He was a

small, slim, clean-shaven, prim-faced man, flaxen-haired and lean-jawed, between thirty and forty years of age, dressed in a grey suit and wearing a straw hat." He was also using yet another of his false names and Holmes remarked about him, "I said it in London, Watson, and I say it again now, that never yet have we helped to hunt down a more dangerous man." *The Hound of the Baskervilles*

*STARK, COLONEL LYSANDER ("FRITZ"). Of Eyford, in Berkshire. He employed Victor Hatherley to come at a very late hour and for a suspiciously large fee to repair his hydraulic press. Hatherley then lost his thumb under unusual circumstances, which brought Sherlock Holmes into the case. *The Engineer's Thumb*

*STARR, DR. LYSANDER. Suspiciously close to the above name. But when speaking to a man who claimed to have been "in the law at Topeka," Sherlock Holmes mentioned that he used to have a correspondent in that city, 'Dr. Lysander Starr', the Mayor in 1890. The supposed lawyer replied that Dr. Starr's name was still honoured in Topeka —a very revealing comment in view of the fact that Holmes had just made the name up. *The Three Garridebs*

STAUNTON, A. H. "A rising young forger" listed in one of Sherlock Holmes' common-place books. *The Missing Three-Quarter*

STAUNTON, GODFREY. "Simply the hinge that the whole team turns on." But Staunton had mysteriously vanished just before Cambridge's important match with Oxford. The team-captain, Cyril Overton, rushed to Scotland Yard, and then to Sherlock Holmes, hoping that the three-quarter could be found before the start of play. But, owing to the obstacles which Staunton's uncle (the parsimonious Lord Mount-James) and a certain Dr. Leslie Armstrong of

Cambridge put in the way, Holmes failed to find this star player in time and Cambridge lost the match. Later, when he did find him, he was confronted with an absolutely over-riding reason why Staunton abandoned his team-mates. *The Missing Three-Quarter*

*STAUNTON, HENRY. The volume of Sherlock Holmes' commonplace book devoted to persons and things whose names began with the letter S was a "mine of varied information." One of the names was Henry Staunton, who the detective had helped to hang. *The Missing Three-Quarter*

STEILER, PETER, THE ELDER. He managed the Englischer Hof in Meiringen, where Holmes and Watson put up on May 3,1891. An intelligent man who spoke excellent English, having served for three years as waiter at the Grosvenor Hotel in London. "At his advice, upon the afternoon of the 4th we set off together with the intention of crossing the hills and spending the night at the hamlet of Rosenlaui." The pair made a detour to see the Reichenbach Falls, with apparently devastating results. *The Final Problem*

*STEINER. An agent of the German spy Von Bork, he was captured before World War I. *His Last Bow*

STENDALS, THE. See the Scowrers.

*STEPHENS. Butler at Shoscombe Old Place. He and the head trainer, John Mason, saw the strange actions of Sir Robert Norberton and as a result Mason went to consult Holmes. *Shoscombe Old Place*

STERNDALE, DR. LEON. The great lion-hunter and explorer had a huge body, a deeply-seamed face, fierce eyes and a hawk-like nose. And was so tall that his grizzled hair nearly touched the ceiling. His beard was "golden at the fringes and white near the lips, save for the nicotine stain from his perpetual cigar." On his Cornish mother's side, he could be called cousin to the Tregennis family. And he had spent so much of his life outside the law that he came at last "to be a law to himself." In love with a member of that same family (who had died as the result of an attempt at mass-murder) Sterndale did take the law into his own hands, forcing the murderer to inhale poisonous fumes and watching while he did so. Holmes followed the same path: on being told that the explorer had intended after this act of revenge to bury himself in Central Africa because his work there was only "half-finished", the detective told him to "Go and do the other half. I, at least, am not prepared to prevent you." *The Devil's Foot,*

*STEVENS, BERT. A "terrible murderer" who had wanted Holmes and Watson to get him off in '87, his name was recalled by Holmes when Watson said that a man's appearance was the important thing in indicating guilt or innocence. The detective, however, reminded him that Bert Stevens had been a most "mild-mannered, Sunday-school young man." *The Norwood Builder*

*STEVENSON. One of the two men on the Cambridge University rugby team who was being considered as a replacement for Godfrey Staunton. *The Missing Three-Quarter*

*STEWART, JANE. Housemaid at 'Lachine', the Barclays' villa in Aldershot, she overheard the argument which took place between Colonel Barclay and his wife shortly before he was found dead, and she unconscious, in their locked morning-room. *The Crooked Man*

*STEWART, MRS. See the town of Lauder. *The Empty House*

STIMSON & CO. Undertakers, of the Kennington Road. Henry Peters and Annie Fraser hired them to carry out the funeral of Rose Spender, and stipulated an unusually deep coffin. *The Disappearance of Lady Frances Carfax*

*****STOCKDALE, BARNEY**. Steve Dixie's boss in the Spencer John gang. *The Three Gables*

STOCKDALE, SUSAN. A maid at Mrs. Maberley's home, The Three Gables, and a member of the Spencer John gang, she was also the wife of Barney Stockdale. *The Three Gables*

STONER, HELEN. Daughter of Major-General and Mrs. Stoner, she consulted Holmes when she feared that she would suffer the same horrible fate as her sister. See also **STONER, JULIA**. The twin of Helen Stoner, she died under mysterious circumstances in 1881. Her last words were. "O, my God! Helen! It was the band! The speckled band!" *The Speckled Band*

*****STONER, MAJOR-GENERAL**. Of the Bengal Artillery, he died in India, leaving a young widow and two infant daughters. *The Speckled Band*

*****STONER, MRS**. Dr. Grimbsby Roylott was her second husband, and shortly after their return to England from India with her two children she was killed in a railway accident near Crewe. *The Speckled Band*

STOPER, MISS. She managed an employment agency ('Westaways') in the West End of London, and Violet Hunter went there seeking a position as governess. *The Copper Beeches*

*****STRAKER, JOHN**. The trainer of the racehorse owned by Colonel Ross at King's Pyland stables, Straker (*alias* William Darbyshire) was found horribly murdered, his head shattered by a savage blow. He was "a retired jockey, who rode in Colonel Ross's colours before he became too heavy for the weighing chair. He has served the Colonel for five years as jockey, and for seven as trainer, and has always shown himself to be a zealous and honest servant." Things began to look very different later, however. *Silver Blaze*

STRAKER, MRS. Wife of the above. *Silver Blaze*

*STRAUBENZEE. A gunsmith who lived in the Minories. He had made the air-gun — "a pretty bit of work, as I understand"—which Count Negretto Sylvius used in an attempt to persuade Holmes to stay off the case of the stolen Crown diamond. *The Mazarin Stone*

*STRAUSS, HERMAN. Jack McMurdo thought that the murderers Lawler and Andrews might be after Strauss. *The Valley of Fear*

SUDBURY. One of the young men at Harold Stackhurst's establishment for coaching students, The Gables, he was also one of the persons who discovered the carcass of Fitzroy Macpherson's Airedale terrier on the edge of the pool where its master had received a fatal blow. *The Lion's Mane*

*SUMNER. A shipping agent in the Ratcliff Highway. Captain Basil (Sherlock Holmes in disguise) had sent for three harpooners from Sumner's office to report to him at Baker Street. He rejected two, but the third man turned out to be the murderer he was looking for. See Cairns. *Black Peter*

SUTHERLAND, MISS MARY. She came to Holmes with the perplexing problem of the disappearance of her husband-to-be Mr. Hosmer Angel, almost on the church steps. Holmes felt that "there was never any mystery in the matter, though, as I said yesterday, some of the details are of interest." *A Case of Identity*

*SUTRO, MR. Mrs. Mary Maberley's lawyer. *The Three Gables*

SUTTON. A member of the Worthingdon bank gang. They stole seven thousand pounds from the Worthingdon bank in 1875, but during the raid the bank's caretaker was murdered. Sutton turned state's evidence when they were arrested, and thus secured the execution of one of the gang, Cartwright, and fifteen years in jail for the rest. See Blessington. *The Resident Patient*

*SWAIN, JOHN. See McCauley. *The Five Orange Pips*

*SWINDON, ARCHIE. He sold out and left the Vermissa Valley. "The old devil left a note for us to say he would rather be a free crossing-sweeper in New York than a large mine-owner under the power of a ring of blackmailers." *The Valley of Fear*

SYLVIUS, COUNT NEGRETTO. He had stolen the great Crown diamond and hoped to persuade Holmes to stay out of the case — which led to his own undoing. Holmes, however, respected his bravery. "A man of nerve. Possibly you have heard of his reputation as a shooter of big game. It would indeed be a triumphant ending to his excellent sporting records if he added me to his bag." *The Mazarin Stone*

T

TANGEY. Commissionaire at the Foreign Office. On the night that a top-secret naval treaty disappeared from Percy Phelps' office there, Tangey (an old soldier) had been asleep at his post. *The Naval Treaty*

TANGEY, MRS. The commissionaire's wife, she did the cleaning at the Foreign Office. After taking Phelps' order for coffee she had then left quickly for home. *The Naval*

TARLTON, SUSAN. A maid at Yoxley Old Place, she was the only person able to say something positive about the immediate circumstances surrounding the murder of Willoughby Smith. *The Golden Pince-nez*

*****THURSTON.** Watson's billiards partner at his club. *The Dancing Men*

*****TIRED CAPTAIN, THE.** One of the cases which took place in the July preceding Watson's marriage, and in which he "had the privilege of being associated with Sherlock Holmes, and of studying his methods." He did not, however, find time to write-up the investigation. *The Naval Treaty*

*****TOBIN.** The caretaker in "the great Worthingdon bank business" who lost his life. *The Resident Patient*

*****TODMAN.** Sold his Vermissa Valley mine to the State and Merton County Railroad Company. *The Valley of Fear*

*****TOLLER.** Groom at the Rucastle house in Hampshire, he was the only person who could handle the savage mastiff, Carlo. *The Copper Beeches*

TOLLER, MRS. A servant of Jethro Rucastle's, and wife of the above. *The Copper Beeches*

*****TONGA.** An Andaman Islander, the loyal companion of the ex-convict, Jonathan Small, who had once saved his life. *The Sign of Four*

*****TREGELLIS, JANET.** Daughter of the head gamekeeper at Hurlstone, the ancestral home of a branch of the Musgrave family in Western Sussex, Brunton (the butler at Hurlstone) took up with her after dropping Rachel Howells. *The Musgrave Ritual*

TREGENNIS, BRENDA. Found dead of fright the morning after she had played cards with her three brothers, she "had been a very beautiful girl, though [now] verging upon middle age. Her dark, clear-cut face was handsome, even in death, but there lingered upon it something of that last convulsion of horror which had been her last human condition." *The Devil's Foot*

TREGENNIS, GEORGE. On a certain spring evening in 1897, he sat down, "in excellent health and spirits," to play cards with his brothers and sister. On the following morning, however, he and his brother Owen were found "laughing, shouting, and singing, the senses stricken clean out of them," while their sister lay dead. His face was "an expression of the utmost horror—a convulsion of terror which was dreadful to look upon." Shortly afterwards, George and Owen were removed to the asylum in Helston. *The Devil's Foot*

TREGENNIS, MORTIMER. "An independent gentleman" who rented rooms from the vicar of the parish in the Cornish hamlet of Tredannick Wollas, he was said to be "a sad-faced, introspective man ...brooding apparently upon his own affairs." Mortimer certainly had reason to be sad-faced, for his sister had been killed and his two brothers driven insane. But when he too died the mystery deepened, and the tale became one of retribution. *The Devil's Foot*

TREGENNIS, OWEN. See George Tregennis. *The Devil's Foot*

TREVELYAN, DR. PERCY. Of 403, Brook Street, he graduated from London University, occupied a research position at King's College Hospital, and won the Bruce Pinkerton Prize and Medal for his monograph on obscure nervous lesions. 'Mr. Blessington', a complete stranger, then set him up in the Brook Street practice in return for three quarters of his earnings. Blessington also demanded to be looked after, and had two rooms on the premises, a bedroom and a sitting room, for himself. He offered to run the whole house, even as far as finding the furniture and paying the maids. All the doctor had to do was wear out his chair in the consulting room. But his strange lodger hardly ever left the house. In spite of building up a lucrative practice, Trevelyan felt compelled to ask Holmes' advice. *The Resident Patient*

*TREVOR, JUSTICE OF THE PEACE. Victor Trevor's father, he was a widower and had been a boxer, a traveller and a prospector for gold. "He was a man of little culture, but with a considerable amount of rude strength both physically and mentally. He knew hardly any books, but he had travelled far, had seen much of the world, and had remembered all that he had learned." In his younger days, he had had a questionable career, which came back to haunt him in the person of a man named Hudson. *The "Gloria Scott"*

*TREVOR, VICTOR. The only friend Sherlock Holmes had made during his two years at college. His invitation to Holmes to come down to his father's place at Donnithorpe, in Norfolk, involved Holmes in his first case. When the truth surrounding the case was fully disclosed, Victor was heartbroken over the facts concerning his father, and went out to the **Terai** tea planting, where Holmes heard that he was doing well. *The "Gloria Scott"*

TURNER, ALICE. The daughter of John Turner, of Boscombe Valley Estate. James McCarthy refused to propose to her, even though there was an obvious attraction between the two young people, because he had earlier, and unknown to everyone else, imprudently married a barmaid. When James was arrested for the murder of his father, Alice felt that he was innocent and retained Inspector Lestrade to find out the truth. Lestrade consulted Holmes when the case seemed hopeless to him. *The Boscombe Valley Mystery*

TURNER, JOHN. He had made his fortune in Australia and retired to the Boscombe Valley area, in Herefordshire. He let a farm on his estate to his old acquaintance, Charles Mc-Carthy, who was later found murdered. See Black Jack of Ballarat. *The Boscombe Valley Mystery,*

*TURNER, MRS. She appeared as Holmes' landlady in place of Mrs. Hudson during his battle of wits with Irene Adler and has since created a mystery all her own. Said Sherlock to Watson. "When Mrs. Turner has brought in the tray I will make it [*A Scandal in Bohemia*] clear to you."

*TUSON, SERGEANT. A member of the City of London Police, he was alert enough to foil the Pinner (*alias* Beddington) robbery of Mawson & Williams. *The Stockbroker's Clerk*

U

*UPWOOD, COLONEL. The full explanation of a famous case had to wait until Holmes concluded two more cases "of the utmost importance." In the first, "he had exposed the atrocious conduct of Colonel Upwood in connection with the famous card scandal of the Nonpareil Club." *The Hound of the Baskervilles*

V

*VAMBERRY. The case of Vamberry, the wine merchant, was one of Watson's untold tales. *The Musgrave Ritual*

*VAN DEHER. Like many another in the area, he sold his Vermissa Valley ironworks to the West Wilmerton General Mining Company. *The Valley of Fear*

*VAN JANSEN. The death of Enoch J. Drebber reminded Holmes "of the circumstances attendant on the death of Van Jansen in Utrecht, in the year '34," for, though no wound appeared on the body, great gouts and splashes of blood lay all around. *A Study in Scarlet*

*VAN SEDDAR. Count Negretto Sylvius felt that Holmes was completely ignorant of Van Seddar, and how he was to get the stolen Crown diamond to Amsterdam. *The Mazarin Stone*

VANDELEUR. One of the assumed names of Rodger and Beryl Baskerville when they ran a school in East Yorkshire. 'Mr. Vandeleur' had a great interest in entomology, and "the name of Vandeleur had been permanently attached to a certain moth which he had, in his Yorkshire days, been the first to describe." *The Hound of the Baskervilles*

*VENUCCI, LUCRETIA. Maid to the Princess of Colonna, she had been suspected of stealing the famous black pearl of the Borgias. *The Six Napoleons*

*VENUCCI, PIETRO. "One of the greatest cut-throats in London," Venucci was from Naples and had ties with the Mafia. He was found brutally murdered on the doorstep of Horace Harker's house. *The Six Napoleons*

*VERNER. Following his epic struggle with Professor Moriarty above the Reichenbach Falls and his subsequent travels, Sherlock Holmes returned to his rooms in 221B Baker Street. After he had been back for some time, he asked Watson to sell his small Kensington practice and move back into Baker Street with him. Watson was astounded when a young doctor named Verner bought the practice, giving almost without argument the highest price he dared to ask. The incident was only explained some years later, when the Doctor discovered that Verner was a distant relative of Holmes and that it was Sherlock who had supplied the money. The similarity between 'Verner' and 'Vernet' (see 'Art' in Props) is certainly suggestive. *The Norwood Builder*

VIBART, JULES. The fiancé of Marie Devine, he connected the sudden departure of her mistress, the Lady Frances Carfax, "with the visit to the hotel a day or two before of a tall, dark, bearded man." *The Disappearance of Lady Frances Carfax*

VON BORK. A German whom Holmes beat in a battle of wits just before the First World War. He was unmatchable among all the Kaiser's agents, something which recommended him for the English mission. Von Bork gathered his information by pretending to be a sports-man, able to associate with British officers and Cabinet Ministers. Besides this particular spy, Holmes had also had dealings with two of his relatives, a cousin and an uncle. *His Last Bow*

*VON HERDER. The blind German mechanic, who constructed a noiseless and tremendously powerful air-gun which fired soft revolver bullets. *The Empty House*

*VON HERLING, BARON. Chief Secretary of the German legation in London, he knew about the operations in England of the German spy, Von Bork. *His Last Bow*

VON KRAMM, COUNT. The hereditary King of Bohemia, Wilhelm Gottsreich Sigismond von Ormstein, came to Holmes disguised as the Count von Kramm. (*A Scandal in Bohemia*) but Sherlock soon guessed who he really was. A very close friend of Irene Adler, which see.

*VON SAXE-MENINGEN, CLOTILDE LOTHMAN. The woman the King of Bohemia planned to marry for dynastic reasons. She was the second daughter of the King of Scandinavia. *A Scandal in Bohemia*

*VON WALDBAUM, FRITZ. Watson retained an almost verbatim report of Holmes' interview with Monsieur Dubuque, of the Paris police, and Fritz von Waldbaum, the well-known specialist of Danzig, in the investigation known as *The Naval Treaty*

WALDRON. Rodger Prescott (which see) used this *alias* to rent the rooms later occupied by Nathan Garrideb. *The Three Garridebs*

*WALKER BROTHERS**. They sent only one hundred dollars to the Scowrers as protection money, with fatal results as five hundred dollars had been demanded. "If [we] do not hear by Wednesday their winding gear may get out of order. We had to burn their breaker last year before they became reasonable." *The Valley of Fear*

WALTER, COLONEL VALENTINE. The younger brother of Sir James Walter, he was a very tall, handsome, light-bearded man of fifty whose "wild eyes, stained cheeks, and unkempt hair" all spoke of the sorrow he felt at his brother's death. *The Bruce-Partington Plans*

*WALTER, SIR JAMES**. The actual official guardian of the stolen Bruce-Partington submarine plans, he was a famous Government expert. One of the two men who had a key to the safe in which the precious plans were kept, he was so proud that it broke his heart to think of the thief's identity. *The Bruce-Partington Plans*

WALTERS, CONSTABLE. The policeman in the Surrey Constabulary who was left in possession of the house of the recently murdered Aloysius Garcia. *Wisteria Lodge*

*WARBURTON, COLONEL**. Watson introduced two cases to Sherlock Holmes. One concerned Victor Hatherley's thumb and the other Colonel Warburton's madness. However, only an account of *The Engineer's Thumb* appeared in print.

*WARDLAW, COLONEL. Ran Pugilist for the Wessex Cup against *Silver Blaze*

*WARNER, JOHN. Ex-gardener of High Gable, who had been "sacked in a moment of temper by his imperious employer," Mr. Henderson. Holmes used Warner to gain information about the staff and the layout of High Gable, and the man was also responsible for rescuing Miss Burnett. *Wisteria Lodge*

*WARREN, MR. A timekeeper at Morton & Waylight's, in Tottenham Court Road, he was the husband of Mrs. Warren, who came to Sherlock Holmes complaining about the unusual habits of one of her lodgers. Even though the husband was just as nervous over the situation as his wife, he quickly became even more nervous "when two men came up behind him, threw a coat over his head, and bundled him into a cab that was beside the kerb," finally tossing him out of the vehicle onto Hampstead Heath. *The Red Circle*

WARREN, MRS. A landlady, she brought her problem to Holmes because he had arranged an affair for a lodger of hers the year previous. Although the detective rebuffed her initially, Mrs. Warren drew upon "the pertinacity, and also the cunning, of her sex" in order to get Holmes to take her case. Which led eventually to the murder of "a devil and a monster." *The Red Circle*

*WARRENDER, MISS MINNIE. Holmes had all the facts concerning the life history of Miss Minnie Warrender in a squat notebook. The notebook was important because it contained details of the entire career of Count Negretto Silvius, who had, among many other crimes, deceived this woman. *The Mazarin Stone*

W[ATSON]. H. From these initials engraved on a family

heirloom, Holmes deduced a number of remarkable things about Dr. Watson's elder brother by studying their father's watch, which had come to Watson on the death of that brother. *The Sign of Four*

[WATSON], JAMES. Kate Whitney had come to ask Mrs. Watson's for help to bring her opium addicted husband home. Seeing Mrs. Whitney's distress Mary Watson asked, "Should you rather that I sent James off to bed?" Later Dr. *John* H. Watson went out looking for the errant man, knowing—one hopes —why his wife had called him "James" or, perhaps, who the other individual in the Watson family was. *The Man with the Twisted Lip*

WATSON, JOHN H. "In the year 1878 I took my degree of Doctor of Medicine of the University of London, and proceeded to Netley to go through the course prescribed for surgeons in the army. Having completed my studies there, I was duly attached to the Fifth Northumberland Fusiliers as Assistant Surgeon. The regiment was stationed in India at the time, and before I could join it, the second Afghan War had broken out. On landing at Bombay, I learned that my corps had advanced through the passes, and was already deep in the enemy's country. I followed, however, with many other officers who were in the same situation as myself, and succeeded in reaching Candahar in safety, where I found my regiment, and at once entered upon my new duties.

The campaign brought honours and promotion to many, but for me it had nothing but misfortune and disaster. I was removed from my brigade and attached to the Berkshires, with whom I served at the fatal battle of Maiwand. There I was struck on the shoulder by a Jezail bullet, which shattered the bone and grazed the subclavian artery.

Worn with pain, and weak from the prolonged hardships which I had undergone, I was removed, with a great train of wounded sufferers, to the base hospital at Peshawar. Here I rallied, and had already improved so far as to be able to walk about the wards, and even to bask a little upon the verandah, when I was struck down by enteric fever, that curse of our Indian possessions. For months my life was despaired of, and when at last I came to myself and became convalescent I was so weak and emaciated that a medical board determined that not a day should be lost in sending me back to England. I was despatched, accordingly, in the troopship *Orontes,* and landed a month later on Portsmouth jetty, with my health irretrievably ruined, but with permission from a paternal government to spend the next nine months in attempting to improve it.

I had neither kith nor kin in England, and was therefore as free as air—or as free as an income of eleven shillings and sixpence a day will permit a man to be. Under such circumstances I naturally gravitated to London, that great cesspool into which all the loungers and idlers of the Empire are irresistibly drained. There I stayed for some time at a private hotel in the Strand, leading a comfortless, meaningless existence, and spending such money as I had, considerably more freely than I ought. So alarming did the state of my finances become, that I soon realized that I must either leave the metropolis and rusticate somewhere in the country, or that I must make a complete alteration in my style of living. Choosing the latter alternative, I began by making up my mind to leave the hotel, and to take up my quarters in some less pretentious and less expensive domicile."

As with Sherlock Holmes, one feels that the Doctor should be itemised no further since, after meeting and sharing lodgings with the detective, Watson pervades almost the entire canon. Is, indeed, largely responsible for its existence. But see *A Study in Scarlet,* etc.

WATSON, MRS. [See also Mary Morstan.] When Kate Whitney, an old school-friend, came asking for help in bringing her husband home from an opium den, Watson said, "Folk who were in grief came to my wife like birds to a lighthouse." *The Man with the Twisted Lip.* See also *The Boscombe Valley Mystery, The Stockbroker's Clerk* and *The Final Problem*

*WEST, ARTHUR CADOGAN. Found dead just outside Aldgate Station, the twenty-seven-year-old West seemed quite a puzzle. A clerk at Woolwich Arsenal who, though hot-headed and impetuous, had been straight and honest, with ten years of good work to his credit, nevertheless pages from the top-secret plans for the Bruce-Partington submarine were found on his dead body. Before Holmes could decide whether West had been either a spy or a good citizen the detective had to solve what had impelled the him to leave his fiancée, Miss Violet Westbury, standing in the fog on the evening before the discovery of his body. *The Bruce-Partington Plans*

WESTBURY, MISS VIOLET. She felt that West was innocent of any wrong-doing in spite of what appeared to be un-chivalrous treatment towards her. *The Bruce-Partington Plans*

*WESTPHAIL, MISS HONORIA. Unmarried sister of Mrs. Stoner [Mrs. Grimsby Rylott] and aunt of Helen and Julia Stoner. Julia met a half-pay major at her house and became engaged to him. *The Speckled Band*

*WHITE, ABEL. An indigo-planter in India, he took pity on Jonathan Small, who had lost a leg to a crocodile in the Ganges River, and offered him a job as overseer on his plantation. White was later killed in the Indian Mutiny. *The Sign of Four*

*WHITNEY, ELIAS. Doctor of Divinity and Principal of the Theological College of St. George's. His brother, Isa Whitney, was an opium addict and had to be rescued from The Bar of Gold by Watson. *The Man with the Twisted Lip*

WHITNEY, KATE. See Mrs Watson

*WHITTINGTON, LADY ALICIA. She was at the wedding of Lord St. Simon and Hatty Doran. *The Noble Bachelor*

WIGGINS. At the time that Holmes was investigating the death of Enoch J. Drebber, Wiggins headed the Baker Street Irregulars. *A Study in Scarlet.* "One of their number, taller and older than the others, [Wiggins] stood forward with an air of lounging superiority which was very funny in such a disreputable little scarecrow." *The Sign of Four*

*WILCOX, CHESTER. Of Marley Creek, Vermissa Valley. In an attempt on his life by the Scowrers one of them, Jim Carnaway, was killed. Wilcox was the chief foreman of the Iron Dyke Company. Jack McMurdo led another unsuccessful attempt on his life. In view of what was revealed later, this attempt was bound to be aborted. *The Valley of Fear*

WILDER, JAMES. Secretary to the Duke of Holdernesse, "he was small, nervous, alert, with intelligent, light blue eyes and mobile features." He also happened to be the Duke's elder (illegitimate) son. *The Priory School*

*WILLABY, ARTHUR. He stood guard with Jack McMurdo outside the editorial offices of the Vermissa *Herald,* while other members of The Ancient Order of Freemen (The Scowrers) attacked the editor. *The Valley of Fear*

WILLIAMS. A prize-fighter, he had been lightweight champion of England. Once employed as a porter by Major John Sholto of Pondicherry Lodge until that man's death, he then went to work for his son, Thaddeus Sholto, as a servant. He drove the vehicle which took Mary Morstan, Sherlock Holmes and Doctor Watson to his employer's house after picking up them up outside the Lyceum Theatre. *The Sign of Four*

*WILLIAMS, JAMES BAKER. His large house, Forton Old Hall, was, like so many others in this tale, near that of Aloysius Garcia. *Wisteria Lodge*

WILLIAMSON, MR. This man's agent was entirely mistaken in thinking that he was a respectable elderly gentleman. In fact, Williamson was an unfrocked clergyman quite willing to trick Violet Smith into an illegal marriage. *The Solitary Cyclist*

*WILLOWS, DR. He felt that John Turner was a wreck, and that his nervous system was shattered after the violent death of his tenant, Charles McCarthy. But as it turned out Turner had murdered the man. *The Boscombe Valley Mystery*

*WILSON. The sham chaplain aboard the barque *Gloria Scott* in 1855, in league with the convict Jack Prendergast. He was instrumental in the convict uprising, shooting the captain. Presumed dead when the ship was destroyed in an explosion. *The "Gloria Scott"*

WILSON. Manager of the district office where the young messenger boy, Cartwright, worked. Holmes employed the youth to run errands and perform other tasks during the investigation into the death of Sir Charles Baskerville but he had earlier helped Wilson in a little case which saved the manager's good name, and perhaps his life. *The Hound of the Baskervilles*

*WILSON. According to Watson, a number of memorable events occurred in 1895. One of these was the "arrest of Wilson, the notorious canary-trainer, which removed a plague-spot from the East End of London." *Black Peter*

WILSON. A Kentish constable, he met Holmes, Watson, and Stanley Hopkins at the garden gate of Yoxley Old Place. This was the country house where Willoughby Smith had been murdered. *The Golden Pince-nez.*

*WILSON. "A mere boy, in his teens," he volunteered to murder Andrew Rae. *The Valley of Fear*

*WILSON, BARTHOLOMEW. District ruler of Lodge 29, Chicago, of The Ancient Order of Freemen. *The Valley of Fear*

WILSON, JABEZ. A pawnbroker, Wilson was fortunate to obtain what seemed like a sinecure with an organisation of red-heads, but came to Holmes one day when he found his 'work' had suddenly stopped without notice. *The Red-Headed League*

WILSON, SERGEANT. Sussex Police. He received first news of the murder of John Douglas. *The Valley of Fear*

*WILSON, STEVE. Of Hobson's Patch. Jack McMurdo claimed that he was the Pinkerton operative on the trail of the Scowrers. *The Valley of Fear*

WINDIBANK, JAMES. Holmes said, "There never was a man who deserved punishment more…That fellow will rise from crime to crime until he does something very bad and ends on a gallows." *A Case of Identity*

WINDIGATE. He was the ruddy-faced landlord of the Alpha Inn who instituted a Christmas Goose Club. *The Blue Carbuncle*

*WINDLE, J. W. He wrote a letter to the Vermissa Lodge

from Merton County Lodge 249, signing himself D.M.A.O.F. [Division Master Ancient Order Freemen] and asking that two men be sent over to eliminate Andrew Rae of Rae and Sturmash, coal owners. The response was, "Windle has never refused us when we have had occasion to ask for the loan of a man or two, and it is not for us to refuse him." *The Valley of Fear*

WINTER, JAMES. See Evans and/or Morecroft.

WINTER, MISS KITTY. A woman "ruined" by the notorious Baron Adelbert Gruner, she vowed to drag him down until he was lower than herself, and she tried to help Holmes by telling Miss Violet de Melville how wicked the Baron was and that she shouldn't think of marrying him. Although her words fell on deaf ears, Kitty finally disfigured the handsome man with vitriol. *The Illustrious Client*

*WOOD, DR. "A brisk and capable general practitioner" from Birlstone, he was called in to examine the dead body of John Douglas, of Birlstone Manor. *The Valley of Fear*

WOOD, HENRY. Once the smartest man in the 117th Foot, and the rival of Sergeant James Barclay for the love of Nancy Devoy, daughter of a colour-sergeant. He was deliberately led into an ambush by Barclay, captured by rebels during the Indian Mutiny and taken to Nepal. Escaping, he wandered in Afghanistan and the Punjab, where he "lived mostly among the natives, and picked up a living by...conjuring tricks." *The Crooked Man*

*WOOD, J. G. A "famous observer" and author. One of Wood's books, *Out of Doors,* described his encounter with the fearsome *Cyanea Capillata. The Lion's Mane*

*WOODHOUSE. A criminal, he was, according to Holmes, one of the fifty men who had "good reason" for taking the detective's life. *The Bruce-Partington Plans*

*WOODLEY, MISS EDITH She had at one time been engaged to Ronald Adair. *The Empty House*

WOODLEY, JACK. "Roaring Jack" had been "the greatest brute and bully in South Africa, a man whose name [is] a holy terror from Kimberley to Johannesburg." He had come back to England with Bob Carruthers who had introduced the innocent Violet Smith into his household as governess to his only daughter as a prelude to fraud. *The Solitary Cyclist*

WRIGHT, THERESA. Lady Brackenstall's maid and occasional nurse. She had served her mistress since she was a baby, and detested the way Lady Brackenstall was being treated by her violent husband whenever he was drunk. *The Abbey Grange*

Y

*YOUGHALL. He belonged to the Scotland Yard Criminal Investigation Department and arrested the thieves who had stolen the Crown diamond. *The Mazarin Stone*

YOUNG, BRIGHAM. Real-life leader of the religious sect known as the Mormons, he welcomed John and Lucy Ferrier into the Faith but later visited the latter to discuss the rumours that John was failing in one of its main tenets, his daughter was engaged to a gentile. She had, said Young, thirty days in which to choose a Mormon husband before one was forced upon her. *A Study in Scarlet*

Z

*ZAMBA. An invalid, and 'sleeping partner' in the firm of Castalotti and Zamba, New York Fruit Importers. *The Red Circle*

PART TWO
(PLACES)

The Old Hereford Jail

"The Boscombe Valley Mystery"

Disregarding such titles as 'The Abbey Grange', 'The Three Gables' etc., there are surprisingly few imagined place or other names in the canon, and those place-names which do occur are occasionally combined with non-imaginary ones. For example Cerne Abbas in Dorset and King's Pyon in Herefordshire (near Clyro Court where Doyle visited his friend Sir Thomas *Baskerville)*, becomes +Abbas Parva in Berkshire and +King's Pyland on Dartmoor. Others are real places, but not in the geographical area of the supposed 'Adventure'. This applies particularly to London, where a name used does exist but not at or near the scene of operations. For example Pinchin Lane, where Sherman the bird-stuffer lives in "a row of shabby two storied brick houses", isn't in "the lower quarter of Lambeth" but across the river in Whitechapel. A location which would have been rather inconvenient for Watson after he had escorted Miss Morstan to Mrs. Forrester's house in Lower Camberwell and then needed to cross London Bridge in the early hours of the morning to borrow a dog.

A

+**ABBAS PARVA**. A small village in Berkshire. It was where Ronder, a showman and lion-tamer, was killed by Leonardo the Circus Strong Man. *The Veiled Lodger*

ABBEY GRANGE. The home of Sir Eustace and Lady Mary Brackenstall in Marsham, Kent. *The Abbey Grange*

ABBEY SCHOOL. Holmes was clearing up the case of the 'Abbey School' - possibly 'The Priory School'- at the time James Dodd asked him to look into the mystery of *The Blanched Soldier*

ABERDEEN. Holmes noted that there was a case parallel to that of Lord St. Simon's in Aberdeen, which he had read about some years earlier. *The Noble Bachelor*

ALDGATE STATION. On the District Railway. Arthur

Cadogan West's body was found here. *The Bruce-Partington Plans*

ALLAHABAD, INDIA. A young man called Edmunds, who belonged to the Berkshire police force, was sent to Allahabad sometime after the tragic events in Abbas Parva. He had consulted Holmes about the case, and certain points about it puzzled both him and the detective. They even smoked a pipe or two together over it. Was he sent to India because, as Sherlock said, he was "A smart lad that!"? *The Veiled Lodger*

+ALLARDYCE'S. Holmes spent a good part of one morning in this butcher's shop trying to transfix a dead pig, hung from the rafters, by a single blow from a harpoon. *Black Peter*

AMERICA. "It is always a joy to me to meet an American, Mr. Moulton, for I am one of those who believe that the folly of a monarch and the blundering of a Minister in far gone years will not prevent our children from being someday citizens of the same world-wide country under a flag which shall be a quartering of the Union Jack with the Stars and Stripes." So said Sherlock in *The Noble Bachelor*

ANDAMAN ISLANDS. Situated 340 miles to the north of Sumatra, in the Bay of Bengal. The men who were bound by 'The Sign of the Four Oath' were imprisoned in that part of the area known as Blair Island. *The Sign of Four*

ANDOVER. A case, similar to the one Miss Mary Sutherland brought to Sherlock Holmes, happened in Andover in 1887. *A Case of Identity*

+ANGLO-INDIAN CLUB. One of the London clubs where Colonel Sebastian Moran was a member. *The Empty House*

APPLEDORE TOWERS. A notorious blackmailer's house in Hampstead. *Charles Augustus Milverton*

ARIZONA. Francis Hay Moulton, the true husband of

Hatty Doran, prospected there after leaving San Francisco. *The Noble Bachelor*

ASTON. The man who called himself John Garrideb excitedly displayed a newspaper advertisement to Nathan Garrideb and said that if they could really find another person of the same name (i.e. three altogether) both would become rich. Nathan saw (or thought he saw) that the advertisement had been placed by "Howard Garrideb, Constructor of Agricultural Machinery," who could be reached at the Grosvenor Buildings, Aston. *The Three Garridebs*

AUSTRALIA. John Turner had made his fortune in Australia, and then come back to England. Charles McCarthy joined him, and, for reasons not revealed until later, was given a fine farm on his estate. *The Boscombe Valley Mystery*. See also *The "Gloria Scott", The Empty House, The Priory School* and *The Disappearance of Lady Frances Carfax*

B

BADEN. Watson traced Lady Frances Carfax to the Englischer Hof in Baden. Only to find she had left the town in the company of a rascally couple calling themselves (for nefarious purposes) Dr. and Mrs. Shlessinger. *The Disappearance of Lady Frances Carfax*

+BAGATELLE CARD CLUB. One of the three clubs of which Ronald Adair was a member. It was known that on the day he died he had played whist here. Colonel Sebastian Moran was also a member of the club. *The Empty House*

BAKER STREET. Both Holmes and Watson were searching for less expensive lodgings when they first met. and Holmes told his new acquaintance that he had his eye on a suite of rooms in Baker Street which would suit them "down to the ground." *A Study in Scarlet*. See also *A Scandal in Bohemia, The Five Orange Pips, The Engineer's Thumb, The Beryl Coronet, The Copper Beeches, The Golden Pince-nez, The Cardboard Box, The Bruce-Partington Plans* and *The Mazarin Stone*

+**BALDWIN CARD CLUB**. See above. *The Empty House*.

BALLARAT. The holes which had been dug in the grounds of Pondicherry Lodge by the Sholto brothers searching for the great Agra treasure reminded Watson of a hill near Ballarat, Australia, where prospectors had been at work. *The Sign of Four*. See also *The Boscombe Valley Mystery*

BARBERTON. Philip Green, in love with Lady Frances, went to this area of South Africa and made his fortune there. *The Disappearance of Lady Frances Carfax*

+**BAR OF GOLD, THE**. An opium den in +Upper Swandam Lane, "between a slop shop and a gin shop, approached by a steep flight of steps leading down to a black gap like the mouth of a cave." Watson went there to retrieve Isa Whitney and send him home to his wife, Kate Whitney. *The Man with the Twisted Lip*

+**BASKERVILLE HALL**. The ancestral home of the Baskervilles, described at some length in *The Hound of the Baskervilles*

+**BEAUCHAMP ARRIANCE**. Dr. Leon Sterndale, who loved and was loved only once in his life, spent his time while in England in a small bungalow buried in the lonely wood of Beauchamp Arriance, on the Cornish Peninsula. *The Devil's Foot*

BELFAST. The cardboard box that Miss Susan Cushing received, and which contained two severed human ears, was posted in Belfast. *The Cardboard Box*

+**BELLIVER TOR**. This was the place where Watson

found the hidden lair of a mysterious man. *The Hound of the Baskervilles*

BENTINCK STREET. As Holmes passed the corner of Bentinck Street and Welbeck Street he was nearly run over by a van drawn by two horses. A little idea of Professor James Moriarty's. *The Final Problem*

BERKELEY SQUARE. The home of Miss Violet de Merville, and her (possibly putative) father General de Melville, at 104 Berkeley Square, was "one of those awful grey London castles which would make a church seem frivolous." *The Illustrious Client*

BERKSHIRE. Colonel Lysander Stark, who hired Victor Hatherley to repair his hydraulic press and was determined the young man would not leave the house alive, lived in Eyford, in Berkshire. *The Engineer's Thumb*. See also *The Speckled Band, The Veiled Lodger* and *Shoscombe Old Place*

+BEVINGTON'S. A silver-and-brilliant pendant of old Spanish design, belonging to the vanished Lady Frances Carfax, was pawned by Henry Peters at this jewellers in Westminster Road. *The Disappearance of Lady Frances Carfax*

BHURTEE. The place where the 117th Foot (later named 'The Royal Mallows' after the reorganisation of the army) were surrounded by insurgents during the Indian Mutiny. It was at this time that a 'love triangle' of James Barclay, Nancy Devoy, and Henry Wood reached its climax. *The Crooked Man*

+BIRLSTONE, MANOR HOUSE OF. "About half a mile from the town, standing in an old park famous for its huge beech trees, is the ancient Manor House of Birlstone. The Manor House, with its many gables and its small, diamond-paned windows, was still much as the builder had left it in the early seventeenth century." *The Valley of Fear*

+**BIRLSTONE, VILLAGE**. Consisting of "A small… cluster of half-timbered cottages on the northern border of the county of Sussex." *The Valley of Fear*

BIRMINGHAM. Holmes and Watson travelled together to Birmingham to investigate Hall Pycroft's odd tale of how he was invited to work for the Franco-Midland Hardware Company. *The Stockbroker's Clerk*. See also *The Three Gables* and *The Three Garridebs*

BLACKHEATH. John Hector McFarlane, accused of murdering Jonas Oldacre, lived with his parents at Torrington Lodge, Blackheath. *The Norwood Builder*. See also *The Missing Three-Quarter* and *The Sussex Vampire*

BLACKHEATH STATION. Watson caught his train there when he returned home from visiting Josiah Amberley's house in Lewisham. Sherlock Holmes' great rival in detection, Barker, took the carriage next to the Doctor's hoping to remain anonymous. But Watson recognized him from a previous sighting. *The Retired Colourman*

+**BLACK TOR**. On the moor in Devonshire, where Watson spotted someone standing. *The Hound of the Baskervilles*

BLAIR ISLAND. Jonathan Small was sent to the prison colony here to serve his life sentence for the murder of the merchant, Achmet. *The Sign of Four*

BLANDFORD STREET. Holmes and Watson, busy stalking Colonel Sebastian Moran (the 'old shikari' who intended to assassinate the detective) came out into Manchester Street and on to Blandford Street, where they turned swiftly down a narrow passage. *The Empty House*

BOMBAY. When as a young newly qualified army doctor Watson arrived in Bombay to join his regiment as an

Assistant Surgeon (Fifth Northumberland Fusiliers), he "learned that my corps had advanced through the passes, and was already deep in the enemy's country." *A Study in Scarlet*

BOND STREET. A hat-shop belonging to Madame Lesurier was situated in this very fashionable and expensive Street. *Silver Blaze*. See also *The Hound of the Baskervilles*

BORDEAUX. Westhouse & Marbank, the great claret importers, had their French offices in Bordeaux. James Windibank was said to be there when his stepdaughter, Mary Sutherland, addressed a letter to him asking permission to marry Hosmer Angel. *A Case of Identity*

+BOSCOMBE POOL. Charles McCarthy was brutally killed on the edge of this body of water. *The Boscombe Valley Mystery*

+BOSCOMBE VALLEY. This was a country district, not far from Ross, in Herefordshire. *The Boscombe Valley Mystery*

BOWERY, THE. A dangerous and run down area of New York City, where Gennaro Lucca saved Tito Castalotte from being set upon by some ruffians. *The Red Circle*

BRADFORD. Holmes was jubilant over his discovery of "an infallible test for blood stains." He felt it would have been decisive in the case of Mason who came from the city of Bradford. *A Study in Scarlet*

+BRADLEY'S. Holmes asked Watson, as the latter was on his way out, to ask Bradley's to send up a pound of the strongest shag tobacco to help him in his study of the salient points arising from the mysterious death of Sir Charles Baskerville. *The Hound of the Baskervilles*

BRAZIL. Jonathan Small and Tonga had booked their passage on the *Esmeralda*, at Gravesend, bound for Brazil, in their attempt to escape from England after the murder of

Bartholomew Sholto. *The Sign of Four*. See also *The Problem of Thor Bridge*

+**BRIARBRAE**. The name of the house in which Percy Phelps lived. *The Naval Treaty*

+**BRIONY LODGE**. Irene Adler's house in St. John's Wood. *A Scandal in Bohemia*

BRITISH MUSEUM. Holmes spent a morning here reading Eckermann's *Voodooism and the Negroid Religions*, among other works, in order to find out what the weird objects found in the kitchen of the house rented by Aloysius Garcia might mean. *Wisteria Lodge*

BRIXTON. The Tangeys, husband and wife, who worked in the Foreign Office as commissionaire and charwoman respectively, lived at 16, Ivy Lane, Brixton. See also *Black Peter, The Disappearance of Lady Frances Carfax, The Three Garridebs* and *The Red Circle*

+**BRODERICK AND NELSON**. The dog Toby followed a false scent by way of Nine Elms and the White Eagle tavern to Broderick and Nelson's large Timber Yard. *The Sign of Four*

BROOK STREET. Dr. Percy Trevelyan had his surgery at 403 Brook Street, where he looked after a very frightened 'Mr. Blessington'. *The Resident Patient*

BROOKLYN. Gennaro and Emilia Lucca lived here after their flight from Italy. *The Red Circle*

BRUSSELS. On their way to the Switzerland, Holmes and Watson landed at Dieppe, and made their way to Brussels. *The Final Problem*. See also *The Stockbroker's Clerk*

BUDA-PESTH [BUDAPEST]. Watson tells us that some months after the conclusion of one of his 'Adventures' with Holmes a "curious" newspaper clipping arrived in Baker Street from here. It revealed what may have happened to three people concerned in the investigation he called *The*

Greek Interpreter. See also *The Devil's Foot*

BUFFALO. Holmes, disguised as Altamont, the Irish-American spy, said that he learned his trade, 'graduated', in an Irish secret society at Buffalo. *His Last Bow*

C

CALCUTTA. Dr. Grimesby Roylott had, by his professional skill and force of character, established a large practice in Calcutta. *The Speckled Band*

CAMBERWELL. Madame Charpentier's boarding-house, where a dead man, Enoch J. Drebber, had stayed, was here in Torquay Terrace. *A Study in Scarlet.* See also *A Case of Identity, The Valley of Fear* and *The Disappearance of Lady Frances Carfax*

CAMBERWELL ROAD. The hat found beside the dead body of Enoch J. Drebber was made by John Underwood and Sons of 129, Camberwell Road. *A Study in Scarlet*

CAMBRIDGE. Sherlock Holmes, who travelled to Cambridge to investigate the mysterious disappearance of Godfrey Staunton, thought it was an "inhospitable town." *The Missing Three-Quarter.* See also *The Naval Treaty*, and *The Golden Pince-nez*

+CAMDEN HOUSE. This very significant unrented dwelling was opposite 221B Baker Street and had "bare planking" and wallpaper "hanging in ribbons." *The Empty House*

+CAMFORD. The name of both "a famous University" and the "charming town" in which it was situated. Obviously a conflation of Cambridge and Oxford, making it intriguing to know which of these two Institutions (if either) Holmes attended. *The Creeping Man*

+CAMPDEN HOUSE ROAD. Where Horace Harker's plaster cast of Devine's bust of Napoleon was found smashed to pieces in the front garden of an empty house.

The Six Napoleons

+CAMPDEN MANSIONS. Louis La Rothiere, of Campden Mansions, Notting Hill, was one of only three (foreign) agents capable of stealing the plans for building a super-submarine. *The Bruce-Partington Plans*

CANDAHAR. The young Dr. Watson, newly attached to the Fifth Northumberland Fusiliers as Assistant Surgeon, says he joined his regiment here after travelling from Bombay. Note the nineteenth century spelling. *A Study in Scarlet*

CANTERBURY. The Continental Express that carried Holmes and Watson away from Victoria Station stopped at Canterbury. There they left the train and made a cross-country journey to Newhaven, and on to Dieppe by boat. *The Final Problem*

+CAPITAL AND COUNTIES BANK. Holmes banked here, at the Oxford Street branch. *The Priory School.* See also *The Man with the Twisted Lip* and *The Bruce-Partington Plans*

+CAPLETON STABLES. Located on the moor, about two miles from the King's Pyland Stables, these were owned by Lord Backwater and managed by Silas Brown. *Silver Blaze*

CARLTON. Holmes received a note from Sir James Damery asking to see the detective. A note which was sent from the Carlton Club. *The Illustrious Client*

+CAVENDISH CARD CLUB. See the Bagatelle and Baldwin card clubs. *The Empty House*

CAVENDISH SQUARE. Dr. Percy Trevelyan noted that "a specialist who aims high is compelled to start in one of a dozen streets in the Cavendish Square quarter, all of which entail enormous rents and furnishing expenses." *The Resident Patient.* See also *The Empty House*

+CEDARS, THE. Near Lee, in Kent, it was the residence of Neville St. Clair, who mysteriously disappeared into the room of the wretched beggar, Hugh Boone, at The Bar of Gold opium den. Watson and Holmes stayed at The Cedars during their investigation of the case. This has led to the supposition that Holmes may have been in love with St. Clair's wife, or entrapped by her, since there seems no obvious reason why he should have left London.[2] *The Man with the Twisted Lip.*

+**CHARLINGTON HALL.** Located between the village of Farnham and +Chiltern Grange, "the house was invisible from the road, but the surroundings all spoke of gloom and decay." An unfrocked clergyman named Williamson lived here with a small staff of servants. *The Solitary Cyclist*

CHARING CROSS HOSPITAL. James Mortimer was a house surgeon at Charing Cross Hospital from 1882 to 1884. He accidently left his commemorative walking stick (presented to him when he quitted the Hospital) at 221B Baker Street. The words engraved on it, "To James Mortimer, M.R.C.S., from his friends of the C.C.H.", enabled Holmes to deduce certain facts, and from some marks that his visitor owned a small terrier. *The Hound of the Baskervilles.* In another investigation, Holmes was first carried to the Charing Cross Hospital and then taken to his rooms in Baker Street after the murderous attack made on him on the orders of the notorious Baron Adelbert Gruner. *The Illustrious Client*

CHEESEMAN'S. Robert Ferguson's home, which was near +Lamberley in Sussex, was an isolated and old farm-house. "The ancient tiles which lined the porch were marked with the rebus of a cheese and a man, after the original builder." *The Sussex Vampire*

---

[2] 'The Little Woman in Kent' by Lars Falk. The Sherlock Holmes Journal   VOL 29 No 4 pp 139-141 (Summer, 2010)

CHESTERFIELD. Neville St. Clair's father had been a schoolmaster in Chesterfield. *The Man with the Twisted Lip.* See also *The Priory School*

CHESTERTON. One of the villages on the north side of Cambridge, it had been explored and found disappointing by Sherlock Holmes when he was searching for Godfrey Staunton. *The Missing Three-Quarter*

CHICAGO. Abe Slaney was known as "the most dangerous crook in Chicago." Although Holmes claimed that he knew something of Chicago criminals, he relied on a friend in the New York Police Bureau to provide him with information about Slaney. *The Dancing Men.* Holmes, disguised as Altamont the Irish-American spy, later went to Chicago to further implement a *persona* which would eventually help him capture the German spy, Von Bork. *His Last Bow.* See also *The Three Garridebs*

+CHILTERN GRANGE. About six miles from the village of Farnham, Chiltern Grange was the home of Bob Carruthers, the not so respectable man who employed Violet Smith as a governess. *The Solitary Cyclist*

CHINA. Holmes deduced that Jabez Wilson had been to China from the tattoo immediately above the old man's right wrist. "That trick of staining the fishes' scales of a delicate pink is quite peculiar to China. When, in addition, I see a Chinese coin hanging from your watch-chain, the matter becomes even more simple." *The Red-Headed League*

CHISWICK. Josiah Brown, whose plaster cast of Napoleon's head was smashed, had his address at Laburnum Lodge, Laburnum Vale, Chiswick. *The Six Napoleons*

CHRISTIE'S. Reclusive collector Nathan Garrideb seldom went out except to "drive down to Sotheby's or Christie's." (Two very famous London Sale Rooms). *The Three*

Garridebs. See also *The Illustrious Client*

CHURCH STREET. Sherlock Holmes, while posing as an elderly, deformed bibliophile, claimed to Watson that he kept a little bookshop on the corner of this street. *The Empty House*. See also *The Six Napoleons*

+CITY AND SUBURBAN BANK, COBURG BRANCH. It lay just around the corner from Jabez Wilson's Coburg Square pawnshop. *The Red-Headed League*

CLAPHAM JUNCTION. As Holmes, Watson, and Colonel Ross returned to London following their visit to the Winchester Races, their train passed through Clapham Junction on its way to Victoria Station. *Silver Blaze*. See also *The Greek Interpreter* and *The Naval Treaty*. It was during this latter investigation that Holmes made his 'beacons of light' speech about the board schools.

+CLEFT TOR. John Barrymore, the butler at Baskerville Hall, got mysterious signals late at night from this spot on an infamous moor. *The Hound of the Baskervilles*

CLEVELAND. In the pocket of Enoch J. Drebber, found dead under mysterious circumstances in an empty house on the Brixton Road, were cards bearing his name and an address in Cleveland, Ohio, where he had formerly lived. *A Study in Scarlet*

COBURG SQUARE. Jabez Wilson's small pawnbroker business was here, most significantly very near a bank. *The Red-Headed League*

CONDUIT STREET. Colonel Sebastian Moran's London address was in Conduit Street. *The Empty House*

COOMBE TRACEY. A town in Devonshire. Inspector Lestrade got off the London train there when he came to help Holmes in his investigation into the mystery of *The Hound of the Baskervilles*

+COPPER BEECHES. The home of Jephro Rucastle and

his wife and son, five miles on the far side of Winchester. *The Copper Beeches*

CORNISH PENINSULA. Sherlock Holmes, recovering from his "constant hard work and occasional indiscretions" [drug-taking? Constantly sitting up all night?] went with Watson to a small cottage near Poldhu Bay "at the farthest extremity of the Cornish Peninsula." It isn't, of course. Poldu Bay is close to the village of Mullion, which in its turn is nearer to The Lizard than to Land's End. *The Devil's Foot*

CORNWALL. The failure of the West Country banking firm, Dawson & Neligan, was the ruin of half the families living in Cornwall. *Black Peter*. See also *The Red-Headed League*

CORPORATION STREET. The temporary 'offices' of the Franco-Midland Hardware Company were at 126B Corporation Street, Birmingham. *The Stockbroker's Clerk*

COSTA RICA. Beryl Garcia, the wife of Jack Stapleton but posing as his sister, was a noted beauty from Costa Rica. *The Hound of the Baskervilles*. See also *Black Peter*

COVENT GARDEN. At the conclusion of one of their investigations together, Sherlock Holmes asked Watson to accompany him to a "Wagner night at Covent Garden." *The Red Circle*

COVENT GARDEN MARKET. Mr. Breckinridge's meat stall was in Covent Garden Market and he sold a goose from there – with interesting gastronomic results. *The Blue Carbuncle*

COVENTRY. At the time of the investigation into the affair which put Violet Smith in such danger, her fiancé Cyril Morton was working for the Midland Electric Company, at Coventry. *The Solitary Cyclist*. See also *The Five Orange Pips*

+**COX & CO**. "Somewhere in the vaults of the bank of Cox & Co., at Charing Cross, there is a travel-worn and battered tin dispatch.box with my name, John H. Watson, M.D., Late Indian Army, painted upon the lid. It is crammed with papers, nearly all of which are records of cases to illustrate the curious problems which Mr. Sherlock Holmes had at various times to examine." Watson, of course, wasn't in an Indian regiment. His box ought to have been labelled 'Late British Army in India'. Not so snappy perhaps but more accurate. *The Problem of Thor Bridge*

+**COXON & WOODHOUSE**. Hall Pycroft used to have a job at Coxon & Woodhouse, of Drapers' Gardens, but "they were let in early in the spring through the Venezuelan loan, as no doubt you remember, and came a nasty cropper." Pycroft eventually found a seemingly good job through Mr. Coxon's testimonial, but the strange circumstances surrounding it prompted him to seek Holmes' advice. *The Stockbroker's Clerk*

CRANE WATER. Near Reading, the home of the Armitage family. *The Speckled Band*

CRAVEN STREET. The Stapletons lodged in a hotel situated in this London street and, wearing a false beard, Jack Stapleton followed Dr. Mortimer to Baker Street, and afterwards to the station and on to the Northumberland Hotel. *The Hound of the Baskervilles*

CREWE. Mrs. Stoner, who had married the fierce Dr. Grimesby Roylott, died some years later in a railway accident near Crewe. *The Speckled Band*

CRENDALL. Three miles from Shoscombe Old Place in Berkshire. Holmes and Watson stayed at the Green Dragon Inn there. *Shoscombe Old Place*

CRITERION BAR. Dr. John H. Watson, recently returned

from the second Afghan War and paying more than he could afford to stay in a hotel in the Strand, ran into 'Young Stamford' (his former dresser at Bart's) when he went into the Criterion Bar. On being told that the old soldier was looking for cheaper lodgings, Stamford offered to introduce him to Sherlock Holmes, who was also looking for digs that he might share with someone. *A Study in Scarlet*

CROYDON. Miss Susan Cushing, who received a parcel containing two severed human ears, lived in Cross Street, Croydon. *The Cardboard Box*

D

DANZIG. See Fritz von Waldbaum. *The Naval Treaty*

DARTMOOR. Site of the mysterious events surrounding the disappearance of a very special racehorse, and the killing of its trainer, John Straker. *Silver Blaze.*

DAUBENSEE. As Holmes and Watson passed over the Gemmi Pass and "walked along the border of the melancholy Daubensee, a large rock which had been dislodged from the ridge upon our right clattered down and roared into the lake behind us." They had travelled from Brussels to Strasburg, then gone on to Geneva, spent a 'charming week' wandering through the Valley of the Rhone and branched off at Leuk. The rock incident showed that Holmes had not exaggerated when he warned Watson of the danger they would be in. *The Final Problem*

+DEEP DENE HOUSE. The residence of one Jonas Oldacre, in the London suburb of Lower Norwood. *The Norwood Builder*

DIEPPE. Having left the Continental Express at Canterbury, Holmes and Watson travelled overland to Newhaven, and from there to Dieppe, on their way to

Switzerland. *The Final Problem*

+**DONNITHORPE**. A little hamlet in Norfolk, it was the setting for Holmes' first case, *The "Gloria Scott"*

DUNDEE. Joseph Openshaw received a very frightening letter from Dundee, with instructions to "Put the papers on the sundial." *The Five Orange Pips*. Also, the steam sealer *Sea Unicorn*, which Captain Peter Carey commanded, sailed out of Dundee. *Black Peter*

E

EDGWARE ROAD. The Church of St. Monica, where Godfrey Norton and Irene Adler were married, with the disguised Sherlock Holmes as a witness, was in the Edgware Road. *A Scandal in Bohemia*. Nathan Garrideb's house agents, Holloway and Steele, had offices in the same Road, and he lived in Little Ryder Street, one of its smaller offshoots. *The Three Garridebs*

ENGLISCHER HOF. On May the 3rd, 1891, Holmes and Watson put up at The Englischer Hof, run by Peter Steiler the elder, in the Swiss village of Meiringen. *The Final Problem*. Lady Frances Carfax had stayed a fortnight at an Englischer Hof in Baden, before she vanished. See Shlessinger. *The Disappearance of Lady Frances Carfax*

ESSEX. The Reverend J. C. Elman's vicarage was in Little Purlington, Essex. *The Retired Colourman*

ETON. John Clay, who claimed to be the grandson of a royal duke and was himself a "murderer, thief, smasher, and forger," had been to Eton. *The Red-Headed League*. Colonel Sebastian Moran, whom Holmes finally bagged with Oscar Meunier's waxen image, was also educated at Eton [and Oxford]. *The Empty House*

EUSTON STATION. Enoch J. Drebber and Joseph Stangerson went to Euston Station to catch the Liverpool express on the night that Drebber was decoyed away and murdered. *A Study in Scarlet*. See also *The Priory School* and *The Blanched Soldier*

+**EYFORD**. A village in Berkshire near the borders of Oxfordshire and nearly seven miles from Reading. *The Engineer's Thumb*

F

+**FAIRBANK**. The "modest residence" of Alexander Holder in the southern suburb of Streatham. A priceless jewel, one of the most precious possessions of the Empire, was stolen from his house. *The Beryl Coronet*

FAREHAM. Joseph Openshaw had left his house to visit his old friend Major Freebody. Returning home from Fareham in the twilight, he met with what a jury afterwards decided (erroneously) was an accident. One which proved fatal. *The Five Orange Pips*

FARNHAM. A village on the borders of Surrey. Sherlock Holmes felt that the area around Farnham was "a beautiful neighbourhood, and full of the most interesting associations." One of these was that he and Watson apprehended Archie Stamford the forger near the town. *The Solitary Cyclist*

FLEET STREET. A certain group of red-heads supposedly had its offices in Pope's Court, Fleet Street. *The Red-Headed League*. See also *The Resident Patient*

FLORENCE. A week after his supposed death at the Reichenbach Falls, Sherlock Holmes found himself in Florence, "with the certainty that no one in the world knew what had become of me." *The Empty House*

FLORIDA. Elias Openshaw emigrated to America as a young man, and became a planter in Florida, where he was said to have done well. *The Five Orange Pips*

+**FOLKESTONE COURT**. Sherlock Holmes said, "It is

suggestive that during the last three years there have been four considerable burglaries in the West country, for none of which was any criminal ever arrested. The last of these, at Folkestone Court, in May, was remarkable for the cold-blooded pistol-ing of the page, who surprised the masked and solitary burglar." A burglar he now thought might have been Jack Stapleton. *The Hound of the Baskervilles*

FORDINGBRIDGE. The mysterious letter which was instrumental in causing the death of Justice of the Peace Trevor bore the postmark 'Fordingbridge'. Trevor's old friend and confederate (now calling himself Beddoes) when they were in Australia, lived in this picturesque town in Hampshire. *The "Gloria Scott"*

+FOULMIRE. A moorland farmhouse in Devonshire, near Baskerville Hall. *The Hound of the Baskervilles*

FRANCE. It was thought that the French or Russian Embassies would pay a very large sum to find out the contents of an important document (foreshadowing Britain's foreign policy in certain circumstances) which disappeared mysteriously from Percy Phelps' office. *The Naval Treaty*. During his wanderings after his supposed death at the Reichenbach Falls, Holmes travelled in France and spent some months doing research into coal.tar derivatives in a Montpellier laboratory. *The Empty House*. See also *A Case of Identity, The Stockbroker's Clerk* and *The Final Problem*

FRANKFORT. [*sic*] Holmes was jubilant over his discovery of "an infallible test for blood stains. There was the case of Von Bischoff at Frankfort last year. He would certainly have been hung had this test been in existence." *A Study in Scarlet*.

FRATTON. Sherlock Holmes, disguised as Altamont the Irish-American spy, claimed to have rooms "down Fratton way." Which is a suburb of Portsmouth. *His Last Bow*.

FRESNO STREET. The offices of the Aberdeen Shipping Company, where Mrs. Neville St. Clair picked up a small parcel of considerable value, were in Fresno Street. *The Man with the Twisted Lip*

FULWORTH. Sherlock Holmes' retirement villa was near the little cove and village of Fulworth in Sussex. *The Lion's Mane*

G

+GABLES, THE. Harold Stackhurst's well-known coaching establishment The Gables was half-a-mile from Holmes' retirement villa. Quite a large place, young fellows preparing for various professions lived there with a staff of several teachers. Two were Fitzroy McPherson and Ian Murdoch and they were both attacked by a marine creature called colloquially *The Lion's Mane*

+GELDER & CO. A sculpting works in Stepney. They had supplied both Morse Hudson and Harding Brothers with their plaster casts of Devine's head of Napoleon. *The Six Napoleons*

GEORGIA. The Ku Klux Klan, which pursued two generations of Openshaws to their deaths, had some of its main branches in Georgia. Significantly, the vessel *Lone Star* sailed out of Savannah, Georgia. *The Five Orange Pips*

GLOUCESTER ROAD STATION. Holmes began his investigation of Hugo Oberstein's house (13, Caulfield Gardens) at Gloucester Road Station, where a helpful railway official showed him how the property overlooked the District Railway. *The Bruce-Partington Plans*

GODOLPHIN STREET. An old-fashioned and secluded row of eighteenth-century houses between the Thames and Westminster Abbey, and very near the Houses of

Parliament. It was of interest to Holmes because Eduardo Lucas lived in it. *The Second Stain*

GORDON SQUARE. Francis Hay Moulton took lodgings there after he arrived in London. *The Noble Bachelor*

GRAVESEND. Jonathan Small and Tonga had booked passage on the *Esmeralda,* at Gravesend, bound for Brazil, in an attempt to escape from England. *The Sign of Four.* See also *The Five Orange Pips* and *The Man with the Twisted Lip*

GREAT ALKALI PLAIN. "In the central portion of the great North American Continent there lies an arid and repulsive desert, which for many a long year served as a barrier against the advance of civilization. From the Sierra Nevada to Nebraska, and from the Yellowstone River in the north to the Colorado upon the south, is a region of desolation and silence." It was upon this Great Alkali Plain that John Ferrier and his adopted daughter, Lucy, were stranded. They were later rescued by the migrating Mormon band on its way to Utah, in a tale within a tale. *A Study in Scarlet*

GREAT ORME STREET. Mrs. Warren, a landlady who came to Sherlock Holmes complaining about the unusual habits of one of her lodgers, lived in "a high, thin, yellow-brick edifice in Great Orme Street, a narrow thoroughfare at the north-east side of the British Museum." *The Red Circle*

+GRIMPEN. A village in Devonshire, where the ghastly events of a particularly vicious plot were played out in *The Hound of the Baskervilles*

+GRIMPEN MIRE. It was said of this that "a false step yonder means death to man or beast." Watson compared his feelings about a giant dog to this Mire, which dominated the countryside around Baskerville Hall. Ever since he'd arrived there he had been conscious of shadows, and "Life has become like…little green patches everywhere into which one may sink and with no guide to point the track." *The Hound of the Baskervilles*

GRODNO. According to Holmes, incidents similar to those played out in one of his cases had occurred in Grodno in 1866. *The Hound of the Baskervilles*

+GROSS & HANKEY'S. Presumably jewellers, in Regent Street. It is thought that Godfrey Norton purchased the ring for his marriage to Irene Adler there. *A Scandal in Bohemia*

+GROSVENOR MANSIONS. Residence of Lord St. Simon. *The Noble Bachelor*

GROSVENOR SQUARE. The area where the little problem of the Grosvenor Square furniture van, "which was now quite cleared up . though, indeed, the solution was obvious from the first", occurred. *The Noble Bachelor.* Isadora Klein's residence was in Grosvenor Square. *The Three Gables.*

H

HAMPSHIRE. Where the 'Adventure' involving the house called Copper Beeches occurred. Said by a cunning Jephro Rucastle to be a "charming rural place." Holmes, however, noted ominously, "You look at these scattered houses, and you are impressed by their beauty. I look at them, and the only thought which comes to me is a feeling of their isolation, and of the impunity with which crime may be committed there. Look at these lonely houses, each in its own fields, filled for the most part with poor ignorant folk who know little of the law. Think of the hellish cruelty, the hidden wickedness which may go on, year in, year out, in such places, and none the wiser." *The Copper Beeches.* See also *The Speckled Band, The "Gloria Scott"* and *The Problem of Thor Bridge*

HAMPSTEAD. An affluent London suburb, where Appledore Towers was located, and where the man Holmes called 'the king of all the blackmailers' and "as cunning as the Evil One" lived. *Charles Augustus Milverton*

HAMPSTEAD HEATH. A region of partly wooded heathland between Hampstead and London. Holmes and Watson had to run a considerable distance across it after escaping from Appledore Towers. *Charles Augustus Milverton*. See also *The Red Circle*

HANOVER SQUARE. The location of St. George's Church, where Lord St. Simon and Miss Hatty Doran went through a wedding ceremony. *The Noble Bachelor*

HARROW. Miss Honoria Westphail, aunt of Julia and Helen Stoner, lived near Harrow. It was at her house that Julia met a half-pay Major of Marines. An event which led eventually to her mysterious death. *The Speckled Band*

HARROW WEALD. The house known as 'The Three Gables' was in Harrow Weald. The owner, Mrs. Mary Maberley, had asked Holmes to come there to investigate the strange demand that she sell it and, even more importantly, almost all its contents. *The Three Gables*

HARWICH. Watson met Holmes at Harwich in his little Ford car and they then went on to the German spy Von Bork's country home, from which the lights of Harwich (an important port and an escape route to the continent) could be clearly seen. *His Last Bow*

+HATHERLEY. The name of the farm, on the Boscombe Valley Estate in Herefordshire, which John Turner gave to Charles McCarthy. *The Boscombe Valley Mystery*

+HAVEN, THE. Josiah Amberley's house in Lewisham. *The Retired Colourman*

+HAVEN, THE. Home of the Bellamy family, in Fulworth. *The Lion's Mane*

HEREFORDSHIRE. Boscombe Valley, the site of Charles

McCarthy's murder, was a country district, not very far from Ross, in Herefordshire. *The Boscombe Valley Mystery*

+**HIGH GABLE**. "One house, and only one, riveted my attention. It is the famous old Jacobean grange of High Gable, one mile on the further side of Oxshott, and less than half a mile from the scene of the tragedy." A description of a building from Sherlock Holmes, when investigating the death of Aloysius Garcia. *Wisteria Lodge*

+**HIGH TOR**. A moorland farmhouse in Devonshire. Not far from Baskerville Hall, it was the place of Sir Charles Baskerville's unexplained death. A death which brought Sir Henry Baskerville from Canada to claim his inheritance. *The Hound of the Baskervilles*

HIMALAYAS. Colonel Sebastian Moran was the author of (among many other works) 'Heavy Game of the Western Himalayas', published in 1881. *The Empty House.*

HISTON. A village north of Cambridge which was explored by Sherlock Holmes in his hunt for the missing Godfrey Staunton, who played rugby for the University. *The Missing Three-Quarter*

HOLBORN, THE. Soon after Watson met Stamford in the Criterion Bar, he invited him to lunch at the Holborn. It was in the cab on the way there that that they discussed Watson's search for cheaper lodgings. *A Study in Scarlet.*

HOLBORN BAR. Steve Dixie killed the man known as 'young Perkins' outside this place. *The Three Gables*

HOLLAND. After the first two adventures they shared together, Holmes got in touch with Watson occasionally, and once told him of a mission he had accomplished for the Royal Family of Holland. *A Scandal in Bohemia*

HOLY LAND. 'Holy' Peters ('Dr. Shlessinger') deceived a lone traveller into thinking he was preparing a map of this area for inclusion in a monograph on the Midianites. *The*

Disappearance of Lady Frances Carfax
HOPE TOWN. A small village on the slopes of Mount Harriet on Blair Island, part of the Andaman group. It was here that Small was given his hut so that he served out his sentence for murder in comparative privacy. *The Sign of Four*

HOTELS.

+**ANERLEY ARMS**. The hotel John Hector McFarlane went to stay for the night after he had visited Jonas Oldacre. *The Norwood Builder*

+**BENTLEY'S PRIVATE HOTEL**. The Cambridge University rugby team stayed here in London before their important match with Oxford. *The Missing Three-Quarter*

+**BLACK SWAN**. In Winchester, where Miss Violet Hunter was staying and where Holmes and Watson went to meet her. *The Copper Beeches*

+**BRAMBLETYE HOTEL**. In Forest Row, Sussex. Rooms were arranged there for Holmes and Watson after they had studied the scene of the particularly sanguinary death of Captain Peter Carey of Woodman's Lee. It was the place where John Hopley Neligan also stayed. *Black Peter*

CHARING CROSS HOTEL. Holmes laid a trap for a certain international spy in the smoking-room of this building. *The Bruce-Partington Plans*

CLARIDGES. Holmes asked Von Bork's servant, Martha, to meet him at this hotel the day after the German spy was captured. *His Last Bow*. See also *The Problem of Thor Bridge*

+**COSMOPOLITAN**. The Countess Morcar was staying here when her precious jewel was stolen. *The Blue Carbuncle*

+**DACRE**. The Borgia black pearl was stolen from

here. *The Six Napoleons*

+**DULONG**. Watson received a telegram from Lyons to say that Holmes was lying ill here. *The Reigate Squire*

+**EAGLE COMMERCIAL**. In Tunbridge Wells where a man named Hargrave, a suspected murderer, had stayed. The Valley of Fear

+**ESCURIAL**. See the Marquess of Maltava. *Wisteria Lodge*

+**GRAND HOTEL**. It was between the Grand Hotel and Charing Cross Station, "where a one-legged newsvendor displayed his evening papers," that Watson saw the headline which so horrified him. "MURDEROUS ATTACK UPON SHERLOCK HOLMES." *The Illustrious Client*

GROSVENOR HOTEL. See Peter Steiler the elder. *The Final Problem*

+**HALLIDAY'S (PRIVATE)**. The establishment in Little George Street where Joseph Stangerson was found stabbed to death in his bedroom. *A Study in Scarlet*

+**HEREFORD ARMS**. Holmes and Watson stayed at the Hereford Arms in Ross while they investigated the facts surrounding the brutal slaying of Charles McCarthy. *The Boscombe Valley Mystery*

+**LANGHAM HOTEL**. Captain Morstan's address when he returned to England in 1878 to visit his daughter, Mary. *The Sign of Four*. See also *A Scandal in Bohemia* and *The Disappearance of Lady Frances Carfax*

+**MEXBOROUGH (PRIVATE)**. See Craven Street.

+**NATIONAL** Susan Dobney last heard from her old employer who was staying here, and Watson travelled to Lausanne to find out why that employer had suddenly vanished. *The Disappearance of Lady Frances Carfax*

+**NORTHUMBERLAND HOTEL**. When he arrived in

London from Canada to claim his inheritance, and before going down to Baskerville Hall, Sir Henry Baskerville stayed here. *The Hound of the Baskervilles*

ST. PANCRAS HOTEL. Hosmer Angel and Mary Sutherland were to be married at St. Saviour's Church, near King's Cross, and later to have their wedding breakfast at the St. Pancras Hotel; but when their cabs pulled up in front of the church, Angel had disappeared. *A Case of Identity*

+UNION HOUSE. Owned by Boss McGinty *The Valley of Fear*

+WESTVILLE ARMS. Holmes, Watson, and Inspector MacDonald all stayed at this hotel in the village of Birlstone while investigating the murder of John Douglas. *The Valley of Fear*

HYDE PARK. Miss Hatty Doran was last seen here walking with a woman who had once been the mistress of her new husband. *The Noble Bachelor*

I

INDIA. Where the young Watson, after studying medicine at London University and then doing extra training for the army, says he was attached to the Fifth Northumberland Fusiliers as an Assistant Surgeon. *A Study in Scarlet*

INNS.

+ALPHA INN, THE. A small public house in Bloomsbury, the favourite drinking place of Mr. Henry Baker, who bought his Christmas goose (a peace-offering to his wife?) from the 'goose club' being run there by the landlord. Holmes and Watson gained valuable information by sitting over a couple of glasses of beer with the latter. *The Blue Carbuncle*

+BULL, THE. Holmes and Watson took rooms at

The Bull inn in Esher, Surrey. This was while they were investigating certain odd happenings brought to their notice by Mr Scott Eccles. *Wisteria Lodge*

+**CHEQUERS**. The inn in Lamberley, Sussex, where Holmes and Watson stayed while investigating the strange behaviour of Robert Ferguson's wife. *The Sussex Vampire*

+**CHEQUERS**. The hostelry in Camford where Holmes and Watson put up while trying to solve the mystery of Professor Presbury's peculiar behaviour. *The Creeping Man*

+**CROWN INN**. Opposite Dr. Grimesby Roylott's ancestral home. Holmes and Watson took rooms there for the night after concluding their investigation into the nasty business of *The Speckled Band*

+**FIGHTING COCK**. On the Chesterfield High Road, in Hallamshire. It was owned by Mr. Reuben Hayes, and Watson described it as a "forbidding and squalid inn." *The Priory School*

+**GREEN DRAGON INN**. Run by Josiah Barnes. It was known to be a fine old-fashioned tavern. *Shoscombe Old Place*

+**IVY PLANT, THE**. A pub near the house in which the international spy Eduardo Lucas was murdered. Constable Macpherson went there to get brandy when the woman he had admitted to the murder-house "dropped on the floor, and lay as if she were dead." *The Second Stain*

+**RAILWAY ARMS**. A country inn in Little Purlington, "the most primitive village in England," where Watson and Josiah Amberley were forced to spend the night. *The Retired Colourman*

+**RED BULL, THE**. Inn on the High Road, near

Mackleton. Its landlady was sick one night and had sent to Mackleton for a doctor. So the patrons of the inn were still there and could swear that no one, including the missing Lord Saltire and the School's German master, Heidegger, had passed in the night. *The Priory School*

+**WHITE EAGLE TAVERN**. Broderick and Nelson's large timber yard, to which Toby initially traced a wrong scent, was just past the White Eagle tavern. *The Sign of Four*

+**WHITE HART**. When Constable John Rance discovered the dead body of Enoch J. Drebber in a lonely suburban London house, he had earlier investigated a fight at the White Hart tavern. *A Study in Scarlet*

INTERLAKEN. Holmes and Watson went from here to Meiringen on the last stage of their journey from Brussels. *The Final Problem*

ITALY. The document which strangely disappeared from Percy Phelps' room in the Foreign Office was drawn up between England and Italy. *The Naval Treaty*. See also *The Red Circle*

J

JAPAN. One of Holmes' deductions that so impressed Justice of the Peace Trevor was that the latter had visited Japan. *The "Gloria Scott"*. See also *The Three Garridebs*

JOHANNESBURG. The South African city in which, according to Bob Carruthers and Jack Woodley, Violet Smith's Uncle Ralph had died quite poverty-stricken. *The Solitary Cyclist*

K

KENNINGTON PARK GATE. John Rance, the constable who found the dead body of Enoch J. Drebber in a lonely suburban London house just off the Brixton Road, lived at 46 Audley Court, Kennington Park Gate. *A Study in Scarlet*

KENNINGTON ROAD. Morse Hudson sold pictures and

statues in the Kennington Road, where the first of a series of plaster busts of Napoleon was smashed. The second was deliberately broken in the same road, within a few yards of Hudson's shop. *The Six Napoleons*

KENSINGTON. Can one assume Dr. Watson was living in this road with his wife at the time of the Jabez Wilson Mystery? It seems obvious from the text of *The Red-Headed League* that he was no longer living in Baker Street. See also *The Greek Interpreter, The Six Napoleons*, *Wisteria Lodge* and *The Bruce-Partington Plans*. By the time Holmes investigated the predicament of the unfortunate John Hector McFarlane, Watson was a widower and had sold his Kensington practice to a young doctor named Verner, before moving back into Baker Street. *The Norwood Builder*

KENT. The Cedars, the home of Neville St. Clair and his wife, was near Lee, in Kent. *The Man with the Twisted Lip*. See also *The Golden Pince-nez, The Abbey Grange* and *The Lion's Mane*

KING'S COLLEGE HOSPITAL. After he graduated from London University, Dr. Percy Trevelyan occupied a minor position in King's College Hospital. *The Resident Patient*

KING'S CROSS STATION. Holmes felt that he and Watson ought to journey to Cambridge by way of King's Cross Station if they were to investigate the sudden disappearance of a brilliant player, Godfrey Staunton, just before the all important rugby match between Cambridge and Oxford Universities. *The Missing Three-Quarter*. See also *A Case of Identity*

+KING'S PYLAND. The training stables of Colonel Ross, on Dartmoor. A champion racehorse disappeared from here. *Silver Blaze*

KINGSTON. Vernon Lodge, where the notorious Baron Adelbert Gruner lived, was near this town. *The Illustrious Client*

L

LA SCALA. Irene Adler, famed as the woman who got the better of Holmes, had sung at La Scala. *A Scandal in Bohemia*

+LABURNUM LODGE. In Laburnum Vale, Chiswick. Mr. Josiah Brown, whose plaster cast of Devine's bust of Napoleon was smashed, lived there. *The Six Napoleons*

+'LACHINE'. Colonel James Barclay's villa at Aldershot. *The Crooked Man*

+LAFTER HALL. On the moor. Home of Mr. Frankland, father of Laura Lyons. *The Hound of the Baskervilles*

LAMBETH. The bird-.stuffer, Sherman, and his 'dog detective', Toby, lived at 3, Pinchin Lane, Lambeth. *The Sign of Four*

LHASSA. From the near disaster of the Reichenbach Falls, Sherlock Holmes "travelled for two years in Tibet" and amused himself by visiting Lhassa and spending some days with the head Llama [sic]. *The Empty House*

LAUDER. Holmes was convinced that Colonel Sebastian Moran was at the bottom of the death of Mrs. Stewart of Lauder, in 1887, although at the time nothing could be proved. *The Empty House*

+LAURISTON GARDENS. Off the Brixton Road, the body of Enoch J. Drebber had been found in an empty house at 3, Lauriston Gardens. Inspector Tobias Gregson sought Holmes' help in untangling the case. *A Study in Scarlet*

LAUSANNE. Watson, acting as Holmes' agent, travelled to Lausanne to search for the missing Lady Frances Carfax. She had last been heard of at the Hotel National there. *The Disappearance of Lady Frances Carfax*

LEADENHALL STREET. Hosmer Angel, who disappeared on his wedding-day, supposedly worked as a cashier in a Leadenhall Street office. He said that he lived on the premises, and received all his mail from Mary Sutherland at the Leadenhall Street Post Office. *A Case of Identity*

LEWISHAM. In 1896, Josiah Amberley retired from business and bought a house at Lewisham. *The Retired Colourman.* See also *The Abbey Grange*.

LIEGE. As Holmes sat down to await the expected arrival of the murderer of Enoch J. Drebber, he took up "a queer old book I picked up at a stall yesterday—De Jure inter Gentes—published in Latin at Liege in the Lowlands, in 1642." *A Study in Scarlet*

LONDON. Recently invalided home from the second Afghan War, Dr. John H. Watson "naturally gravitated to London, that great cesspool into which all the loungers and idlers of the Empire are irresistibly drained." He said, after meeting Stamford, "The sight of a friendly face in the great wilderness of London is a pleasant thing indeed to a lonely man." *A Study in Scarlet*. See also *The Red-Headed League The Norwood Builder* and *The Six Napoleons*

LONDON BRIDGE. The Bar of Gold opium den was situated in Upper Swandam Lane, in "a vile alley lurking behind the high wharves which line the north side of the river to the east of London Bridge." *The Man with the Twisted Lip*. See also *The Retired Colourman*

LONDON BRIDGE STATION. John Hector McFarlane came to ask Sherlock Holmes for help in proving his innocence in the murder of Jonas Oldacre. He knew the police were already on his trail and told Holmes, "I have been followed from London Bridge Station, and I am sure that they are only waiting for the warrant to arrest me." *The Norwood Builder*. See also *The Bruce Part-tington Plans*

LONDON LIBRARY. See Lomax. *The Illustrious Client*

LONDON, UNIVERSITY OF. As he tells us at the beginning of his account of his first meeting with Sherlock Holmes, Dr. Watson took his degree of Doctor of Medicine at the University of London in the year 1878. *A Study in Scarlet*. Dr. Percy Trevelyan, who came to Holmes with a curious problem which ended in tragedy, had graduated from the University of London where his "student career was considered by [his] professors to be a very promising one." *The Resident Patient*

LOWER BRIXTON ROAD. Dr. Barnicot, a well-known London medical practitioner, had his branch surgery and dispensary there. *The Six Napoleons*

LOWER BURKE STREET. Mr. Culverton Smith, the planter and prominent resident of Sumatra, had his house at 13, Lower Burke Street. *The Dying Detective*

+LOWER GILL MOOR. A great rolling moor, extending for ten miles, that lay between the Priory School, Holdernesse Hall and the Chesterfield high road. *The Priory School*

LOWER NORWOOD. The London suburb of which Jonas Oldacre had been a well-known resident, as a result of his having carried on his business as a builder for many years there. *The Norwood Builder*

LOWTHER ARCADE. It was to the Strand end of the Lowther Arcade that Watson directed his cab in his mad dash to join Holmes aboard the Continental Express at Victoria Station. *The Final Problem*

LUCERNE. The luggage of the dead Douglas Maberley was labelled "Milano" and "Lucerne." *The Three Gables*. See also *The Final Problem*

LUXEMBOURG. Holmes and Watson slowly made their way to Switzerland, during their visit to Europe, by way of Luxembourg. *The Final Problem*

LYCEUM THEATRE. Mary Morstan received a mysterious note asking her to "Be at the third pillar from the left outside the Lyceum Theatre tonight at seven o'clock. If you are distrustful bring two friends. You are a wronged woman, and shall have justice. Do not bring the police. If you do, all will be in vain. Your unknown friend." The two 'friends' she brought with her were Sherlock Holmes and Dr. Watson. *The Sign of Four*

+LYON PLACE, CAMBERWELL. Mary Sutherland, who lived here with her mother and step-father at No. 31, came to Holmes after her fiancé disappeared on the way to their wedding. *A Case of Identity*

LYONS, FRANCE. Watson writes, "I see it was on the 14th of April that I received a telegram from Lyons, which informed me that Holmes was lying ill in the Hotel Dulong." *The Reigate Squire*

M

+MACKLETON. Dr. Thorncycroft Huxtable's Priory School, from which the young Lord Saltire disappeared, was near this town in the north of England. *The Priory School*

MAIWAND. Dr. Watson admitted to Holmes that the murder of Enoch J. Drebber had upset him, even though "I ought to be more case-hardened after my Afghan experiences. I saw my own comrades hacked to pieces at Maiwand without losing my nerve." Watson himself had received a serious wound (or, perhaps, two as he refers in later investigations to both a dicky shoulder and a gammy leg) at Maiwand. *A Study in Scarlet*

MANAOS. Maria Pinto Gibson, the ill-fated wife of Neil Gibson the Gold King, was the daughter of a Government official in Manaos, Brazil. *The Problem of Thor Bridge*

+MCQUIRE'S CAMP. Aloysius Doran worked a mining claim near the Rockies. It was the place where Francis Hay Moulton met Hatty Doran and the two young people became engaged to be married, not something her father wanted. *The Noble Bachelor*

MADRID. Don Juan Murillo, the Tiger of San Pedro, escaped to Madrid after a revolution in his country. But he met his death there some time later, when both he and his secretary were murdered in their rooms at the Hotel Escurial. *Wisteria Lodge*

MARYLEBONE LANE. The van which narrowly missed hitting Holmes at the corner of Bentinck Street and Welbeck

Street rushed round from Marylebone Lane and was gone in an instant. *The Final Problem*

MAURITIUS, ISLAND OF. After his marriage to Alice Rucastle, the girl her father persuaded an unknowing Violet Hunter to periodically imitate, Mr. Fowler took a Government appointment in Mauritius. *The Copper Beeches*

MECCA. After his supposed death at the Reichenbach Falls, Sherlock Holmes "travelled for two years in Tibet." Shortly after that he "looked in at Mecca." *The Empty House*

MEIRINGEN. While trying to escape from Professor Moriarty, Holmes and Watson paused at Meiringen, and spent the night at the Englischer Hof there. It was, however, all part of Holmes' determination to settle his account with the Professor once and for all. *The Final Problem*

+MERRIPIT HOUSE. Home of the Stapletons, on the moor in Devonshire. *The Hound of the Baskervilles*

+MERTON COUNTY. An agricultural county on the railway line running through the Gilmerton Mountains and Vermissa Valley, otherwise a coal and iron producing area. *The Valley of Fear*

MIDDLESEX. Mrs. Effie Hebron had a maiden aunt at Pinner, in Middlesex. She stayed with this woman after she returned to England following the death of her husband in America. *The Yellow Face*. See also *The Man with the Twisted Lip*

+MILLER HILL. Ill.-kept public park in the very centre of Vermissa, where Jack McMurdo and Brother Morris met to exchange information dangerous to both in a more frequented area. *The Valley of Fear*

MONTAGUE PLACE. Miss Violet Hunter had her lodgings in Montague Place. From there she wrote Holmes the note which in-volved him in one of his 'Adventures'. *The Copper Beeches*

MONTAGUE STREET. Holmes said, "When I first came up to London I had rooms in Montague Street, just round the corner from the British Museum, and there I waited, filling in my too abundant leisure time by studying all those branches of science which might make me more efficient." *The Musgrave Ritual*

MONTANA. Francis Hay Moulton travelled there after his marriage to Hatty Doran in order to make his fortune. *The Noble Bachelor.*

MONTPELLIER. Holmes thought that his discovery of "an infallible test for blood stains" would have been decisive in the case of the notorious Muller, and Lefevre of Montpellier. *A Study in Scarlet*. The detective also carried out some research into coal.tar derivatives at a laboratory in Montpellier during the Great Hiatus. *The Empty House*. See also *The Disappearance of Lady Frances Carfax*

MORTIMER STREET. After discussing their plans to escape Professor Moriarty by a mad dash to the Continental express and thence through Europe, Holmes clambered over the garden wall of Watson's house into this street. *The Final Problem*

MOUNTS BAY. From the windows of their little whitewashed holiday cottage in Cornwall, Holmes and Watson "looked down upon the whole sinister semicircle of Mounts Bay, that old death trap of sailing vessels, with its fringe of black cliffs and surge-swept reefs on which innumerable seaman met their end." *The Devil's Foot*

MUNICH. Holmes noted that there was a case similar to that of *The Noble Bachelor* in Munich, the year after the Franco-Prussian War.

MUTTRA. Where Abel White had an indigo plantation, and Jonathan Small was employed as an overseer. *The Sign of Four*

+MYRTLES, THE. At the time Mr. Melas was asked to leave his lodgings in Pall Mall to travel to Beckenham late at night, (and in a closed carriage) to ply his trade, Sophy Kratides was staying at Mr. Harold Latimer's house, The Myrtles, in that town. *The Greek Interpreter*

N

NAPLES. Pietro Venucci, "one of the greatest cut.throats in London," was from Naples. *The Six Napoleons*. See also *The Red Circle*

NETLEY. After graduating from the University of London, John H. Watson "proceeded to Netley to go through the course prescribed for surgeons in the army." *A Study in Scarlet*

NEW BRIGHTON. Mary Browner and her man friend took tickets for a trip to New Brighton, thinking that her husband was still at sea. *The Cardboard Box*

NEW FOREST. On a blazing hot day in August when Holmes began an investigation which Watson was later to call *The Cardboard Box*, the Doctor "yearned for the glades of the New Forest". Having a depleted bank account, however, meant he had to postpone his holiday.

NEW JERSEY. Irene Adler, famed as the woman reluctantly admired by Holmes because she had managed to fool him, was born in New Jersey in 1858. *A Scandal in Bohemia*

NEW MEXICO. Francis Hay Moulton was said to have been killed in an Apache attack on a miners' camp in New Mexico. He was later to turn up at a most inopportune moment for Lord Robert de Vere St. Simon. *The Noble Bachelor*

NEW YORK. The two letters found in the pockets of the dead Enoch J. Drebber were both from the Guion Steamship Company and referred to the sailing of Drebber's and Joseph Stangerson's ship from Liverpool. Holmes concluded, "It is clear that this unfortunate man was about to return to New York." *A Study in Scarlet*. See also *The Hound of the Baskervilles, The Abbey Grange, The Red Circle* and *His Last Bow*

NEW ZEALAND. One of Holmes' deductions that so impressed Justice of the Peace Trevor was that the latter had been to New Zealand. *The "Gloria Scott"*. See also *A Case of Identity* and *The Stockbroker's Clerk*

NEWHAVEN.   Holmes and Watson, after leaving the Continental Express at Canterbury, travelled overland to Newhaven, and from there to Dieppe. *The Final Problem*

NORFOLK. The father of Victor Trevor, Holmes' only friend at college, had a house in Norfolk. See Donnithorpe. *The "Gloria Scott".* See also *The Dancing Men*

NORTH CAROLINA. The Anderson murders, similar to the case which Holmes investigated in *The Hound of the Baskervilles,* happened here.

NORTHUMBERLAND AVENUE. This was where Holmes and Watson took a Turkish Bath at the beginning of an adventure involving *The Illustrious Client.* See also *The Noble Bachelor* and *The Greek Interpreter*

NORWAY. Neligan, of the ruined banking firm Dawson & Neligan, had set off in his private yacht for Norway, where he hoped by judicious investment of the securities which he took with him to overturn the effect on others of the failure of his firm. He was thought lost at sea. Later, the true circumstances of Neligan's death came to light after Watson and Holmes travelled to Norway. *Black Peter*

NOTTING HILL. Louis La Rothiere, of Campden Mansions, Notting Hill, was one of only three foreign agents in England capable of handling as large an affair as the stealing of some submarine plans. *The Bruce-Partington Plans.* See also *The Red Circle*

O

ODESSA. Holmes, in analyzing his successful investigation of the mysterious death of Enoch J. Drebber, cited the case of Dolsky in Odessa. *A Study in Scarlet.* At the time of *A Scandal in Bohemia,* Watson had occasionally heard some vague account of Holmes' doings, such as his summons to Odessa to investigate the Trepoff murder.

OLD DEER PARK 'Big Bob Ferguson' once threw Watson over the ropes into the crowd at the Old Deer Park at Richmond during one of their "athletic contests". They were to meet again during what was a most mysterious case. *The Sussex Vampire*

OLD JEWRY. The London street in which Robert Ferguson's lawyers, Morrison, Morrison, and Dodd, had their offices. *The Sussex Vampire*

OXFORD. John Clay's *alma mater. The Red-Headed League.* Colonel Sebastian Moran, Moriarty's right-hand man, also went to this university. *The Empty House.* Godfrey Staunton, the crack three-quarter of the Cambridge rugby team, disappeared just before their match with the Oxford team which, presumably because of his absence, Oxford won by a goal and two tries. *The Missing Three-Quarter*

OXFORD STREET. Holmes went out at midday to conduct some business in Oxford Street, when Professor Moriarty's hired agents made the first of a series of promised attacks on Sherlock's life. *The Final Problem.* See also *The Red-Headed League, The Resident Patient, The Greek Interpreter, Charles Augustus Milverton, The Golden Pince-nez* and *The Disappearance of Lady Frances Carfax*

+**OXSHOTT COMMON.** The brutally beaten body of Aloysius Garcia was found on Oxshott Common, about a mile from his home. *Wisteria Lodge*

+**OXSHOTT TOWERS.** Sir George Folliott's large house, Oxshott Towers, although in the vicinity, was further away from the one rented by Aloysius Garcia than others in the area. A relevant fact when it came to working out what had happened to him. *Wisteria Lodge*

P

PADDINGTON STATION. Sherlock Holmes was pacing up and down the platform here, in his long grey travelling-cloak, waiting for Watson to join him. They were on their way to Herefordshire to investigate the murder of Charles McCarthy. *The Boscombe Valley Mystery.* See also *The Engineer's Thumb, Silver Blaze* and *The Stockbroker's Clerk*

PALL MALL. Mycroft Holmes' rooms were in Pall Mall, just across the street from the Diogenes Club, which he had helped to found and which formed one of the limits of his sedentary life.style. *The Greek Interpreter.* See also *The Solitary Cyclist, The Abbey Grange* and *The Bruce-Partington Plans*

PARIS. Enoch Drebber and Joseph Stangerson managed to evade Jefferson Hope, when he reached St. Petersburg in pursuit of them, by fleeing to Paris. When Hope arrived in Paris, they had just left for Copenhagen. *A Study in Scarlet.* See also *The Stockbroker's Clerk, he Second Stain* and *The Bruce-Partington Plans.*

PARK LANE. Lady Maynooth lived at 427, Park Lane with her second son, Ronald Adair, and her daughter, Hilda Adair. This was also the popular name given in the press to the mystery solved by Holmes. *The Empty House.*

PENNSYLVANIA. Ezekiah Hopkins, the supposed founder of a particular company, was said to have come from the town of Lebanon, Pennsylvania. *The Red-Headed League*

PENTONVILLE. James Ryder's friend Maudsley was released from this notorious prison at the time of the investigation which Watson labelled *The Blue Carbuncle*

PERNAMBUCO, BRAZIL. Isadora Klein's people had been notable here. *The Three Gables*

PHILADELPHIA. Jephro Rucastle claimed (falsely) that his daughter, Alice, had left England on a trip to this part of America. *The Copper Beeches*

PERSIA. Holmes "passed through Persia" during his wanderings after his supposed death above the Reichenbach Falls. Also, Sir Augustus Moran, father of the notorious Colonel Sebastian Moran, was once British Minister to Persia. *The Empty House*

PERU. Bob Ferguson's devoted wife (although her actions seemed to belie her affection) was a Peruvian lady. *The Sussex Vampire*

PESHAWAR. Dr. John H. Watson, seriously wounded at the battle of Maiwand during the Second Afghan War was, according to his own account, removed to the base hospital at Peshawar.[Wounded soldiers from that area were normally sent to Karachi] *A Study in Scarlet*

PETERSFIELD. Lord Backwater had a residence near here, where Lord and Lady St. Simon were to have spent their honeymoon. *The Noble Bachelor*

PINCHIN LANE. The bird-stuffer Sherman, and his hound Toby, lived here. *The Sign of Four*

PINNER. In Middlesex. Mrs. Effie Hebron had a maiden aunt there, with whom she had stayed after she returned to England following the death of her husband in America. *The Yellow Face*

PITT STREET. "...a quiet little backwater just beside one of the briskest currents of London life." A man was found brutally knifed on the steps of No. 131, the home of Mr. Horace Harker who owned one of the plaster casts of Devine's bust of Napoleon. *The Six Napoleons*

PLYMOUTH. As one of his ploys, Holmes claimed falsely that he had seen Mrs. John Straker in Plymouth, at a garden-party, in an expensive costume of dove-coloured silk with ostrich-feather trimming. She replied that he was mistaken. *Silver Blaze.* See also *The Hound of the Baskervilles* and *The Devil's Foot*

POLDHU BAY. See the Cornish Peninsula. *The Devil's Foot*

POPE'S COURT. The offices of a particular body of men were at 7 Pope's Court, Fleet Street. *The Red-Headed League*

PORTLAND. Jack James, an American citizen, was sentenced to a term in this prison for spying for the Germans before the First World War. *His Last Bow*

+PORTSDOWN HILL. See Major Freebody. *The Five Orange Pips*

PORTSMOUTH. Dr. John H. Watson, after being seriously wounded and recovering from a severe bout of enteric fever contracted at the base hospital in Peshawar, was invalided home aboard the troopship *Orontes*, which berthed at Portsmouth jetty a month later. *A Study in Scarlet.* See also *The Naval Treaty* and *His Last Bow*

POSILIPPO. A town near Naples, it produced two vastly dissimilar persons. Emilia Barelli Lucca and Giuseppe Gorgiano. *The Red Circle*

+POTTER'S TERRACE. Hall Pycroft, whose strange new job prompted him to consult Sherlock Holmes, had his rooms "out Hampstead way —17 Potter's Terrace." *The Stockbroker's Clerk*

POULTNEY SQUARE. Annie Fraser and Henry ("Holy") Peters' residence was 36 Poultney Square, Brixton. *The Disappearance of Lady Frances Carfax*

PRAGUE. Wilhelm Gottsreich Sigismond von Ormstein had come incognito from Prague in order to consult Holmes in a "matter... so delicate that I could not confide it to an agent without putting myself in his power." *A Scandal in Bohemia*. Concerning Baron Adelbert Gruner and the death of his wife in the Splugen Pass, Holmes felt, "Who could possibly have read what happened at Prague and have any doubts as to the man's guilt! It was a purely technical legal point and the suspicious death of a witness that saved him!" *The Illustrious Client*. Professor Presbury of Camford University broke his lifelong habits and went away on a journey without telling anyone where he was going. Later, Holmes' client, Mr. Bennett, received a letter from a fellow student saying that he was glad to have seen the Professor in Prague, but he had not been able to talk with him. It was discovered later that Presbury had visited the infamous H. Lowenstein, a man who dealt in unlicensed drugs, of that city. *The Creeping Man*

PRINCETOWN. The prison on Dartmoor from which Selden, the murderer, had escaped. *The Hound of the Baskervilles*

+PRIORY SCHOOL, THE. Preparatory school near Mackleton, in Hallamshire, it was founded by Dr. Thorneycroft Huxtable and was one of the most select schools in England, boasting some of the best names in the kingdom among its students. The Duke of Holdernesse's son, Lord Saltire, was entrusted to Dr. Huxtable's care, but he mysteriously disappeared, and Holmes was called in to investigate. *The Priory School*

PUNJAB, THE. After travelling through Nepal and Afghanistan, Henry Wood went back to the Punjab, where he "lived mostly among the natives, and picked up a living by the conjuring tricks [he] had learned." *The Crooked Man*

+PURDEY PLACE. Purdey Place, the large house of Mr. Hynes, a Justice of the Peace, lay near Aloysius Garcia's house in Surrey. *Wisteria Lodge*

Q

QUEEN ANNE STREET. At the time of the investigation into Baron Gruner's questionable activities, Dr. Watson was living in his own rooms in Queen Anne Street. *The Illustrious Client*

R

+RAGGED SHAW. A grove of trees between the Priory School and Lower Gill Moor, in Hallamshire. Lord Saltire disappeared through the Ragged Shaw. *The Priory School*

RATCLIFF HIGHWAY. Sumner, the shipping agent whom Captain Basil (Sherlock Holmes in disguise) asked for three harpooners, had offices there. *Black Peter*

READING. Mr. Sandeford, whose plaster cast of Devine's bust of Napoleon was the last to be smashed, lived in Lower Grove Road, Reading. *The Six Napoleons.* See also *The Boscombe Valley Mystery, The Speckled Band, The Engineer's Thumb,* and *Silver Blaze*

REGENT CIRCUS. As Holmes and Watson strolled out into the London evening streets to take in two of the city's great 'curiosities' (Mycroft Holmes and the Diogenes Club) they found themselves walking toward Regent Circus. *The Greek Interpreter.* See also *Charles Augustus Milverton*

REGENT STREET. Holmes spotted a man with a bushy black beard and a pair of piercing eyes trailing Dr. Mortimer and Sir Henry Baskerville in a cab as they strolled down Regent Street. *The Hound of the Baskervilles.* See also *A Scandal in Bohemia, The Boscombe Valley*

REICHENBACH FALLS. Watson said. "It is, indeed, a fearful place. The torrent, swollen by the melting snow, plunges into a tremendous abyss, from which the spray rolls up like the smoke from a burning house. The shaft into which the river hurls itself is an immense chasm, lined by glistening, coal.black rock, and narrowing into a creaming, boiling pit of incalculable depth, which brims over and shoots the stream onward over its jagged lip. The long sweep of green water roaring for ever down, and the thick flickering curtain of spray hissing for ever upwards, turn a man giddy with their constant whirl and clamour." Holmes and Watson arrived there by making a detour on their way to visit Rosenlaui from Meiringen, and it was against this wild backdrop that the fateful struggle between the detective and Professor Moriarty took place. There is more than a hint that Holmes engineered the confrontation. *The Final Problem*

REIGATE. Where, on a visit to an old army man, Holmes and Watson became involved with *The Reigate Squire*

RHONE, VALLEY OF THE. Holmes and Watson spent "a charming week" wandering up the Valley of the Rhone in their attempted escape from Professor Moriarty. *The Final Problem*

+RIDLING THORPE MANOR. The home of the Hilton Cubitts, and the scene of the curious incident of the childish stick figures, followed by a tragedy of immense proportions. *The Dancing Men*

RIGA. Francois le Villard consulted Holmes about a case which "was concerned with a will, and possessed some features of interest." Holmes "was able to refer him to two parallel cases," one of which occurred "at Riga in 1857." *The Sign of Four.*

RIPLEY. A "pretty little village" near Woking. While investigating the disappearance of the top-secret naval treaty from Percy Phelps' office, Holmes stopped for tea in Ripley, filled a flask and bought a packet of sandwiches. *The Naval Treaty*

RIVIERA. Holmes had all the facts in that squat notebook, concerning the robbery in the *train-de-luxe* to the Riviera on February 13,1892, which apparently implicated Count Negretto Sylvius in a dastardly crime. *The Mazarin Stone.* See also *The Three Gables*

ROBERT STREET. Holmes, Watson, and Mary Morstan passed Robert Street and **ROCHESTER ROW** on their way to Thaddeus Sholto's house. *The Sign of Four*

ROME. Douglas Maberley had been Attaché at Rome before he died there of pneumonia. *The Three Gables*

ROSENLAUI. See The Reichenbach Falls *The Final Problem*

ROTHERHITHE. Mrs. Hudson reported that Holmes had been working at a case down at Rotherhithe, in an alley near the river, and had brought an illness back with him to Baker Street. The case had involved some Chinese sailors down on the docks, the implication being that he had somehow caught the sickness from them. *The Dying Detective*

ROTTERDAM. Sherlock Holmes, pretending to be Altamont the Irish-American spy, said that he was hoping to catch a boat from Rotterdam to New York. *His Last Bow.* See also *The Boscombe Valley Mystery*

RUSSELL SQUARE. Hilton Cubitt came up to London for Queen Victoria's Jubilee and stopped at a boarding-house in Russell Square because Parker, the vicar of his parish, had been staying there. Here he met the woman who was to become his wife, Elsie Patrick. *The Dancing Men*

RUSSIA. Holmes' investigation into the tragedy of Yoxley Old Place revealed the many intrigues which originated in Russia due to the proclivities of the Russian Nihilists. *The Golden Pince-nez*. See also *The Naval Treaty* and *The Second Stain*

RUTLAND ISLAND. In the Andaman Islands. In return for a share of the great Agra treasure, Major John Sholto was to leave a small yacht there provisioned for a sea voyage, for the men bound by a particular oath. *The Sign of Four*

S

ST. GEORGE'S. The fashionable Church in Hanover Square where Lord St. Simon and Miss Hatty Doran were married. *The Noble Bachelor*

+ST. GEORGE'S, THEOLOGICAL COLLEGE OF. See Elias Whitney. *The Man with the Twisted Lip*

ST. JAMES'S HALL. The famous (real-life) violinist, Sarasate, was playing at St. James's Hall, and Holmes invited Watson to accompany him to the performance. They were "off to violin land", where there were no red-headed clients to annoy them. *The Red-Headed League*

ST. JAMES'S SQUARE. Where Watson obtained a book on Chinese Pottery from the London Library. *The Illustrious Client*.

ST. JAMES'S STREET. See Langdale Pike. *The Three Gables*

ST. JOHN'S WOOD. Irene Adler's house, called Briony Lodge, was in St. John's Wood. *A Scandal in Bohemia*

+ST. LUKE'S, COLLEGE OF. Hilton Soames, who came to Holmes over a very painful problem surrounding the Fortescue Scholarship examination, was a tutor and lecturer at this College which was situated in one of England's great university towns. *The Three Students*

ST. LOUIS. Jefferson Hope, Senior, and John Ferrier had been good friends in St. Louis. *A Study in Scarlet*. See also *The Sign of Four*

ST. MONICA, CHURCH OF. See Edgware Road. *A Scandal in Bohemia*

+ST. OLIVER'S PRIVATE SCHOOL. In York, it was run for a time by 'Mr. and Mrs. Vandeleur'. *The Hound of the Baskervilles*

ST. PETERSBURG. Enoch Drebber and Joseph Stangerson fled from Jefferson Hope to St. Petersburg. *A Study in Scarlet*

ST. SAVIOUR'S. See St. Pancras Hotel, The. *A Case of Identity*

SALT LAKE CITY. John Ferrier prospered so much that there were not half a dozen men in the whole of Salt Lake City who could be compared to him in prosperity. *A Study in Scarlet*

SAN FRANCISCO. Aloysius Doran took his daughter there to try to prevent her marrying against his wishes. *The Noble Bachelor*

SAN PAULO. One of the headings in a notebook, containing Stock Exchange securities, found on the floor of Captain Peter Carey's cabin after his violent death. *Black Peter*

SAVANNAH. The *Lone Star*, commanded by the villain James Calhoun, was out of Savannah, Georgia. *The Five Orange Pips*

SCOTLAND YARD. Holmes sent Watson to Lausanne to see if he could find out what had happened to Lady Frances Carfax. The detective felt that he could not leave London himself because "Scotland Yard feels lonely without me, and it causes an unhealthy excitement among the criminal classes." *The Disappearance of Lady Frances Carfax.* See also *The Norwood Builder, The Lion's Mane* and *The Empty House*

SENEGAMBIA. Holmes felt that the murder of Bartholomew Sholto was paralleled by cases from India and Senegambia. *The Sign of Four*

SERPENTINE. Lestrade had been dragging the Serpentine for the body of Lady St. Simon (Hatty Doran), who had mysteriously disappeared. *The Noble Bachelor*

+SERPENTINE AVENUE. Irene Adler's address in St. John's Wood. It was in Serpentine Mews that Holmes, dressed as an unemployed groom, hoped to gain the information which would help him recover the compromising photo of Adler and the hereditary King of Bohemia. It was also in this Avenue, outside the house, that the detective, with the help of Watson, staged the ruse which gained him access to the woman's sitting.room. *A Scandal in Bohemia*

SEVERN. After "passing through the beautiful Stroud Valley and over the broad and gleaming Severn," Holmes and Watson found themselves at Ross, where they were to investigate the facts in the brutal slaying of Charles McCarthy. *The Boscombe Valley Mystery*

+SHOSCOMBE OLD PLACE. Residence of Lady Beatrice Falder, who received the earnings from this Berkshire estate. Lady Beatrice had only a "life interest" in the property. On her death, it would revert to her late husband's brother. Her brother, Sir Robert Norberton, also lived in the house. S*hoscombe Old Place*

SIAM. With conditions as they were in Siam, it was awkward for Mycroft Holmes to be away from the Foreign Office. But, even so, he came round to_Sherlock's rooms to press him for help in solving the mystery of the death of Arthur Cadogan West. *The Bruce-Partington Plans*

SIBERIA. After Sergius ('Professor Coram') betrayed his Nihilist comrades in Russia, many of them were sent to Siberia to work in the salt mines. *The Golden Pince-nez*

+SILVESTER'S. Lady Frances Carfax banked here. Holmes glanced through her account in an effort to discover any clues as to her whereabouts. "Single ladies must live, and their pass-books are compressed diaries." *The Disappearance of Lady Frances Carfax*

SKIBBAREEN (*Sic*). Holmes, in disguise, gave serious trouble to the official police in Skibbareen. *His Last Bow*

SOTHEBY'S. See Christie's. *The Three Garridebs*

SOUTH AFRICA. Sir Charles Baskerville had made his fortune in South African speculation before returning to England and retiring to the family estate, Baskerville Hall. *The Hound of the Baskervilles.* See also *The Solitary Cyclist, The Three Students, The Disappearance of Lady Frances Carfax, The Blanched Soldier,* and *The Dancing Men*

SOUTH AMERICA. Selden, the Notting Hill murderer, planned to escape to South America. *The Hound of the Baskervilles.* See also *The Cardboard Box* and *The Disappearance of Lady Frances Carfax*

SOUTH AUSTRALIA. Mary Fraser was brought up in the free atmosphere of Adelaide, in South Australia. *The Abbey Grange*

SOUTH BRIXTON. Mrs. Merrilow, Eugenia Ronder's landlady, had her lodging house in South Brixton. *The Veiled Lodger*

SOUTH DOWNS. Watson said, "But you had retired, Holmes. We heard of you as living the life of a hermit among your bees and your books in a small farm upon the South Downs." *His Last Bow* **SOUTHAMPTON**. Mr. Fowler and Alice Rucastle were married there by special license on the day after he rescued her from her forced imprisonment in her father's house. *The Copper Beeches*. See also *The Abbey Grange* and *The Blanched Soldier*

SPLUGEN PASS. Holmes was sure that Baron Adelbert Gruner had killed his wife "when the so.called 'accident' happened in the Splugen Pass." *The Illustrious Client*

STAMFORD'S. Holmes had sent down to Stamford's for an Ordnance map of Devonshire. His spirit had "hung over it all day" as he mentally went over the scene of the mysterious death of Sir Charles Baskerville. *The Hound of the Baskervilles*

STEPNEY. Gelder & Co., which had supplied both Morse Hudson and Harding Brothers with their plaster casts of the head of Napoleon, was located in Church Street, Stepney. It was "a river-side city of a hundred thousand souls, where the tenement houses swelter and reek with the outcasts of Europe." *The Six Napoleons*

+STOKE MORAN. Site of the ancestral home of the Roylotts, in western Surrey. *The Speckled Band*

STRAND, THE. Dr. John H. Watson, when he came back from Afghanistan and travelled to London, stayed for some time at a private hotel in this area. *A Study in Scarlet*. See also *The Red-Headed League, The Resident Patient, The Final Problem* and *The Missing Three-Quarter*

STRASBURG. After spending two days in Brussels, Holmes and Watson pushed on to Strasburg. There Holmes received word that, although Professor Moriarty's gang had been rounded up in London, the man himself had escaped the police. Almost immediately, Holmes and Watson left for Geneva. *The Final Problem*

STREATHAM. A suburb of London where 'Fairbank', the home of the unfortunate banker, Alexander Holder, was situated. *The Beryl Coronet*

SUMATRA. In one of his investigations, Holmes apparently contracted a 'coolie' disease from Sumatra. Culverton Smith, who also appears in the account, was a well-known resident of that island. *The Dying Detective*

SURREY. Holmes was ravenous when he came back to Baker Street after his investigation into the mystery of the missing naval treaty. This was because he had just "breathed thirty miles of Surrey air." Obviously very invigorating, although the detective had the reputation of going without food for days when on a hot scent. *The Naval Treaty*. See also *The Man with the Twisted Lip, The Speckled Band, The Solitary Cyclist* and *The Retired Colourman*

SUSSEX. Sherlock Holmes retired to a little home in Sussex where he gave himself up entirely to the soothing life of Nature, for which he said he had often yearned during the long years he spent amid the gloom and fogs of London. His villa was situated on the southern slope of the Downs and commanded a fine view of the English Channel. Anderson, a constable from the neighbouring village, was of "solid Sussex breed — a breed which covers much good sense under a heavy, silent exterior." *The Lion's Mane*. See also *The Five Orange Pips, The Sussex Vampire, The Musgrave Ritual* and *The Second Stain*

SWINDON. On their way to Ross to investigate the facts surrounding the death of Charles McCarthy, Holmes and Watson's train stopped at Swindon for lunch. *The Boscombe*

Valley Mystery

SWITZERLAND. On their Continental journey, Holmes and Watson made their way at their leisure into Switzerland, via Luxembourg and Basel. *The Final Problem*

SYDENHAM. The Lewisham gang, suspected of killing Sir Eustace Brackenstall, had pulled a job at Sydenham a fortnight before. See Randall. Captain Jack Croker of the *Bass Rock* who knew Lady Brackenstall, lived in Sydenham. *The Abbey Grange*

T

TAVISTOCK. Inspector Gregory and Colonel Ross met Holmes and Watson's train when it arrived in Tavistock. The two friends had come down to King's Pyland stables from London to investigate the disappearance of a racehorse and the death of its trainer. *Silver Blaze*

TERAI. Young Victor Trevor, heartbroken over the disclosures of his father, went out to the Terai tea planting, where Holmes had heard that he was doing well. *The "Gloria Scott"*

+THOR BRIDGE. Maria Gibson, neé Pinto, wife of Neil Gibson, the Gold King, was found shot to death on Thor Bridge on their Hampshire estate. *The Problem of Thor Bridge*

+THOR PLACE. Neil Gibson's Hampshire estate. *The Problem of Thor Bridge*

+THORSLEY. James Mortimer, who asked for Holmes' help in *The Hound of the Baskervilles,* was Medical Officer for Grimpen, Thorsley, and High Barrow.

THREADNEEDLE STREET. Every day the supposed beggar, Hugh Boone, took up his position on this street very near The Bank of England. An excellent pitch, helped by good acting skills and repartee –as well as appearance. *The Man with the Twisted Lip.* See also *The Beryl Coronet*

+THREE GABLES, THE. Mrs. Mary Maberley's residence in Harrow Weald. A depressing house, this made it all the more mysterious why someone was so anxious to buy it. *The Three Gables*

THROGMORTON STREET. James Dodd's card revealed to Sherlock Holmes that his visitor was "a stockbroker from Throgmorton Street." *The Blanched Soldier*

TIBET. Knowing that two of the most dangerous members of the Moriarty gang were still at liberty following his supposed death at the Reichenbach Falls (and that they knew he was still alive), Sherlock Holmes travelled for two years in Tibet. *The Empty House*

TOPEKA. The man who claimed to be John Garrideb also claimed to have been "in the law at Topeka." Holmes found he was false by mentioning a fictitious mayor of that town. *The Three Garridebs*

TORQUAY TERRACE. Madame Charpentier's boarding-house, where the late Enoch J. Drebber had stayed, was in Torquay Terrace, Camberwell. *A Study in Scarlet*

TORRINGTON LODGE. See John Hector McFarlane *The Norwood Builder*

TOTTENHAM COURT ROAD. The late Mr. Sutherland (Mary's father) had his plumber's business in Tottenham Court Road. *A Case of Identity.* See also *The Cardboard Box* and *The Red Circle*

TRAFALGAR SQUARE. John Clayton picked up a fare in Trafalgar Square who paid him to shadow two men, Sir Henry Baskerville and Dr. James Mortimer. *The Hound of the Baskervilles.* See also *The Noble Bachelor*

TRANSYLVANIA. Holmes had an entry under "Vampires in Transylvania" in his one of his great index volumes. *The Sussex Vampire*

+TREDANNICK WARTHA. The home of the Tregennis family, it was situated outside a Cornish hamlet (see below). *The Devil's Foot*

+TREDANNICK WOLLAS. The Cornish hamlet nearest the small cottage to which, in the spring of 1897, Sherlock Holmes had gone for "a complete change of scene and air." *The Devil's Foot*

TRINCOMALEE. At the time *of A Scandal in Bohemia,* Watson had, from time to time, heard some vague account of Holmes' doings, such as his clearing up of the singular tragedy of the Atkinson brothers at Trincomalee. *A Scandal in Bohemia*

TRINITY COLLEGE. One of the colleges of Cambridge University, it was where Jeremy Dixon, owner of the canine "detective" Pompey, could be found. Pompey worked in collaboration with Sherlock Holmes to discover the whereabouts of Godfrey Staunton, the missing star of Cambridge University's rugby team. Cyril Overton, who sent Holmes the telegram which brought the detective into the investigation was also of Trinity College. *The Missing Three-Quarter*

TRUMPINGTON. A village, south of Cambridge, where Sherlock Holmes finally found Godfrey Staunton. See above. *The Missing Three-Quarter*

TUNBRIDGE WELLS. After pinning Peter Carey to the wall of his cabin like a beetle on a card, the culprit walked ten miles to Tunbridge Wells, where he caught a train to London. *Black Peter*

+TUXBURY OLD PARK. The Emsworth family's

residence, near Bedford. *The Blanched Soldier*

U

UPPER NORWOOD. Major Sholto's house, Pondicherry Lodge, was situated here. *The Sign of Four*

+UPPER SWANDAM LANE. Site of the Bar of Gold opium den. *The Man with the Twisted Lip*

UPPINGHAM. A public school in Rutland. Willoughby Smith, murdered secretary to the man who called himself 'Professor Coram', was a pupil there before going up to Cambridge. *The Golden Pince-nez*

UTAH. There was not one of the wandering Mormon band under the leadership of Brigham Young "who did not sink upon his knees in heartfelt prayer when they saw the broad valley of Utah bathed in the sunlight beneath them, and learned from the lips of their director that this was the promised land, and that these virgin acres were to be theirs evermore." *A Study in Scarlet*

UTRECHT. The death of Enoch J. Drebber reminded Holmes of the death of Van Jansen in Utrecht, "in '34" Although no wound could be found on the body, "great gouts and splashes of blood lay all around." *A Study in Scarlet*

V

VERE STREET. As Holmes walked through Vere Street, a brick came down from the roof of one of the houses and was shattered to fragments at his feet. Moriarty (or one of his henchmen) was at work, and this was the second of his promised attacks on Sherlock's life. *The Final Problem*

+VERMISSA. The central township which lay at the head of the Vermissa Valley, known for its coal and iron production. *The Valley of Fear*

+VERNON LODGE. Near Kingston, home of the notorious

Baron Adelbert Gruner. *The Illustrious Client*

VICTORIA STATION. The train on which Holmes, Watson, and Colonel Ross were returning to London after the successful conclusion of an important horse race pulled into Victoria Station. *Silver Blaze.* See also *The Sussex Vampire*

VICTORIA STREET. Victor Hatherley, an hydraulic engineer, had his office at 16A Victoria Street. He came to Watson with one thumb "hacked or torn right out from the roots." *The Engineer's Thumb*

+VIXEN TOR. "The sun was already sinking when I reached the summit of the hill, and the long slopes beneath me were all golden-green on one side and grey shadow on the other. A haze lay upon the farthest skyline, out of which jutted the fantastic shapes of Belliver and Vixen Tors." This was the setting in which Watson sought the hidden lair of the mysterious man he had seen standing on one of the tors. *The Hound of the Baskervilles*

W

WALES. The Duke of Holdernesse had mineral holdings in Wales and sometimes resided at Carston Castle, Bangor. *The Priory School.* See also *The Missing Three-Quarter*

WALLINGTON. Sarah Cushing lived in New Street, Wallington. *The Cardboard Box*

WALSALL. Wrote Watson at the end of a most odd case, "As to Miss Violet Hunter, my friend Holmes, rather to my disappointment, manifested no further interest in her when once she had ceased to be the centre of one of his problems, and she is now the head of a private school at Walsall, where I believe that she has met with considerable success." *The Copper Beeches*

WANDSWORTH COMMON. Mr. Melas, after his strange, late.night experience with Harold Latimer, was evicted from a closed carriage onto Wandsworth Common. *The Greek Interpreter*

WARSAW. During a visit to Warsaw, the King of Bohemia met Irene Adler, at one time a *prima donna* of the Imperial Opera there. *A Scandal in Bohemia*

WATERBEACH. One of the villages on the north side of Cambridge, Sherlock Holmes had explored it searching for Godfrey Staunton and found it disappointing. *The Missing Three-Quarter*

WATERLOO BRIDGE. Jefferson Hope trailed Enoch Drebber's cab through miles of streets, until, to his surprise, he found himself back where he started, in the terrace where Drebber had lodged. *A Study in Scarlet.* See also *The Five Orange Pips*

WATERLOO STATION. John Openshaw intended to return to his Horsham estate from Waterloo Station, but met his death near Waterloo Bridge. *The Five Orange Pips.* See also *The Crooked Man, The Naval Treaty, The Hound of the Baskervilles* and *The Solitary Cyclist*

WHITEHALL. Every morning Mycroft Holmes walked around the corner from his rooms in Pall Mall into Whitehall, where he was thought to hold a position auditing the books in some of the Government departments. *The Greek Interpreter.* See also *The Naval Treaty, The Bruce-Partington Plans* and *The Mazarin Stone*

WHITEHALL TERRACE. The Right Honourable Trelawney Hope and his wife Lady Hilda had a house in Whitehall Terrace. *The Second Stain*

WINDSOR. After his successful recovery of the stolen submarine plans, Holmes "spent a day at Windsor, whence he returned with a remarkably fine emerald tie.pin." *The Bruce-Partington Plans*

+**WISTERIA LODGE**. Near Esher, in Surrey, it had been rented by the mysterious Aloysius Garcia, who invited Scott Eccles to stay with him. But Garcia then disappeared, along with his house staff, before the next morning. He was later found horribly murdered. The house was about two miles on the south side of Esher. *Wisteria Lodge*

WOKING. The unfortunate Percy Phelps' residence, Briarbrae, was "among the fir-woods and the heather of Woking." *The Naval Treaty*

+**WOODMAN'S LEE**. Captain Peter Carey's Sussex home, where his death was surrounded by some very obscure (as well as horrific) circumstances. *Black Peter*

WOOLWICH ARSENAL. Arthur Cadogan West, who was found dead with stolen submarine plans stuffed in his pocket, was a clerk at the Woolwich Arsenal. *The Bruce-Partington Plans*

WORCESTERSHIRE. Jonathan Small was born near the town of Pershore, in Worcestershire. *The Sign of Four*

YORK. The 'Vandeleurs' ran a private school in this famous English City. *The Hound of the Baskervilles*

YORK COLLEGE. One of the many 'billets' the American Jefferson Hope had during his wanderings included being a janitor and sweeper-out of a laboratory in this College. It was from here that he somehow obtained the deadly South American poison he hoped to use on Drebber and Stangerson. *A Study in Scarlet*

+**YOXLEY OLD PLACE**. 'Professor Coram's' [Sergius the Nihilist] Country House in Kent. *The Golden Pince-nez*

PART THREE
PROPS

A

+ABERDEEN SHIPPING COMPANY. Mrs. Neville St. Clair had received a telegram to say that a small but valuable parcel which she had been expecting was waiting for her at the offices of the Aberdeen Shipping Company in Fresno Street, just off Upper Swandam Lane. It was while she was walking through Swandam Lane that she spotted her husband Neville St. Clair. *The Man with the Twisted Lip*

+ADDLETON TRAGEDY. This was one of the many cases Holmes dealt with in 1894. It involved, rather intriguingly, an 'Ancient British Barrow'. *The Golden Pince-nez*

AFGHAN WAR (2nd). As soon as his course at Netley had finished, Watson went to India in preparation for his part in this conflict. He was attached to the Fifth Northumberland Fusiliers (then stationed in India) as an Assistant Surgeon. He later went with his regiment up one of the Passes (he was never sure which) into Afghanistan and participated in the second Afghan War. Wounded in battle (again, he wasn't certain in which part of the body) Watson contracted enteric fever and, 'his health despaired of', eventually had to be sent home. *A Study in Scarlet.* He refers to the Afghan Campaign when speaking of the wound (caused by a jezail bullet) which kept him indoors in cold weather. *The Noble Bachelor* and *The Sign of Four*

AGONY COLUMNS. Sherlock Holmes read these "bleatings" and kept a collection of them in a large book. *The Red Circle* He also made use of the agony columns himself, *The Bruce-Partington Plans*, and mentions "the apocrypha of the agony column" in *The Valley of Fear*

AIR GUNS. Holmes was afraid Professor Moriarty would try to kill him with air guns. *The Final Problem.* See also *The Empty House* and *The Mazarin Stone*

+ALICIA. One of Holmes' unfinished tales, mentioned by

Watson, involved "the cutter *Alicia,* which sailed one spring morning into a small patch of mist from where she never emerged, nor was anything further ever heard of herself and her crew." *The Problem of Thor Bridge*

+ALUMINIUM CRUTCH. One of Watson's untold tales was the singular story of the aluminium crutch. *The Musgrave Ritual*

+AMATEUR MENDICANT SOCIETY. Dr. Watson said that this club met in the lower vault of a furniture warehouse. But one would have to guess what made them amateurs in a city of importunate and very experienced beggars. *The Five Orange Pips*

AMATI. As Holmes and Watson went together to number three Lauriston Gardens to investigate the mysterious death of Enoch J. Drebber in an empty house, the Great Detective "was in the best of spirits, and prattled away about Cremona fiddles, and the difference between a Stradivarius and an Amati." *A Study in Scarlet*

ANCIENT BRITISH BARROW. See The Addleton Tragedy. *The Golden Pince-nez*

+ARNSWORTH CASTLE BUSINESS. "When a woman thinks that her house is on fire, her instinct is at once to rush to the thing that she values most. It is a perfectly overpowering impulse, and I have more than once taken advantage of it. In the case of the Darlington Substitution Scandal it was of use to me, and also in the Arnsworth Castle business." So said Sherlock in *A Scandal in Bohemia*

ART. Holmes, who said he was descended from the French artist Vernet, felt that "art in the blood is liable to take the strangest forms," and that heredity was the one source of both his faculty of observation and his facility at deduction. *The Greek Interpreter.* See also *The Copper Beeches*

ASHES, TOBACCO. "He had even smoked there. I found

the ash of a cigar, which my special knowledge of tobacco ashes enabled me to pronounce as an Indian cigar. I have, as you know, devoted some attention to this, and written a little monograph on the ashes of 140 different varieties of pipe, cigar, and cigarette tobacco." Holmes again, in *The Boscombe Valley Mystery*. See also *The Crooked Man* and *A Study in Scarlet*

ASTRONOMY. In Watson's catalogue of "Sherlock Holmes—his limits," he rated the Great Detective's knowledge of astronomy as "Nil." *A Study in Scarlet*

AUGUST 1914. The word "August" and the numbers "1914" were the codes to Von Bork's safe. *His Last Bow*

+THE AURORA. Mordecai Smith's steam launch, chartered by Jonathan Small. *The Sign of Four*

B

BABOON. Not remarkable for neighbourliness or good nature and influenced by his time in Calcutta, Doctor Grimsby kept a baboon in his establishment at Stoke Moran. *The Speckled Band*

BALZAC, HONORE DE. Hosmer Angel quoted Balzac in one of his letters to Mary Sutherland. *A Case of Identity*

BARITSU. More properly bujitsu, 'Japanese Martial Arts', which includes wrestling. The Japanese system of wrestling had proved very useful to Sherlock Holmes more than once, and he found his knowledge of baritsu most useful when struggling with Professor Moriarty at the Reichenbach Falls. *The Empty House*

+BASS ROCK. The new ship of the Adelaide-Southampton line, to be captained by Jack Croker. *The Abbey Grange*

+BAYARD. King's Pyland stables were running two horses in the Wessex Cup, Bayard and Silver Blaze. Silver Blaze was a strong favourite, but Fitzroy Simpson asked the stable boy if it was a fact that, at the weights, Bayard could give Silver Blaze a hundred yards in five furlongs, and if the stable had its money on him. That very night, the latter horse disappeared. *Silver Blaze*

BEECHER, HENRY WARD. Watson admired this brother of Harriet Beecher Stowe (the author of *Uncle Tom's Cabin*) and kept an unframed portrait of him on top of his books in Baker Street. *The Cardboard Box*

BEES. After Watson spoke of the South Downs, Holmes then showed him his "magnum opus of my latter years!" This was a *Practical Handbook of Bee Culture, with some Observations upon the Segregation of the Queen*. Said Sherlock, "Alone I did it. Behold the fruit of pensive nights and laborious days, when I watched the little working gangs as once I watched the criminal world of London." *His Last Bow*

+BENGALORE PIONEERS, THE. Colonel Sebastian Moran's old regiment. *The Empty House*

BERKSHIRES, THE. A regiment Watson says he joined after being transferred from The Northumberland Fusiliers. Also known (before regiments were given names) as The 66th Regiment of Foot. *A Study in Scarlet*

BERTILLON, ALPHONSE. (1853-1914). Head of the Prefecture of Police in Paris, he classified certain bodily measurements as unique to an individual. These remained constant throughout life and, since they didn't change, could be used to identify habitual criminals. Shortly after his death his ideas became obsolete with the wide-spread adoption of finger-printing. *The Naval Treaty*. See also *The Hound of the Baskervilles*

BOCCACCIO. When the pockets of Enoch J. Drebber, who was found dead in an empty house in Brixton, were searched the police found a pocket edition of Boccaccio's

Decameron, with the name of Joseph Stangerson on the fly-leaf. Had Drebber borrowed the book because he thought it was racy? Did Stangerson read it for the same reason? He was seen, outwardly at least, as a little less coarse in his attitudes and behaviour, and more gentlemanly, than the man who ostensibly employed him as his 'secretary'. *A Study in Scarlet*

BIBLE, THE. Holmes said to Watson, "You remember the small affair of Uriah and Bathsheba? My Biblical knowledge is a trifle rusty, I fear, but you will find the story in the first or second of Samuel." *The Crooked Man.* See also *The Valley of Fear*

BINOMIAL THEOREM. Professor Moriarty wrote a treatise upon the binomial theorem at the age of twenty-one which had a European vogue. On the strength of it, he won the Mathematical Chair at one of Britain's smaller universities. *The Final Problem*

+**BISHOPGATE JEWEL CASE.** Holmes thought that concentrating on causes, inferences and effects made this particular case one of "very simple reasoning", and he put Inspector Athelney Jones on the right track to solve it. *The Sign of Four*

BOER WAR. James M. Dodd, who sought Holmes' help in trying to find out what had happened to his old army pal, was (like his lost friend) a veteran of the Boer War. *The Blanched Soldier*

+**BOGUS LAUNDRY AFFAIR.** Aldridge, who was something like Jim Browner, big, clean-shaven, swarthy, and powerful, had helped Lestrade and Holmes in something called the bogus laundry affair. *The Cardboard Box*

+**BOOK OF LIFE, THE.** Watson once sat reading an essay

called 'The Book of Life'. He called it "ineffable twaddle," not realising that the man who wrote it, Sherlock Holmes, was sitting opposite him at the breakfast table in Baker Street. *A Study in Scarlet*

BOTANY. In Watson's famous catalogue of "Sherlock Holmes—his limits," he rated the Great Detective's knowledge of botany as "Variable. Well up in belladonna, opium, and poisons generally. Knows nothing of practical gardening." *A Study in Scarlet.* Holmes was later to show, or appear to show to distract attention from something he was studying, a marked interest in a rose. *The Naval Treaty*

BOXER CARTRIDGES. "When Holmes in one of his queer humours would sit in an arm-chair, with his hair-trigger and a hundred Boxer cartridges, and proceed to adorn the opposite wall with a patriotic V.R. done in bullet-pocks," the good Dr. Watson felt strongly "that neither the atmosphere nor the appearance of our room was improved by it." *The Musgrave Ritual*

BOXING. Watson's catalogue of "Sherlock Holmes —his limits," noted that the Great Detective was "an expert singlestick player, boxer, and swordsman." *A Study in Scarlet.* See also *The Yellow Face, The "Gloria Scott"* and *The Solitary Cyclist*

BRADSHAW (RAILWAY GUIDE). Holmes asked Watson to look up the trains in Bradshaw when he contemplated meeting Miss Violet Hunter at the Black Swan Hotel in Winchester. *The Copper Beeches.* See also *The Valley of Fear*

+BRIGGS, MATILDA. Sherlock Holmes had been successful in the case of Matilda Briggs, but *Matilda Briggs* was not the name of a young woman. Rather, it was a ship associated with the giant rat of Sumatra. "A story for which the world [was] not yet prepared." *The Sussex Vampire*

BRITISH GOVERNMENT. Holmes said that Watson was correct in thinking that his brother Mycroft was under the British Government. "You would also be right in a sense if you said that occasionally he is the British Government." *The Bruce-Partington Plans*

+THE BROTHERHOOD. One of the two names used by the Russian Nihilist group of which Anna, her estranged husband and "the friend of her heart," Alexis, had once been members. *The Golden Pince-nez*

+BRUCE-PARTINGTON SUBMARINE. A weapon so powerful that it was said naval warfare would become impossible within the radius of its operation. Once Holmes learned of the theft of the submarine's plans, he had to figure out why seven of the ten stolen papers ended up "in the pockets of a dead junior clerk in the heart of London." And also where the other three sheets were. *The Bruce-Partington Plans*

+BRUCE PINKERTON PRIZE. Dr. Percy Trevelyan, while at King's College Hospital, won the Bruce Pinkerton prize and medal for his monograph on obscure nervous lesions. *The Resident Patient*

BULL PUP. Watson confessed to Holmes, upon their first meeting, that one of his shortcomings was that he kept a bull pup. This mysterious communication, since the dog was never mentioned again, has been interpreted as Anglo-Indian slang for 'a short temper'.[3] *A Study in Scarlet*

BULL-TERRIER. Holmes' only friend during his two years at college was Victor Trevor, whom he met "only through the accident of his bull-terrier freezing on my

---

[3] *The Encyclopaedia Sherlockiana.* A Universal Dictionary of Sherlock Holmes and his Biographer John H. Watson M.D. by Jack Tracy. NEL 1977

ankle one morning as I went down to chapel." *The "Gloria Scott"*

BORGIAS. The black pearl of the Borgias had been stolen from the Prince of Colonna's bedroom at the Dacre Hotel, and was later rather ingeniously hidden. *The Six Napoleons*

BOSWELL, JAMES. As Holmes was about to receive a rather severe looking personage, Watson offered to leave the room; but Holmes replied, "Stay where you are. I am lost without my Boswell. And this promises to be interesting. It would be a pity to miss it." *A Scandal in Bohemia*

BOUGUEREAU, ADOLPHE WILLIAM. No doubt could have been thrown on the authenticity of the painting by Bouguereau that hung in Thaddeus Sholto's house. *The Sign of Four*

BUDDHA. After Eugenia Ronder contacted him at the beginning of an investigation, "Sherlock Holmes threw himself with fierce energy upon the pile of commonplace books in the corner [of his sitting-room in Baker Street]. So excited was he, he did not rise, but sat upon the floor like some strange Buddha, with crossed legs, the huge books all round him, and one open upon his knees." *The Veiled Lodger*. See also *The Sign of Four*

C

+CAMBERWELL POISONING CASE. Watson writes that "The year '87 furnished us with a long series of cases of greater or less interest, of which I retain the records." One of them concerned a poisoning in Camberwell. By handling the victim's watch, Holmes was able to prove when the man had gone to bed, a deduction of paramount importance in this particular investigation. *The Five Orange Pips*

+CARINA. Holmes suggested to Watson, "Let us escape from this weary workaday world by the side door of music.

Carina sings to-night at the Albert Hall." *The Retired Colourman*

CARLYLE, THOMAS. Watson felt that Holmes' "ignorance was as remarkable as his knowledge. Of contemporary literature, philosophy and politics he appeared to know next to nothing. Upon my quoting Thomas Carlyle, he inquired in the naivest way who he might be and what he had done." *A Study in Scarlet*. See also *The Sign of Four*

CATULLUS. One of the three books which Sherlock Holmes, in the guise of an elderly, deformed bibliophile, offered to sell Watson shortly after the two had collided outside the house in which Ronald Adair had been found murdered. *The Empty House*

+CENTRAL PRESS SYNDICATE. Mr Horace Harker, who saw a man killed on his doorstep, was so agitated he didn't think he could write up the story for this Syndicate which employed him as a journalist. *The Six Napoleons*

CHALDEAN. Sherlock Holmes' study of the subject showed, in his opinion, that the Cornish language contained Chaldean roots. *The Devil's Foot*

CHARLES I. He entrusted his crown to the Musgrave family so that they could pass it on to Charles II when he came to the throne. *The Musgrave Ritual*

CHARLES II. Sir Ralph Musgrave had been "a prominent Cavalier, and the right-hand man of Charles II in his wanderings." *The Musgrave Ritual*

CHEETAH. Another of Doctor Grimsby Roylott's exotic pets. *The Speckled Band*

CHESS. Holmes said of Josiah Amberley that he excelled at chess, which the detective thought showed the mark "of a scheming mind." *The Retired Colourman*

CHOPIN, FREDERIC. Holmes looked forward to spending

the afternoon in a concert hall listening to the violinist Madame Wilma Norman Neruda and mentions a "little thing" by Chopin to Watson. *A Study in Scarlet*

CIGAR. Holmes reasoned that the murderer of Enoch J. Drebber must have smoked a Trichinopoly cigar. "I gathered up some scattered ash from the floor. It was dark in colour and flakey — such an ash as is only made by a Trichinopoly. I have made a special study of cigar ashes— in fact, I have written a monograph upon the subject. I flatter myself that I can distinguish at a glance the ash of any known brand either of cigar or of tobacco." *A Study in Scarlet*

+COAL AND IRON POLICE. A body of men raised by the railways and colliery owners of Vermissa Valley to supplement the largely ineffectual efforts of the ordinary civil police force, helpless against the band of men (known informally as Scowrers) who terrorized the district. *The Valley of Fear*

COCAINE. "Sherlock Holmes took his bottle from the corner of the mantelpiece, and his hypodermic syringe from its neat morocco case. With his long, white, nervous fingers he adjusted the delicate needle, and rolled back his left shirt-cuff. For some little time his eyes rested thoughtfully upon the sinewy forearm and wrist, all dotted and scarred with innumerable puncture marks. Finally, he thrust the sharp point home, pressed down the tiny piston, and sank back into the velvet-lined armchair with a long sigh of satisfaction." Poor Watson felt he ought to make a protest against the use of the drug. But all he got from Holmes for his pains was the question, "Would you like to try it?" [A 7% solution of cocaine] *The Sign of Four*. See also *The Yellow Face*

+CONK-SINGLETON FORGERY CASE, THE. After the

successful conclusion of the investigation into the disappearance of the Borgia Pearl, Holmes asks Watson to get out the papers concerning this case. *The Six Napoleons*

COOK'S, THOMAS (TRAVEL AGENT). Lady Frances booked her journey to Baden through her local travel agent. The manager told Watson where she had gone after leaving Lausanne. *The Disappearance of Lady Frances Carfax*

COPERNICAN THEORY. Once again Watson felt that Holmes' "ignorance was as remarkable as his knowledge" and was amazed to find that his friend knew nothing of "the Copernican Theory and of the composition of the Solar System." *A Study in Scarlet*

COPTIC MONASTERIES. Professor Coram's *magnum opus* was an analysis of the documents found in the Coptic monasteries of Syria and Egypt, a work which, he believed, would "cut deep at the very foundations of revealed religion." *The Golden Pince-nez.* At the time of *The Retired Colourman,* Holmes was "preoccupied with this case of **The Two Coptic Patriarchs**, which should come to a head today."

CORNISH LANGUAGE. According to Holmes, the ancient Cornish language was very similar to the Chaldean, and had been largely derived from the Phoenician traders in tin who are known to have visited the area. *The Devil's Foot*

CREDIT LYONNAIS. A cheque to Miss Marie Devine, from a woman who subsequently couldn't be found, had been cashed at the Credit Lyonnais at Montpelier some weeks after *The Disappearance of Lady Frances Carfax*

CREMONA VIOLINS. See Amati

CRIMEAN WAR. An ill-fated ship, 'The Gloria Scott', left England from Falmouth, bound for Australia with her cargo of criminals, at the height of the Crimean War. *The "Gloria Scott".* See also *The Crooked Man, The Golden Pince-nez,*

The Disappearance of Lady Frances Carfax and *The Blanched Soldier*

CROCKFORD. Holmes looked up the vicar, J. C. Elman, in his copy of this Church of England Directory. *The Retired Colourman*

CYANEA CAPILLATA. A curious, waving, vibrant and hairy creature with streaks of silver among its yellow tresses, its bite was more painful and dangerous than a cobra's. *The Lion's Mane*

D

+DAILY GAZETTE. One of several popular London journals whose "agony columns" were filed by Sherlock Holmes in a great book. His compilation proved useful on many occasions as he was able to use these columns for various purposes.

DAILY TELEGRAPH. Concerning the murder of Enoch J. Drebber, "the Daily Telegraph remarked that in the history of crime there had seldom been a tragedy which presented stranger features." *A Study in Scarlet.* See also *The Norwood Builder, The Second Stain* and *The Bruce-Partington Plans*

+DARLINGTON SUBSTITUTION SCANDAL. A woman's instinct to rescue the object she values most if she thinks the house is on fire, as Irene Adler did, was taken advantage of more than once by Sherlock Holmes. He said that it was of use to him in the case of the Darlington Substitution Scandal. *A Scandal in Bohemia*

DARWIN, CHARLES. Holmes remembered his afternoon at one of Sir Charles Hallé's concerts listening to Wilma Norman Neruda [Hallé's second wife] play the violin, and remarks to Watson, "Do you remember what Darwin says about music? He claims that the power of producing and appreciating it existed among the human race long before the power of speech was arrived at. Perhaps that is why we are so subtly influenced by it. There are vague memories in our souls of those misty centuries when the world was in its childhood." *A Study in Scarlet*

DE CROY, PHILIPPE. He printed a seventeenth-century book which Holmes saw and commented upon. *A Study in Scarlet*

DE QUINCEY, THOMAS. Isa Whitney, the man Watson found in The Bar of Gold, "was much addicted to opium. The habit grew upon him from some foolish freak when he was at college, for having read De Quincey's description of his dreams and sensations, he had drenched his tobacco with laudanum in an attempt to produce the same effects." *The Man with the Twisted Lip*

DE RESZKES, THE. [JEAN AND EDOUARD, OPERA SINGERS]. Holmes invited Watson to hear them after wrapping up an investigation. *The Hound of the Baskervilles*

+DEVINE. Supposedly, a French sculptor. Casts of his head of Napoleon were being systematically smashed in London. However, no sculptor by this name is known to have existed at the time Watson wrote up the investigation. It's possible that he meant Canover, or one of the other three men best known to have made busts of the Emperor. *The Six Napoleons*

+DESBOROUGH. Lord Backwater's racehorse, quartered at the Capleton stables, on Dartmoor, was second favourite in the race for the Wessex Cup. *Silver Blaze*

+DETECTIVE CONSULTING, A. Holmes explained his profession to Watson by saying, "Well, I have a trade of my own. I suppose I am the only one in the world. I'm a consulting detective, if you can understand what that is. Here in London we have lots of Government detectives and lots of private ones. When these fellows are at fault, they come to me, and I manage to put them on the right scent." *A Study in Scarlet*

+DIOGENES CLUB. Mycroft Holmes, who had "better powers of observation" than Sherlock himself, was a member of the Diogenes Club. Sherlock said, "The Diogenes Club is the queerest club in London, and Mycroft one of the queerest men...There are many men in London, you know, who, some from shyness, some from misanthropy, have no wish for the company of their fellows. Yet they are not averse to comfortable chairs and the latest periodicals. It is for the convenience of these that the Diogenes Club was started, and it now contains the most unsociable and un-clubbable men in town. No member is permitted to take the least notice of any other one. Save in the Strangers' Room, no talking is, under any circumstances, permitted, and three offences, if brought to the notice of the committee, render the talker liable to expulsion." *The Greek Interpreter.* See also *The Bruce-Partington Plans*

DOGS. Holmes had serious thoughts of writing a small monograph on the uses of dogs in detective work. Watson queried this but said much about canines in his accounts of the 'Adventures', including what Sherlock said about dogs and family life. "Whoever saw a frisky dog in a gloomy family, or a sad dog in a happy one? Snarling people have snarling dogs, dangerous people have dangerous ones. And their passing moods may reflect the passing moods of others." *The Creeping Man.* Fitzroy Macpherson's faithful Airedale terrier suffered the same fate as his master, causing Holmes to reflect, "That the dog should die was after the beautiful, faithful nature of dogs." *The Lion's Mane.* **CARLO.** The mastiff guard.dog at a house in

Hampshire. Only Toller, the groom, could handle him. *The Copper Beeches* CARLO. A spaniel owned by Robert Ferguson. The animal walked with difficulty. Its hind legs moved irregularly and its tail was on the ground. Though a veterinarian had diagnosed Carlo's malady as spinal meningitis, Holmes understood that the beast's infirmity had been brought about by unnatural causes. Which hints at possible ill-treatment by Ferguson's son, Jack. *The Sussex Vampire*. There was also **POMPEY**, who in Sherlock Holmes' opinion was a detective with a great talent for tracking. Physically, he was "a squat, lop-eared, white-and-tan dog, something between a beagle and a foxhound." He was also the pride of the Cambridge drag hounds. His build meant that he couldn't be called a great flier, but he was nevertheless a staunch hound when once he caught the scent. With the assistance of such a dog, Holmes was finally able to discover the whereabouts of Godfrey Staunton. *The Missing Three-Quarter.* **ROY**. Professor Presbury's faithful wolfhound, he had, seemingly without reason, twice attempted to bite his master. *The Creeping Man.* **SHOSCOMBE SPANIELS.** "The most exclusive breed in England. They are the special pride of the lady of Shoscombe Old Place." This was Lady Beatrice Falder. When Sir Robert Norberton gave away her pet spaniel, it aroused the suspicions of John Mason, who came to Holmes with the problem. *Shoscombe Old Place.* **TOBY**. Old Sherman's sleuth-hound, who assisted Holmes in trailing the murderers of Bartholomew Sholto. The dog was an ugly, long-haired, lop-eared creature, half spaniel and half lurcher, brown and white in colour, with a very clumsy, waddling walk. *The Sign of Four.* And, of course, there's the fierce hound sold to Jack Stapleton, a vicious animal who figured in one of the most famous

'Adventures' of all. *The Hound of the Baskervilles*

+**DUNDAS SEPARATION CASE.** Watson, in his discussion with Holmes as to whether commonplace occurrences held any interest, showed him an article about the ill-treatment of a wife by her husband and said that there was half a column of print, but that he knew without reading any further that it would all be perfectly familiar to him. The other woman, the drink, the push, the blow, the bruise, the sympathetic sister or landlady. In the Doctor's opinion the crudest of writers could invent nothing more crude. Holmes' reaction was, "Indeed, your example is an unfortunate one for your argument…This is the Dundas separation case, and, as it happens, I was engaged in clearing up some small points in connection with it. The husband was a teetotaller, there was no other woman, and the conduct complained of was that he had drifted into the habit of winding up every meal by taking out his false teeth and hurling them at his wife, which you will allow is not an action likely to occur to the imagination of the average story-teller." *A Case of Identity*

DUPIN. Watson told his colleague in fighting crime that the detective reminded him of Edgar Allan Poe's Dupin. Holmes replied stiffly, "Now, in my opinion, Dupin was a very inferior fellow. That trick of his of breaking in on his friends' thoughts with an apropos remark after a quarter of an hour's silence is really very showy and superficial. He had some analytical genius, no doubt; but he was by no means such a phenomenon as Poe appeared to imagine." Which completely ignores the times when Sherlock broke into Watson's thoughts. *A Study in Scarlet*

+**DYNAMICS OF AN ASTEROID, THE.** Holmes said of Moriarty. "Is he not the celebrated author of The Dynamics of an Asteroid— a book which ascends to such rarefied heights of pure mathematics that it is said that there was no man in the scientific press capable of criticizing it?" *The Valley of Fear*

E

EAR. "As a medical man, you are aware, Watson, that there is no part of the body which varies so much as the human ear. Each ear is as a rule quite distinctive, and differs from all other ones. In last year's Anthropological Journal you will find two short monographs from my pen upon the subject." *The Cardboard Box*

EAR-FLAPPED TRAVELLING-CAP. This distinctive headgear was worn by Holmes on his way down to Dartmoor to investigate the murder of a trainer and the disappearance of a racehorse, *Silver Blaze*.

EARLY ENGLISH CHARTERS. At the time that Mr. Hilton Soames came to Holmes with the problem of the three students, Holmes and Watson were residing in furnished lodgings in one of the great university towns of Britain where Holmes was doing library research "in Early English charters —researches which led to results so striking that they may be the subject of one of my future narratives." *The Three Students*

ECHO. The "newspaper of the day" which gave the police all the credit for solving the mystery of *A Study in Scarlet*

EGRIA. The German-speaking country which was not far from Carlsbad. "Remarkable as being the scene of the death of Wallenstein, and for its numerous glass factories and paper mills." *A Scandal in Bohemia*

ELEY'S NO.2. Holmes said to Watson, "I should be very much obliged if you would slip your revolver into your pocket. An Eley's No. 2 is an excellent argument with gentlemen who can twist steel pokers into knots." He meant, of course, Doctor Grimesby Roylott. *The Speckled Band*

F

FATE. At the conclusion of his investigation of the brutal slaying of Charles McCarthy, Holmes philosophized. "Why does Fate play such tricks with poor helpless worms? I never hear of such a case as this that I do not think of Baxter's words, and say, 'There, but for the grace of God, goes Sherlock Holmes.'" *The Boscombe Valley Mystery* The Great Detective showed to the once-beautiful Eugenia Ronder such sympathy as he was seldom known to exhibit. "Poor girl! Poor girl! The ways of Fate are indeed hard to understand. If there is not some compensation hereafter, then the world is a cruel jest." *The Veiled Lodger*

FENCING. Apart from fencing and boxing, Holmes had few athletic tastes during his two years at college. *The "Gloria Scott"*

+FERGUSON & MUIRHEAD. Tea brokers, of Mincing Lane. Ferguson was the part-owner who asked Sherlock Holmes for help in finding the reason for his wife's strange behaviour. *The Sussex Vampire*

FERRERS DOCUMENTS.[4] Holmes initially felt that he and Watson were too busy, having been retained in the case of the Ferrers Documents, and with the Abergavenny murder coming up for trial, to investigate the problem that Dr. Thorneycroft Huxtable brought to them. *The Priory School*

FOOTSTEPS. Holmes mentioned that he had "been guilty of several monographs," among which was one "upon the tracing of footsteps, with some remarks upon the uses of

---

[4] These documents may have been suggested by the real-life case of Earl Ferrers, a Peer of the Realm hanged at Tyburn in 1760.

plaster of Paris as a preserver of impresses." *The Sign of Four* See also *A Study in Scarlet*

+FRANCO-MIDLAND HARDWARE COMPANY LIMITED. Supposedly, it had 134 branches in the towns and villages of France, not counting one in Brussels and one in San Remo. *The Stockbroker's Clerk*

FREEMASON. Holmes knew that Jabez Wilson, the man with the fiery red hair, was a Freemason from his arc-and-compass breast-pin. *The Red-Headed League.*

+FRIESLAND, THE STEAMSHIP. Sherlock Holmes felt that his first few months back in London following the death of Professor Moriarty were uneventful. Watson, who at Holmes' request had moved back into his old rooms in Baker Street, disagreed and cited "the shocking affair of the Dutch steamship, Friesland." An affair which had nearly cost them both their lives. *The Norwood Builder*

FLAUBERT, GUSTAVE. Holmes, bored as usual after completing a case, derived some solace from Gustave Flaubert's comment to George Sand: "The man is nothing, the work is everything." *The Red-Headed League*

G

GABORIAU, EMILE. Watson asked his new friend if he had ever read Gaboriau's works, or if Lecoq was his idea of a detective. Sherlock Holmes' reply to this is that "Lecoq was a miserable bungler. He had only one thing to recommend him, and that was his energy. That book made me positively ill." *A Study in Scarlet*

"GAME IS AFOOT, THE". On a bitterly cold and frosty morning during the winter of 1897 Watson was woken up by someone tugging at his shoulder. He says, "It was Holmes. The candle in his hand shone upon his eager, stooping face, and told me at a glance that something was amiss. 'Come, Watson, come!' he cried. 'The game is afoot.

Not a word! Into your clothes and come!'" But as Sebastian Faulks says, "Too much of the action [in the canon] is given in speech...but the danger is that it can put the action at arm's length...we have inverted commas within Holmes's inverted commas. This obviously has a distancing effect."[5] For Faulks the best stories are those where action is prioritised over speech. But maybe too much of that might have resulted in another 'Sexton' rather than a 'Sherlock'. *The Abbey Grange*.

GASOGENE. A gadget for carbonating soda water using 'sparklet bulbs'. Similar in action to a soda siphon. "With hardly a word spoken, but with a kindly eye, he waved me to an arm-chair, threw across his case of cigars, and indicated a spirit case and a gasogene in the corner." *A Scandal in Bohemia*

GEOLOGY. In Watson's famous catalogue of "Sherlock Holmes—his limits," he rated the Great Detective's knowledge of geology as "Practical, but limited. Tells at a glance different soils from each other. After walks has shown me splashes upon his trousers, and told me by their colour and consistence in what part of London he had received them." *A* Study *in Scarlet*. See also *The Five Orange Pips*

GHAZIS. Fanatical Moslems dedicated to killing 'Infidels'. They followed the army, and the seriously wounded Watson at the Battle of Maiwand during the Second Afghan War "would have fallen into the hands of the murderous Ghazis had it not been for the devotion and courage shown by Murray, my orderly, who threw me across a packhorse, and succeeded in bringing me safely to the British lines." *A Study in Scarlet*

---

[5] "Faulks on Fiction." BBC Books 2011, pp 59-60

+GIANT RAT OF SUMATRA, THE. The story for which the world was "not yet prepared" at the time Sherlock Holmes undertook a particular case. *The Sussex Vampire*

+"GLORIA SCOTT", THE. A vessel which, in 1855, became a convict ship and was sent to Australia. A relic of the Chinese tea-trade, the craft was old-fashioned, heavy-bowed, broad-beamed and easily outclassed by the new clippers. Weighing 500 ton, she had on board thirty-eight convicts, four warders, twenty six crew members with their Captain, eighteen soldiers, three mates, a doctor and a chaplain. She was said to have been lost at sea that same year. *The "Gloria Scott".* See also *The Musgrave Ritual* and *The Sussex Vampire*

+GREAT MOGUL, THE. Said to be the second largest diamond in existence, it was part of the great Agra treasure stolen by the men bound by the oath 'The Sign of the Four'. *The Sign of Four*

GOETHE, JOHANN WOLFGANG VON. Holmes quotes him twice in *The Sign of Four*

GORDON, GENERAL. As Sherlock Holmes observed him, Watson's "eyes fixed themselves upon [his] newly framed picture of General Gordon...." *The Cardboard Box*

GREUZE, JEAN BAPTISTE. A French artist who flourished between 1750 and 1800. According to Holmes, "Modern criticism has more than endorsed the high opinion formed of him by his contemporaries." A portrait by Greuze, "a young woman with her head on her hands, peeking at you sideways," as Inspector MacDonald said, hung on the wall of Professor Moriarty's study. *The Valley of Fear*

H

HAFIZ. Holmes said that if he told Mary Sutherland who her fiancé really was she would not believe him and (to Watson) "You may remember the old Persian saying, 'There is danger for him who taketh the tiger cub, and danger also for whoso snatches a delusion from a woman.' There is as much sense in Hafiz as in Horace, and as much knowledge of the world." However, this quotation hasn't yet been found in either poet's works, nor yet anywhere else. *A Case of Identity*

HALLÉ, SIR CHARLES. Holmes wanted to speed up his investigation into the death of Enoch J. Drebber so that he could go to a Hallé concert to hear Wilma Norman Neruda play the violin that afternoon. Madame Norman Neruda performed only on Saturdays and Mondays during the season. Something which seriously compromises the chronology of the first of Holmes' investigations to be written up by Watson. *A Study in Scarlet*

+HOLDER & STEVENSON. They were the second largest private banking firm in the City and had their offices in Threadneedle Street. *The Beryl Coronet*

HUNGARIAN POLICE. The Hungarian police were of the opinion that the stabbing deaths of Wilson Kemp and Harold Latimer were the result of a quarrel between themselves. Sherlock Holmes thought differently, however. *The Greek Interpreter*

I

IMPERIAL OPERA OF WARSAW. Irene Adler, famed as someone Holmes called *the* woman, had been prima donna of the Imperial Opera of Warsaw. *A Scandal in Bohemia*

IMPERIAL THEATRE. Violet Smith's father, the late James Smith, had conducted the orchestra at the old Imperial Theatre. *The Solitary Cyclist*

INDIAN MUTINY. James Barclay rose in the service from

private to full colonel by the bravery he showed in the Indian Mutiny. The Royal Mallows regiment, which he later commanded, also distinguished itself in action there. *The Crooked Man*

+IRIS. The horse run by the Duke of Balmoral for the Wessex Cup, it came in a bad third.

ISONOMY. Speaking of a famous fictional racehorse, a favourite for the Wessex Cup, Holmes told Watson that the animal was from Isonomy stock. This latter was a real-life horse who won the Ascot Gold Cup in two consecutive years, 1879-80. *Silver Blaze*

J

+JACKSON PRIZE FOR COMPARATIVE PATHOLOGY. Dr. .James Mortimer won this Prize with his essay "Is Disease a Reversion?" *The Hound of the Baskervilles*

JEZAIL BULLET. Dr. John H. Watson, newly attached to the Berkshires after being removed from The Northumberland Fusiliers, says that he took part in "the fatal battle of Maiwand. There I was struck on the shoulder by a Jezail bullet, which shattered the bone and grazed the subclavian artery." *A Study in Scarlet*. At one point during his second investigation with Holmes (*The Sign of Four*) Watson sits nursing his wounded leg. "I had had a Jezail bullet through it sometime before, and though it did not prevent me from walking, it ached wearily at every change of the weather." In a later investigation Watson said, "I had remained indoors all day, for the weather had taken a sudden turn to rain, with high autumnal winds, and the jezail bullet which I brought back in one of my limbs as a relic of my Afghan campaign, throbbed with dull persistency." *The Noble Bachelor*. These remarks have led to much speculation as to where, physically, Watson was wounded. Did the bullet pass through him and strike both the shoulder and the leg? Was he wounded twice?

K

KU KLUX KLAN. Holmes traced the series of mysterious letters that foreshadowed the death of two generations of Openshaws to the Ku Klux Klan and referred to his American Encyclopaedia for specific information about the Organisation. He read that the name was "derived from a fanciful resemblance to the sound produced by cocking a rifle. This terrible secret society was formed by some ex-Confederate soldiers in the Southern States after the Civil War, and it rapidly formed local branches in different parts of the country, notably Tennessee, Louisiana, the Carolinas, Georgia, and Florida. Its power was used for political purposes, principally for the terrorizing of the negro voters, and the murdering or driving from the country of those who were opposed to its views." *The Five Orange Pips*

L

LASSUS, ROLAND DE. Sherlock Holmes wrote a monograph on the Polyphonic Motets of Lassus, which when printed for private circulation was said by experts to be the last word on the subject. *The Bruce-Partington Plans*

+LATIMER'S. Watson had bought his boots from Latimer's, in Oxford Street. Holmes, however, wasn't interested in the boots. He simply wanted to see how the laces were tied. *The Disappearance of Lady Frances Carfax*

LAW. In Watson's catalogue, mentioned above, of "Sherlock Holmes —his limits," he noted that his new friend had "a good practical knowledge of British law. *A Study in Scarlet*. See also *The Five Orange Pips*

LECOQ. See Gaboriau. *A Study in Scarlet*

LEGION OF HONOUR, ORDER OF THE. See Huret. *The Golden Pince-nez*

LITERATURE. In Watson's famous catalogue he rated the Great Detective's knowledge of literature as "Nil." But in the same place Holmes' knowledge of sensational literature is said to be "immense." *A Study in Scarlet*

M

MAFIA. The secret political society, which used murder to make sure its decrees were obeyed. Pietro Venucci was a member of this terrible organisation. *The Six Napoleons*

MALINGERING.Holmes said, "The best way of successfully acting a part is to be it. I give you my word that for three days I have tasted neither food nor drink until you were good enough to pour me out that glass of water . Three days of absolute fast does not improve one's beauty For the rest, there is nothing which a sponge may not cure. With vaseline upon one's forehead, crusts of beeswax around one's lips, a very satisfying effect can be produced. Malingering is a subject upon which I have sometimes thought of writing a monograph." *The Dying Detective*. See also *The Reigate Squire*

MALTHUS, THOMAS. (1766-1864). His famous essay on population argued that the human capacity for reproduction exceeded the rate at which subsistence from the land can be increased. There were natural checks on population growth such as famine, disease and war. Artificial constraints included late marriage and chastity. But living standards were reduced by the decrease in the supply of food, leading to some kind of 'poverty trap'. *A Study in Scarlet*

'MARQUESS DE BRINVILLIERS'. The Daily Telegraph cited this woman as an arch-poisoner when writing about the death of Enoch J. Drebber. Described as quiet, mousey and much given to good works, she poisoned her father and her two brothers. She also attempted to poison her husband but he recovered. A regular visitor to hospitals, de Brinvilliers tried out her poisons on patients, often with fatal results. She was beheaded, and her body burnt, in

1676. A famous drawing by Charles Le Brun shows her on her way to execution.[6] *A Study in Scarlet*

+**MARX & CO.** (See also the Scowerers) Of High Holborn. A good deal of clothing bearing their stamp had been left behind in the house of Aloysius Garcia, who was found brutally murdered. They said they knew nothing of their customer, save that he paid well. *Wisteria Lodge*

+**MAWSON & WILLIAMS.** A giant stock-broking firm in Lombard Street. Hall Pycroft, who had lost his job at Coxon & Woodhouse owing to the failure of the Venezuelan loan, managed to obtain a job here. He was persuaded, however, not to show up for his first day's work, and the strange circumstances surrounding this event prompted him to consult Sherlock Holmes. *The Stockbroker's Clerk*

+**MEUNIER, MONSIEUR OSCAR**. An artist of Grenoble, who spent some days in doing the moulding of a bust of Sherlock Holmes in wax, a bust so like the detective that even Watson was deceived until he threw out his hand to make sure his friend was still next to him. *The Empty House*

+**MORTON & WAYLIGHT'S.** The firm in Tottenham Court Road at which Mr. Warren was employed as a timekeeper. Mrs. Warren had come to Sherlock Holmes, saying that her husband was as nervous over the actions of one of their lodgers as she was. *The Red Circle*

MANOR HOUSE CASE. Mycroft Holmes had expected his brother Sherlock to consult him over the Manor House case. Both Sherlock and Mycroft had come to the same conclusion that the guilty party was Adams. *The Greek Interpreter*

+**MCFARLANE'S.** This carriage-building depot lay just around the corner from Jabez Wilson's Coburg Square pawnshop. *The*

---

[6] "The Sun King" by Nancy Mitford. Hamish Hamilton, 1966. Page 82

Red-Headed League

MENDELSSOHN, FELIX. Watson knew that Holmes could perform pieces, and difficult ones at that, on the violin because (at his request) Holmes had played some of Mendelssohn's Lieder; which were a favourite of the Doctor. *A Study in Scarlet*

MEREDITH, GEORGE. Holmes had already decided upon the major points in the death of Charles McCarthy so he wished to talk about George Meredith, leaving minor points until the next day. *The Boscombe Valley Mystery*

MONGOOSE. See Teddy. *The Crooked Man*

MORMONS. It was the migrating Mormon band of nearly ten thousand souls searching for a place where they could practice their religion unimpeded by State Law which rescued John and Lucy Ferrier upon the Great Alkali Plain. They joined the group and Ferrier became a successful farmer in Utah. *A Study in Scarlet*

MORRISON, MORRISON, AND DODD. Robert Ferguson's lawyers. They suggested he go to see Sherlock Holmes about some domestic trouble. *The Sussex Vampire*

N

NAPOLEON. Plaster casts of the famous head of Napoleon supposedly by a French sculptor Devine (thought to be a fictitious name chosen by the writer) were being systematically smashed. Lestrade came to Holmes thinking that there was some "queer madness" behind the whole affair. *The Six Napoleons*

+NEALE, OUTFITTER, VERMISSA, U.S.A. A tailor's tab found on the neck of an overcoat that Holmes fished out of the shallow moat which surrounded the Manor House of Birlstone, where John Douglas had apparently been murdered. *The Valley of Fear*

THE NEGRO. See Newton

NEW YORK POLICE BUREAU. Holmes cabled his friend

Wilson Hargreave, of the New York Police Bureau. A man "who has more than once made use of my knowledge of London crime." *The Dancing Men*

NORAH CREINA, THE. Three members of the Worthingdon Bank Gang (who killed Blessington in what was popularly known as 'The Brook Street Mystery') were thought to have drowned when this ship was lost at sea. *The Resident Patient*

NORTHUMBERLAND FUSILIERS, FIFTH. After completing his training at Netley, the young Dr. Watson "was attached to the Fifth Northumberland Fusiliers as Assistant Surgeon." The regiment, at that time, was stationed in India. *A Study in Scarlet*

NORMAN NERUDA. Holmes' reason for speeding up a particular investigation was because he wanted to go to Hallé's concert to hear Madame Norman Neruda that afternoon. "Her attack and her bowing are splendid. What's that little thing of Chopin's she plays so magnificently. Tra-la-la-lira-lira-lay." *A Study in Scarlet*

O

OYSTERS. Holmes said to Athelney Jones, "I insist upon your dining with us. It will be ready in half an hour. I have oysters and a brace of grouse, with something a little choice in white wines." *The Sign of Four*. Much later he was to use this bivalve when feigning an illness to deceive Watson. "Indeed, I cannot think why the whole bed of the ocean is not one solid mass of oysters, so prolific the creatures seem. No doubt there are natural enemies which limit the increases of the creatures. You and I, Watson, we have done our part. Shall the world, then, be overrun by oysters? No, no; horrible!" *The Dying Detective*

P

PAGANINI, NICCOLO. After telling Watson how he had bought his Stradivarius at a ridiculously low price, Holmes went on to talk about Paganini. "We sat for an hour over a bottle of claret while he told me anecdote after anecdote of that extraordinary man." *The Cardboard Box*

PALMER. Holmes said, "When a doctor does go wrong he is the first of criminals. He has nerve and he has knowledge. Palmer and Pritchard were among the heads of their profession." This last observation, however, is something of an exaggeration. *The Speckled Band*

PARAPHERNALIA. The cigars in the coal-scuttle, the tobacco in the toe of a Persian slipper, the unanswered correspondence transfixed by a jack-knife into the very centre of a wooden mantelpiece. *The Musgrave Ritual.*

PAUL, JEAN. Pseudonym of J. P. F. Richter. Holmes said, "He makes one curious but profound remark. It is that the chief proof of man's real greatness lies in his perception of his own smallness. It argues, you see, a power of comparison and of appreciation which is in itself a proof of nobility." *The Sign of Four*

PEACE, CHARLIE. Holmes thought that Baron Adelbert Gruner had, "like all great criminals", a complex mind and compared him to Charlie Peace, who was what the detective called "a violin virtuoso." *The Illustrious Client*

PENANG LAWYER. "It was a fine, thick piece of wood, bulbous-headed, of the sort known as a 'Penang Lawyer'." A stout cane made of wood imported from that region: and very like a 'life preserver', which was a short stick with a heavily loaded end which many gentlemen carried as protection against thugs. *The Hound of the Baskervilles*

PENNSYLVANIA SMALL ARMS COMPANY. A label for this Company, italicised and abbreviated to *PEN*, was on the fluting between the barrels of the sawn-off shotgun that supposedly killed John Douglas of Birlstone Manor. *The Valley of Fear*

PETRARCH. After discussing some of the facts of the murder of Charles McCarthy with Watson, Holmes refused to say another word and read his 'pocket Petrarch' until they arrived at the scene of the crime. *The Boscombe Valley Mystery*

PINKERTON'S. The private detective agency employed by large railroad and steel companies to break the hold of the Scowrers on the coal mining districts of the Gilmerton area. A disguised Birdy Edwards was their most important agent engaged in a particular effort there. The *Valley of Fear.* In an earlier investigation, Mr. Leverton of Pinkerton's had been sent over from New York to London by the detective agency to find a vicious killer and had been close to him for a week, waiting some excuse to get (as he said) a hand on his collar. It should be noted that this wasn't a fictional agency. It was real and very active in America. *The Red Circle*

PIPES. The short clay, the long cherry wood and the old brier. *The Blue Carbuncle, The Copper Beeches* and *The Man With the Twisted Lip*

POE, EDGAR ALLAN. Watson said Holmes reminded him of Edgar Allan Poe's fictional detective, Dupin. But in Sherlock's opinion "Dupin was a very inferior fellow. That trick of his of breaking in on his friends' thoughts with an apropos remark after a quarter of an hour's silence is really very showy and superficial. He had some analytical genius, no doubt; but he was by no means such a phenomenon as Poe appeared to imagine." *A Study in Scarlet*. This trick, however, was one which Holmes was to employ himself. *The Cardboard Box*

+**THE POLITICIAN, THE LIGHTHOUSE, AND THE TRAINED CORMORANT.** Even though Watson assured his readers that "no confidence [would] be abused" in the memoirs which Sherlock Holmes allowed to be published, at least one reader made efforts to get at and destroy something related to this case. Watson was compelled to state that the source of such an outrage was known, and if they were repeated he had Holmes' "authority for saying that the whole story concerning the politician, the light-house, and the trained cormorant [would] be given to the public." Eventually it was, but by other hands. *The Veiled Lodger*

PONCHO. It was the stampeding of her horse, Poncho, in a herd of cattle that first introduced Lucy Ferrier to Jefferson Hope. *A Study in Scarlet*

POPE, HIS HOLINESS THE. In his anxiety to oblige the Pope in the little affair of the Vatican cameos, Holmes had overlooked the newspaper reports of the mysterious death of Sir Charles Baskerville. *The Hound of the Baskervilles.* Still with the Vatican, one of Holmes' cases in the year 1895 was an investigation into the sudden death of Cardinal Tosca, an investigation which the Pope himself desired the detective to carry out. *Black Peter*

PRACTICAL HANDBOOK OF BEE CULTURE, WITH SOME OBSERVATIONS UPON THE SEGREGATION OF THE QUEEN. Holmes passed the small blue book over to Von Bork, who thought it contained the British naval signals. *His Last Bow.* See also the entry on **Bees.**

+**PUGILIST.** Horse run by Colonel Wardlaw against Silver Blaze for the Wessex Cup. *Silver Blaze.*

R

RATCLIFF HIGHWAY MURDERS. The Daily Telegraph mentioned these when it attributed the death of Enoch J. Drebber to political refugees and revolutionaries. *A Study in Scarlet*

+ROCK OF GIBRALTAR. The "largest and best boat" of the Adelaide-Southampton line. On board the *Rock of Gibraltar*, sailing out of Adelaide, Mary Fraser and Jack Croker began the friendship which, over eighteen months later, would figure prominently in one of Holmes' cases. *The Abbey Grange*

RED INDIAN. Watson wrote of Sherlock Holmes, "For an instant the veil had lifted upon his keen, intense nature, but for an instant only. When I glanced again his face had resumed that Red Indian composure which had made so many regard him as a machine rather than a man." *The Crooked Man.* See also *The Naval Treaty*

RED LEECH, THE. One of the many cases Sherlock Holmes handled in 1894 was "the repulsive story of the red leech and the terrible death of Crosby the banker." These may or may not be separate investigations. *The Golden Pince-nez*

RELIGION. Holmes said that there was nothing is which deduction was so necessary than in religion. It could be built up as an exact science by the reasoner. "Our highest assurance of the goodness of Providence seems to me to rest in the flowers. All other things, our powers, our desires, our food, are really necessary for our existence in the first instance. But this rose is an extra. Its smell and its colour are an embellishment of life, not a condition of it. It is only goodness which gives extras, and so I say again that we have much to hope from the flowers." *The Naval Treaty*

RHODISIAN POLICE, THE. After his disgrace in the affair of the Fortescue Scholarship, the guilty student accepted the offer of a commission in the Rhodesian Police and left for South Africa at once. *The Three Students*

RESTAURANTS. **+Goldoni's.** A "garish Italian restaurant" to which Holmes summoned Watson during a certain investigation. He asked his old friend to join him in a coffee and curacao and to try one of the proprietor's cigars, which were "less poisonous than one would expect." *The Bruce-Partington Plans.* **+Marcini's.** Holmes suggested to Watson that they have a little supper here before going on to a concert. *The Hound of the Baskervilles.* **Simpson's.** "When we have finished at the police-station I think that something nutritious at Simpson's would not be out of place," said Holmes to Watson. *The Dying Detective*

+RASPER. One of the horses entered for the Wessex Cup. *Silver Blaze*

READE WINWOOD. Holmes recommended that Watson read this author's *Martyrdom of Man*. Meanwhile, Holmes would be out investigating the facts surrounding the Agra Treasure Mystery. Later, when Watson suggested that someone had called man "a soul concealed in an animal," Holmes replied, "Winwood Reade is good upon the subject. He remarks that, while the individual man is an insoluble puzzle, in the aggregate he becomes a mathematical certainty." *The Sign of Four*

REYNOLDS, SIR JOSHUA. While dining with Sir Henry Baskerville, Sherlock Holmes thought he recognized a painting by Reynolds in the family gallery. *The Hound of the Baskervilles*

RICHTER. The real name of "Jean Paul." Holmes felt that "there is much food for thought in Richter." *The Sign of*

Four

+RICOLETTI OF THE CLUB FOOT AND HIS ABOMINABLE WIFE, THE CASE OF. One more of Watson's intriguingly untold tales. *The Musgrave Ritual*

ROBERTS, LORD. A real-life military man as esteemed in his field as was Watson's Sir James Saunders in medical circles. Holmes believed that were a "raw subaltern" to have been granted an interview with Lord Roberts, the subaltern's "wonder and pleasure" could not have exceeded that expressed by Mr. Kent when that country surgeon met Sir James. *The Blanched Soldier*

ROSA, SALVATOR. A connoisseur might have thrown a doubt on the Salvator Rosa that hung in Thaddeus Sholto's small house in South London. *The Sign of Four*.

+ROSS AND MANGLES. Animal dealers, in Fulham Road, they sold the "strongest and most savage" dog in their possession to Sir Henry Baskerville's neighbour. *The Hound of the Baskervilles*

ROYAL ARTILLERY. The "very small, dark fellow, with his hat pushed back and several packages under his arm" that both Mycroft and Sherlock Holmes saw from the window of the Strangers' Room of the Diogenes Club, revealed certain facts to the brothers in a kind of friendly rivalry in the art of observation. The man had been a non-commissioned officer of the Royal Artillery, since he still wore his 'ammunition boots', and had served in India. Retired, he had lost his wife and now had the care of a young family, etc. *The Greek Interpreter*

+ROYAL MALLOWS. The old 117th was "one of the most famous Irish regiments in the British Army. It did wonders both in the Crimea and the Mutiny, and has since that time distinguished itself upon every possible occasion." Its commanding officer was Colonel James Barclay, "a gallant veteran, who started as a full private, was raised to commissioned rank for his bravery at the time of the Mutiny, and so lived to command the regiment in which he had once carried a musket." He was found dead in his locked morning-room. *The Crooked Man*

ROYAL MARINE LIGHT INFANTRY. Holmes deduced that the commissionaire who delivered Inspector Gregson's summons was a retired sergeant of Marines. Shortly thereafter, the man identified himself to an astonished Watson as "A sergeant, sir. Royal Marine Light Infantry, sir." *A Study in Scarlet*

RUGBY. Watson had played rugby for Blackheath when Big Bob Ferguson was three-quarter for Richmond. *The Sussex Vampire* .

RUSSELL, CLARK. "It was in the latter days of September, and the equinoctial gales had set in with exceptional violence. All day the wind had screamed and the rain had beaten against the windows, so that even here in the heart of great hand-made London we were forced to raise our minds for the instant from the routine of life, and to recognise the presence of those great elemental forces which shriek at mankind through the bars of his civilisation, like untamed beasts in a cage. As evening drew in the storm grew louder and louder, and the wind cried and sobbed like a child in the chimney. Sherlock Holmes sat moodily at one side of the fireplace cross-indexing his records of crime, whilst I at the other was deep in one of Clark Russell's fine sea stories, until the howl of the gale from without seemed to blend with the text, and the splash of the rain to lengthen out into the long swash of the sea waves." *The Five Orange Pips.*

S

+**SAHARA KING**. Ronder's wild beast show had among its exhibits a very fine North African lion named Sahara King. *The Veiled Lodger*

SAND, GEORGE. Holmes, once more experiencing ennui after unravelling the mystery surrounding Jabez Wilson, found some comfort in Gustave Flaubert's comment to George Sand, *"L'homme n'est rien, l'oeuvre tout."* *The Red-Headed League*

SANGER. "One of the greatest showmen of his day," he was the (real-life) rival of the (real-life) Wombwell and the fictional Ronder. *The Veiled Lodger*

SARASATE, PABLO DE. See St. James's Hall. *The Red-Headed League*

SLOANE, HANS. A real-life collector of antiquities, he was an exemplar of the reclusive collector Nathan Garrideb. *The Three Garridebs*

SCANDINAVIA, KING OF. The hereditary King of Bohemia's marriage to Clotilde Lothman von Saxe-Meningen, second daughter of the King of Scandinavia, was threatened by a compromising photograph in Irene Adler's possession. *A Scandal in Bohemia.* See also *The Noble Bachelor*

SCANDINAVIA, ROYAL FAMILY OF. By the time of the supposed tragedy at The Reichenbach Falls, Holmes had been of some assistance to the Royal Family of Scandinavia, and he hinted to Watson that this had earned him a great deal of cash. *The Final Problem*

SINGLESTICK. In Watson's famous catalogue of "Sherlock Holmes — his limits," he noted that the Great Detective was "an expert singlestick player, boxer, and swordsman," *A Study in Scarlet*. See also *The Illustrious Client*

+**ST. PANCRAS CASE**. Holmes said. "In the St. Pancras case you may remember that a cap was found beside the dead policeman. The accused man denies that it is his. But he is a picture-frame maker who habitually handles glue." Holmes had positively identified the glue using his microscope. The case was brought to him by Merivale of the Yard. *Shoscombe Old Place*

ST. VITUS'S DANCE. Old Mr. Farquhar, from whom Watson purchased a medical practice in the Paddington district, had seen that practice decline because of his age and "an affliction of the nature of St. Vitus' dance from which he suffered." *The Stockbroker's Clerk*. See also *The Greek Interpreter*

+**SEA UNICORN**. The steam whaler commanded by Captain Peter Carey. Peter Cairns came on board as spare harpooner. *Black Peter*

+**SHOSCOMBE PRINCE**. Racehorse that Sir Robert Norberton ran in the Derby and which won the race. Sir Robert had been taking the Prince's half-brother, who was much slower on the track, out for spins in order to fool the touts. Shoscombe Prince was the favourite of Lady Beatrice Falder, but recently she had been paying him no attention, a clue to something rather sinister. *Shoscombe Old Place*

+**SILVER BLAZE**. Racehorse from Colonel Ross's stable who disappeared mysteriously before the race for the Wessex Cup, which he was the favourite to win. His trainer was found murdered but at least Holmes was able to find the animal in time for it to run, even though it had been 'christened'- that is, disguised . *Silver Blaze*

+**SMITH-MORTIMER**. One of the many investigations

Sherlock Holmes handled in 1894 was the famous Smith-Mortimer succession case. *The Golden Pince-nez*

SMITH, JOSEPH. One of the young Mormons who first spoke to John Ferrier identified himself as a "persecuted [child] of God...We are of those who believe in those sacred writings, drawn in Egyptian letters on plates of beaten gold, which were handed unto the holy Joseph Smith at Palmyra." The migrant Mormon band was led by Brigham Young, who "spoke with the voice of Joseph Smith, which is the voice of God." *A Study in Scarlet*

+**SOPHY ANDERSON**. "The year '87 furnished us with a long series of cases of greater or less interest, of which I retain the records." One related to the loss of this sea-going vessel. *The Five Orange Pips*

+**SPECKLED BAND, THE**. Julia Stoner's last words were. "O, my God! Helen! It was the band! The speckled band!" Helen Stoner speculated to Holmes, "Sometimes I have thought that it was merely the wild talk of delirium, sometimes that it may have referred to some band of people, perhaps to these very gipsies in the plantation. I do not know whether the spotted handkerchiefs which so many of them wear over their heads might have suggested the strange adjective which she used." *The Speckled Band*

+**SPENCER JOHN GANG, THE**. Steve Dixie, Barney Stockdale, and Susan Stockdale were members of this gang, which specialized in assaults, intimidation, and the like. *The Three Gables*

+**STATE AND MERTON COUNTRY RAILROAD CO.** Responsible for the railroad that went through the Vermissa Valley, where the Company also owned several mines. *The Valley of Fear*

+**STAUNTON, ARTHUR H.** The volume of Sherlock

Holmes' commonplace book devoted to persons and things whose names began with the letter S was a "mine of varied information." One of the entries referred to an "Arthur H. Staunton, the rising young forger." *The Missing Three-Quarter*

STRADIVARIUS. "We had a pleasant little meal together, during which Holmes would talk about nothing but violins, narrating with great exultation how he had purchased his Stradivarius, which was worth at least five hundred guineas, at a Jew broker's in Tottenham Court Road for fifty-five shillings." There is a possibility, however, that the Great Detective may have deceived himself since violin makers in all parts of the world were making instruments labelled 'Stradivari' at that time: some of them indistinguishable in tone from the real thing. *The Cardboard Box.* See also *A Study in Scarlet* and *The Sign of Four*

SUNG DYNASTY. During the research into Chinese pottery he had undertaken at Holmes' request, Watson learned of the glories of the primitive period of the Sung and the Yuan dynasties. *The Illustrious Client*

SWORDS. In Watson's ubiquitous catalogue of "Sherlock Holmes—his limits," he noted that the Great Detective was "an expert singlestick player, boxer, and swordsman." *A Study in Scarlet*

T

+TANKERVILLE CLUB SCANDAL. John Openshaw had heard of Holmes from Major Prendergast, whom Holmes had saved from ostracism in the Tankerville Club Scandal. The Major had been wrongfully accused of cheating at cards. *The Five Orange Pips*

+**TAPANULI FEVER**. Said Holmes to Watson, "What do you know, pray, of Tapanuli fever? What do you know of the black Formosa corruption?" "I have never heard of either," replied the Doctor. *The Dying Detective*

+**TARLETON MURDERS**. One of Holmes' untold cases. *The Musgrave Ritual.*

+**TAVERNIER**. The French modeller who made the wax image of Holmes which was used to fool Count Negretto Sylvius. *The Mazarin Stone*

TEDDY. Henry Wood's pet mongoose, which he had trained how to entertain certain soldiers every night. *The Crooked Man*

THOREAU, HENRY DAVID. "Circumstantial evidence is occasionally very convincing, as when you find a trout in milk, to quote Thoreau's example," said Holmes in *The Noble Bachelor*

THREE MONTHS IN THE JUNGLE. This was one of Colonel Sebastian Moran's publications, brought out in 1884. *The Empty House*

THUCYDIDES. A chapter of Thucydides was to be given as the first examination paper in the competition for the Fortescue Scholarship. *The Three Students*

TIMES, THE. It was in *The Times* that Violet Smith and her mother saw an advertisement inquiring about their whereabouts. As they were very poor then, they became quite excited, for they thought that someone had left them a fortune. *The Solitary Cyclist*

TOBACCO. Holmes smoked 'Arcadia Mixture'. Watson smoked 'Ships'. *A Study in Scarlet*

TRICHINOPOLY. Holmes reasoned that the murderer of Enoch J. Drebber had smoked a Trichinopoly cigar. "I gathered up some scattered ash from the floor. It was dark in colour and flakey — such an ash as is only made by a Trichinopoly. I have made a special study of cigar ashes — in fact, I have written a monograph upon the subject. I flatter myself that I can distinguish at a glance the ash of any known brand either of cigar or of tobacco. *A Study in Scarlet.* See also *The Sign of Four*

THE TRIPLE ALLIANCE BETWEEN GERMANY, AUSTRIA-HUNGARY AND ITALY). The naval treaty which disappeared from the unfortunate Percy Phelps' office "defined the position of Great Britain towards the Triple Alliance, and foreshadowed the policy this country would pursue in the event of the French fleet gaining a complete ascendency over that of Italy in the Mediterranean." *The Naval Treaty*

TURKEY, SULTAN OF. Holmes had a commission from this man which, if neglected, would lead to dire political results. *The Blanched Solider*

TURKISH BATH. Watson admitted that both he and Holmes had a weakness for the Turkish bath. "It was over a smoke in the pleasant lassitude of the drying.room that I have found him less reticent and more human than anywhere else." They lay together on two couches in the Northumberland Avenue establishment at the opening of one 'Adventure'. *The Illustrious Client.* See also *The Disappearance of Lady Frances Carfax*

TYPE. "The detection of types is one of the most elementary branches of knowledge to the special expert in crime." And so Holmes (having written a monograph on the subject) could correctly identify that the letters of the warning message sent to Sir Henry Baskerville were cut from an article in *The Times* newspaper. *The Hound of the Baskervilles*

TYPEWRITER. The typewriter provided a number of clues in Holmes' solution of the disappearance of Miss Mary Sutherland's fiancé on the way to their wedding. "It is a curious thing that a typewriter has really quite as much individuality as a man's handwriting. Unless they are quite new, no two of them write exactly alike. Some letters get more worn than others and some wear only on one side. I think of writing another little monograph some of these days on the typewriter and its relation to crime. It is a subject to which I have devoted some little attention." *A Case of Identity*

TYRES. Holmes was able to use his extensive knowledge of different types of bicycle tyre to track down what had happened to the young Lord Saltire. *The Priory School*

U

"UPON THE DISTINCTION BETWEEN THE ASHES OF THE VARIOUS TOBACCOS". Holmes told Watson, "I have been guilty of several monographs. They are all upon technical subjects. Here, for example, is one 'Upon the Distinction Between the Ashes of the Various Tobaccos.' In it I enumerate a hundred and forty forms of cigar, cigarette, and pipe tobacco, with coloured plates illustrating the difference in the ash. It is a point which is continually turning up in criminal trials, and which is sometimes of supreme importance as a clue." *The Sign of Four*

"UPON THE POLYPHONIC MOTETS OF LASSUS". The day before the recovery of some stolen submarine plans, Holmes "lost himself in a monograph which he had undertaken upon the Polyphonic Motets of Lassus." *The Bruce-Partington Plans*

V

VAMPIRES. Sherlock Holmes' index contained records of old cases, mixed with the accumulated information of a lifetime; and the volume devoted to letter twenty-two was especially interesting. One of the entries concerned Vampires in Transylvania and another Vampirism in Hungary. *The Sussex Vampire*

VANDERBILT AND THE YEGGMAN. The volume devoted to the letter V in Sherlock Holmes' "Good Old Index" was especially interesting. One of its items concerned "Vanderbilt and the Yeggman." *The Sussex Vampire*

VATICAN CAMEOS. Holmes had been preoccupied with the little affair of the Vatican cameos at the time of the newspaper reports of the mysterious death of Sir Charles Baskerville; and for this reason he had not taken much interest in the case at first. *The Hound of the Baskervilles*

VEHNGERICHT. A secret society dedicated to eliminating its dissidents, choosing by lot who would be the member to accomplish this. *A Study in Scarlet*. See also *The Red Circle*

VENOMOUS LIZARD OR GILA. Sherlock Holmes found that the volume devoted to a certain letter in his Index concerned this animal, which had featured in a case which he thought of as "remarkable." It also contained an entry about vipers. *The Sussex Vampire*

VENNER & MATHESON. A well-known engineering firm of Greenwich. Victor Hatherley had been apprenticed to them for seven years, which gave him enough experience to go into business for himself. *The Engineer's Thumb*

VERNET, EMILE JEAN HORACE. A distinguished French artist, his sister was the grandmother of Sherlock

Holmes. See **Art.** *The Greek Interpreter*

VIGOR. Sherlock Holmes' ubiquitous index had a section devoted to the letter V which, again like the other letters already mentioned, was especially interesting. one of its items concerned "Vigor, the Hammersmith wonder." *The Sussex Vampire*

VIOLIN. In Watson's catalogue of "Sherlock Holmes—his limits," he noted that the Great Detective played the violin well, although he also had other things to say about his newly acquired companion's skills on that instrument. "These were very remarkable, but as eccentric as all his other accomplishments. That he could play pieces, and difficult pieces, I knew well, because at my request he has played me some of Mendelssohn's Lieder, and other favourites. When left to himself, however, he would seldom produce any music or attempt any recognized air." *A Study in Scarlet.* See also *The Sign of Four, The Red-Headed League* and *The Illustrious Client*

VITTORIA. Another item under the heading V in Sherlock Holmes' Index concerned "Vittoria, the circus belle." *The Sussex Vampire*

VON BISCHOFF. Holmes, when rejoicing over that "infallible test for blood stains" mentioned Von Bischoff at Frankfort, who "would certainly have been hung had this test been in existence." *A Study in Scarlet*

V.R. See Boxer Cartridges. *The Musgrave Ritual*

W

WAGNER, RICHARD. Sherlock Holmes so enjoyed the musical compositions of this German composer that, at the conclusion of *The Red Circle,* he asked Watson to join him at a Wagner night at Covent Garden, even though he knew that they had already missed the first act.

WAINWRIGHT. "A complex mind," said Holmes of the notorious Baron Adelbert Gruner. "All great criminals have that. My old friend Charlie Peace was a violin virtuoso. Wainwright was no mean artist. I could quote many more." *The Illustrious Client*

WALLENSTEIN, ALBRECHT VON. Born 1583. The German commander of the Imperial Forces in the Thirty Years War. Successful at first but distrusted later. Assassinated in 1634. *A Scandal in Bohemia*

WHITAKER'S ALMANACK. This volume held the key to Fred Porlock's cipher message. *The Valley of Fear*

WHOLE ART OF DETECTION, THE. Holmes intended to devote his declining years to the composition of a one-volume textbook on this topic. *The Abbey Grange*

WHYTE, WILLIAM. As Holmes sat down to wait for the expected arrival of the murderer of Enoch J. Drebber, he took up "a queer old book I picked up at a stall yesterday — *De Jure inter Gentes*—published in Latin at Liege in the Lowlands, in 1642." *A Study in Scarlet*

WIGMORE STREET POST OFFICE. Observation told Holmes that Watson had been to the Wigmore Street Post Office earlier in the morning, while deduction let him know that his friend had been there to send a telegram. *The Sign of Four*

WILD, JONATHAN. Holmes said, "He was a [real-life] master criminal, and he lived last century —1750 or thereabouts." *The Valley of Fear*

WOMBWELL. He was "one of the greatest showmen of his day," and the rival of Sanger and Ronder. *The Veiled Lodger*

WOMEN. According to Holmes, "Women have seldom been an attraction to me, for my brain has always governed my heart." But he was so struck by the beauty and composure under great stress of Maud Bellamy that he concluded that she would "always remain in my memory as a most complete and remarkable woman." *The Lion's Mane*

WORTHINGDON BANK GANG. Five conspirators, Biddle, Hayward, Moffat, Sutton, and Cartwright, robbed the Worthingdon bank in 1875, but killed a caretaker in making their getaway. All five were eventually caught. Sutton turned informer and, on his evidence, Cartwright was hanged and the other three got fifteen years in jail. When the men were finally released, they vowed to take revenge on Sutton. See Blessington. *The Resident Patient*

Also from MX Publishing

Close To Holmes

A Look at the Connections Between Historical London, Sherlock Holmes and Sir Arthur Conan Doyle.

Eliminate The Impossible

An Examination of the World of Sherlock Holmes on Page and Screen.

The Norwood Author

Arthur Conan Doyle and the Norwood Years (1891 - 1894) – Winner of the 2011 Howlett Literary Award (Sherlock Holmes book of the year)

www.mxpublishing.com

Also From MX Publishing

In Search of Dr Watson

Wonderful biography of
Dr.Watson from expert Molly
Carr – 2nd edition fully updated.

Arthur Conan Doyle, Sherlock
Holmes and Devon

A Complete Tour Guide and
Companion.

The Lost Stories of Sherlock Holmes

Eight more stories from the pen of John
H Watson – compiled by Tony
Reynolds.

www.mxpublishing.com

Also From MX Publishing

Watsons Afghan Adventure

Fascinating biography of Watson's time in Afghanistan from US Army veteran Kieran McMullen.

Shadowfall

Sherlock Holmes, ancient relics and demons and mystic characters. A supernatural Holmes pastiche.

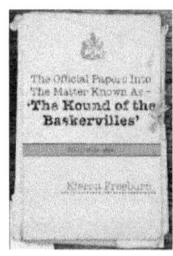

Official Papers of The Hound of The Baskervilles

Very unusual collection of the original police papers from The Hound case.

www.mxpublishing.com

Also From MX Publishing

The Sign of Fear

The first adventure of the 'female Sherlock Holmes'. A delightful fun adventure with your favourite supporting Holmes characters.

A Study in Crimson

The second adventure of the 'female Sherlock Holmes' with a host of sub-plots and new characters joining Watson and Fanshaw

The Chronology of Arthur Conan Doyle

The definitive chronology used by historians and libraries worldwide.

www.mxpublishing.com

Also From MX Publishing

Aside Arthur Conan Doyle

A collection of twenty stories from ACD's close friend Bertram Fletcher Robinson.

Bertram Fletcher Robinson

The comprehensive biography of the assistant plot producer of The Hound of The Baskervilles

Wheels of Anarchy

Reprint and introduction to Max Pemberton's thriller from 100 years ago. One of the first spy thrillers of its kind.

www.mxpublishing.com

Also From MX Publishing

Bobbles and Plum

Four playlets from PG Wodehouse 'lost' for over 100 years – found and reprinted with an excellent commentary

The World of Vanity Fair

A specialist full-colour reproduction of key articles from Bertram Fletcher Robinson containing of colour caricatures from the early 1900s.

Tras Las He huellas de Arthur Conan Doyle (in Spanish)

Un viaje ilustrado por Devon.

www.mxpublishing.com

Also From MX Publishing

The Outstanding Mysteries of
Sherlock Holmes

With thirteen Homes stories and
illustrations Kelly re-creates the
gas-lit, fog-enshrouded world of
Victorian London

Rendezvous at The Populaire

Sherlock Holmes has retired,
injured from an encounter with
Moriarty. He's tempted out of
retirement for an epic battle with
the Phantom of the opera.

Baker Street Beat

An eclectic collection of articles,
essays, radio plays and 'general
scribblings' about Sherlock Holmes
from Dr.Dan Andriacco.

www.mxpublishing.com

Also From MX Publishing

The Case of The Grave Accusation

The creator of Sherlock Holmes has been accused of murder. Only Holmes and Watson can stop the destruction of the Holmes legacy.

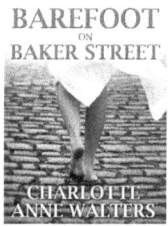

Barefoot on Baker Street

Epic novel of the life of a Victorian workhouse orphan featuring Sherlock Holmes and Moriarty.

Case of Witchcraft

A tale of witchcraft in the Northern Isles, in which long-concealed secrets are revealed -- including some that concern the Great Detective himself!

www.mxpublishing.com

Also From MX Publishing

The Affair In Transylvania

Holmes and Watson tackle Dracula
in deepest Transylvania in this
stunning adaptation by film director
Gerry O'Hara

The London of Sherlock Holmes

400 locations including GPS co-
ordinates that enable Google Street
view of the locations around
London in all the Homes stories

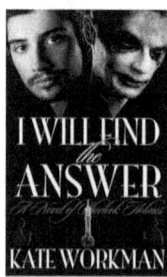

I Will Find The Answer

Sequel to Rendezvous At The
Populaire, Holmes and Watson tackle
Dr.Jekyll.

www.mxpublishing.com

Also From MX Publishing

The Case of The Russian Chessboard

Short novel covering the dark world of Russian espionage sees Holmes and Watson on the world stage facing dark and complex enemies.

An Entirely New Country

Covers Arthur Conan Doyle's years at Undershaw where he wrote Hound of The Baskervilles. Foreword by Mark Gatiss (BBC's Sherlock).

Shadowblood

Sequel to Shadowfall, Holmes and Watson tackle blood magic, the vilest form of sorcery.

www.mxpublishing.com

Also From MX Publishing

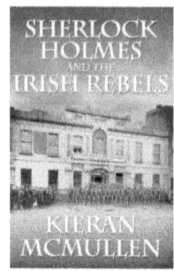

Sherlock Holmes and The Irish Rebels

It is early 1916 and the world is at war. Sherlock Holmes is well into his spy persona as Altamont.

The Punishment of Sherlock Holmes

"deliberately and successfully funny"

The Sherlock Holmes Society of London

No Police Like Holmes

It's a Sherlock Holmes symposium, and murder is involved. The first case for Sebastian McCabe.

www.mxpublishing.com

Also From MX Publishing

In The Night, In The Dark

Winner of the Dracula Society Award
– a collection of supernatural ghost
stories from the editor of the Sherlock
Holmes Society of London journal.

Sherlock Holmes and
The Lyme Regis Horror

Fully updated 2nd edition of this
bestselling Holmes story set in Dorset.

My Dear Watson

Winner of the Suntory Mystery Award
for fiction and translated from the
original Japanese. Holmes greatest
secret is revealed – Sherlock Holmes is
a woman.

www.mxpublishing.com

Also From MX Publishing

Mark of The Baskerville Hound

100 years on and a New York policeman faces a similar terror to the great detective.

A Professor Reflects On Sherlock Holmes

A wonderful collection of essays and scripts and writings on Sherlock Holmes.

Sherlock Holmes On The Air

A collection of Sherlock Holmes radio scripts with detailed notes on Canonical references.

www.mxpublishing.com

Also From MX Publishing

Sherlock Holmes Whos Who

All the characters from the entire canon catalogued and profiled.

Sherlock Holmes and The Lyme Regis Legacy

Sequel to the Lyme Regis Horror and Holmes and Watson are once again embroiled in murder in Dorset.

Sherlock Holmes and The Discarded Cigarette

London 1895. A well known author, a theoretical invention made real and the perfect crime.

www.mxpublishing.com

Also From MX Publishing

Sherlock Holmes and The Whitechapel Vampire

Jack The Ripper is a vampire, and Holmes refusal to believe it could lead to his downfall.

Tales From The Strangers Room

A collection of writings from more than 20 Sherlockians with author profits going to The Beacon Society.

The Secret Journal of Dr Watson

Holmes and Watson head to the newly formed Soviet Union to rescue the Romanovs.